JUSTICE LEAGUE of AMERICA™
EXTERMINATORS

CHRISTOPHER GOLDEN

D0827126

POCKET STAR BOOKS

New York   London   Toronto   Sydney

An *Original* Publication of POCKET BOOKS

 A Pocket Star Book published by
POCKET BOOKS, a division of Simon & Schuster, Inc.
1230 Avenue of the Americas, New York, NY 10020

Cover painting by Alex Ross
Series cover design by Georg Brewer

ISBN: 0-7434-1715-1

First Pocket Books printing July 2004

10 9 8 7 6 5 4 3 2 1

www.dccomics.com

Manufactured in the United States of America

For information regarding special discounts for bulk purchases, please contact Simon & Schuster Special Sales at 1-800-456-6798 or business@simonandschuster.com.

With a glance around the roof and then across the street, Batman mentally calculated the distance and the wind speed, working out what it would take for him to get across to the other building and down into the street with J'onn without being too conspicuous. He reached for his belt and unclipped the grapple-gun, already eyeing the ledge he would have to target to swing out over the street, and the parked SUV whose roof he would land on, breaking some of his momentum before somersaulting to the ground only feet from where J'onn stood. There was a chance he'd been seen, but very little that Graff would witness this move. And it would be better if he and J'onn worked together on this.

The circumstances needed to be controlled.

Batman rose up from his place beside the vent column and extended his hand, thumb on the trigger of the grapple-gun.

Zachary Graff's bedroom window exploded outward in the blast from a shotgun, the report from the weapon echoing off the faces of buildings up and down the street.

Batman was in motion before the echo died.

*For Jean-marc Joseph, who dragged me back into
reading comics after I had lost faith. You cost me a lot
of money, my friend.*

Acknowledgments

The author would like to thank: Marco Palmieri and Scott Shannon at Pocket Books, Charles Kochman at DC Comics, Tom Sniegoski, and Geoff Johns.

JUSTICE LEAGUE of AMERICA™
EXTERMINATORS

Ten years ago . . .

Dark clouds hung heavy across the United Kingdom, pregnant with the coming storm. Gray skies were hardly unusual in this part of the world; in truth, they were merely ordinary. But on this cold spring day there was something more than ordinary in the sky, in the rain. Those who looked up at the storm saw within its gunmetal clouds a faint tinge of sickly yellow, and the heavens roiled like the churning sea.

In Glasgow, a museum curator named Roger Vandal scurried down the scuffed wooden stairs of his flat, nearly tripping before he reached the door that led to the street. The building had been there for centuries and the steps were lopsided. He had been up and down hundreds of times and yet somehow he had not mastered the process of navigating those warped stairs. Hurriedly, Roger opened the door and stepped out into the rain. He cursed loudly, scowling up at the storm as though it were a personal insult, and turned up his collar as he hurried along the block toward his car.

Damned alarm clock, he thought to himself, though he knew the fault was his own rather than a technical failing. He had known the alarm clock was not working properly but usually did not need to rely upon it. There had just been something about the storm this morning, something that made him want to pull up his covers and hide his head. It was one of those rainy days when he could barely open his eyes in the morning and wanted nothing more than to spend the day with a book and a pot of tea.

Roger could not recall the last time he had been late for work. He was not really concerned about being dismissed from his position; after all, it was only this once. He was the curator, the boss, and he had several trusted employees who also held keys to the museum and were certain to have opened the doors on time. Still, he was ever conscious of the example he set for his staff.

The rain felt slick and almost greasy and he shivered with a chill as it ran down the back of his neck. He held his lapels tightly together, pulling his collar closer around his throat, and muttered another curse under his breath. He had been outside all of ten seconds before he began to wish he had never gotten out of bed at all. A creaking old truck trundled by on the street and Roger had to sidestep to avoid being soaked as its tires splashed through a puddle. The cobblestone sidewalk was slick under his shoes. It was a miserable day, there was no doubt about that. Halfway along the next block he at last reached his car, a nondescript blue sedan of the type most commonly driven by bankers, accountants, and museum curators.

Squinting his eyes against the rain Roger fumbled in his pocket for his keys. It was not until he had opened the door that he noticed his front left tire was completely flat.

"Bloody Hell!" Roger snarled, thumping his hand against the door.

He sighed loudly and for a moment even considered returning home. But he had a spare tire in the trunk and his hair and his jacket were already soaked with rain. Though he was shivering, he set himself to the task, searching in the trunk for his jack.

Roger wiped the rain out of his eyes. He could taste it on his lips and there was something unpleasantly metallic in it.

On a farm in Swansea, Julia Williams staggered across the muddy field with a lamb in her arms. It weighed little and yet enough that her boots squelched in the rain-soaked earth. Julia was fourteen years old and the last thing that she had wanted to do today was stagger about in the rain in search of a wandering lamb. But her father would hear none of it. He himself was busy repairing the fence where the lamb had gotten through, and so she knew she ought not to complain. But she was cold and soaked through. Even the lamb in her arms shuddered with the chilly rain.

As she trudged toward him, Julia could hear her father curse loudly as he hammered new boards into place, a temporary patch on the fence at best. But it would do until the storm passed.

A thick raindrop slipped down her cheek and it was strangely warm, as though she had cut her scalp and it was blood dripping down her face instead of rain. This time when Julia shuddered it was not from the cold.

Ian Partington was in love.

His house was all the way on the other side of Norwich; he had walked miles in the rain just to stand here at the counter and order himself a cup of coffee. The Culture Shock Café was trendy enough to draw college students who sat and smoked and talked politics and football, but it was also far enough off the beaten path that most of the tourists who came to Norwich to gawk at the cathedral never stumbled upon it. Which was a pity for them, for if they had, they might have had a chance to gaze upon the porcelain, delicate features of the prettiest girl in all of England.

Her name was Sara. Ian had first spotted her several weeks earlier in a bookstore just up the hill. She had been browsing and chatting with a girlfriend and Ian had felt himself pulled along in their wake, as if

Sara had created some sort of undertow that he could not escape. He found himself breathless as he snuck glances at her eyes, ringed by dark circles of makeup that made her appear almost ghostly. She wore a small, simple steel ring through her nose and blood-red lipstick. In all his life, Ian had never felt so completely helpless. He had overheard the two girls talking and learned both Sara's name and that she worked at Culture Shock.

Now here he was standing at the counter for the fourth time since that day. The woman in front of him got her coffee and turned to walk back to a table. Ian was next but when Sara asked what he would like he could only look at her for a moment. Her black-dyed hair was pulled into a wild tangle at the back of her head; she wore a black top and a skirt the color of pumpkins. You would have thought it was Halloween.

"Have you not decided yet?" she prodded.

He smiled. "Sorry. Bit of a brain freeze there. Cappuccino please. Pinch of cinnamon'd be lovely as well."

Sara raised one eyebrow. "That's a new one for you."

Ian blinked, hoping she didn't recognize the look on his face as utter stupefaction. It was the first time he'd ordered cappuccino at Culture Shock, and Sara knew it. She recognized him. Remembered him from other times he'd been in.

It took him a moment to recover himself. When he

did, he offered her a nonchalant smile. "Yeah," he agreed with a nod of his head. "That's me, though. Gotta try new things in life, or what's the use, right?"

She tilted her head to one side, regarding him as if trying to decipher something about his face. Then she nodded with an air of approval.

"Too right," she agreed.

When she turned away to fetch his cappuccino it was all Ian could do not to pump his arm and whoop in victory. He felt giddy. Butterflies fluttered happily in his stomach. A sigh of amused satisfaction slipped out between his lips and he became suddenly aware of a couple at a table off to his left watching him.

Embarrassed, he glanced away.

Sara returned momentarily with a frothy cappuccino, sprinkled on top with cinnamon he could smell even before she set it down. The two of them were all business as he paid her. The entire time, as she took his money and counted out his change, a furious, impatient voice snarled at him in his head to do it, to speak up, that he was never going to get a better chance than this.

He pocketed the money, caught her eyes, and lost his nerve. Ian turned and took two steps away from the counter. In that moment it was as though someone else had control of his body, or perhaps it was only that his most profound desire overrode his anxiety. He spun and marched back to the counter. Sara glanced up, both eyebrows raised now in curiosity.

"Forget something?"

Ian nodded. "I did, yeah. Do you think you might

like to go out sometime? Not . . . well, not for coffee, of course. But do you think you might like to see a film or . . . or have dinner?"

Her eyes sparkled as a sweet smile spread across her face. She gave him a single, almost imperceptible nod. "I might," she said. "I just might at that."

Breathless, he stared at her. "That's . . . that's tremendous. Really, it's . . . right, then. I'll see you, then."

He turned and walked out of the café, take-out cappuccino cup hot in his grip, though he barely felt it. Sara had not even mentioned how drenched he was from the storm, had not even seemed to notice it. Back out in the rain, coffee steaming in the cold, Ian walked an entire block before he had realized that he had been so startled by Sara's reply that he had not even made a plan with her. He considered going back, but realized it did not matter. Tomorrow would be soon enough, and less embarrassing. He'd go in for coffee—maybe an espresso this time—and firm things up. Take her out to dinner, not just down to the pub with his mates, but someplace nice.

With a laugh, he threw back his head and let the rain spatter his face, sluicing down his cheeks. Ian thrust out his tongue and tasted the water on his tongue.

The rain was bitter. There was a metallic, chemical tinge to it that made him frown and close his mouth, wiping his face with his sodden sleeve. The unpleasant taste remained in his mouth, but even that could do nothing to dim his spirits.

An image of that sweet smile on Sara's face was burned into his mind, and he held that picture there for all the hours until he saw her again.

And all across the United Kingdom, from Norwich to Glasgow to Swansea, the bitter rain continued to fall.

CHAPTER ONE

Now . . .

Keystone City was awash with the warmth and color of spring. At the Citywalk outdoor marketplace, street vendors sold lemonade and Italian ice and hot pretzels. A juggler on a unicycle drew a small crowd of lawyers and software salesmen on their lunch breaks. From somewhere nearby came the sound of voices raised in song, an a cappella group from one of the local colleges. Across the street, where a historic building was being renovated to become the new Keystone Children's Museum, construction workers sat on scaffolding eating lunch and watching as women walked by in light cotton dresses that had just emerged from a long winter at the back of their closets.

It really was a glorious day. The whole city had an infectious, upbeat vibe. But Wally West wasn't catching the infection.

The truth was, he *had* caught it—after lunch with his Aunt Iris he had passed by a vendor selling long-stemmed roses cash-and-carry on the sidewalk and wanted to bring some home to his wife—but the good feeling had worn off. He did not have any cash on him and had to stand in line at the ATM behind half a dozen people who obviously weren't in any rush.

Wally's impatience fought it out with his desire to get roses for Linda, and the roses won, but only barely. At the front of the line was a fiftyish woman with the look and carriage of a school teacher; she stared, befuddled, at the screen for long seconds each time new options presented themselves, as if she had never used an ATM before.

Come on, Wally mentally prodded her, bouncing on his heels.

He tried to be patient. He really did. Linda was always telling him to slow down and the truth was, most of the time he only ever did it for her. To take her dancing or out to dinner or even to a movie he had to force himself to relax, to take a breath and savor what life had to offer him, not what might happen in the next few seconds.

Linda was worth it. Even thinking about her right now was enough to calm him down a little, to dilute his frustration with the woman at the cash machine who could not seem to figure out how to enter the amount of her deposit. Long-stemmed roses for Linda. He pictured in his mind the smile they would bring to her stunning features, thinking if he could slow down this long, maybe they ought to do dinner out tonight as well. His first thought was Rocco's in Chicago, then he thought better of it. Something right here in Keystone. Maybe Dixie Kitchen, the little Cajun café on Bridge Boulevard.

Wally did his best to suppress his nervous energy. The woman at last finished with her eternal deposit and the next person in line—a bespectacled guy in a well-tailored suit—seemed to be just making a withdrawal.

There we go, Wally thought. *It isn't forever. It only feels like it.*

He tried to be patient. It just wasn't easy. Not when you were the fastest man alive.

Not when you were the Flash.

Eventually, after a great many sighs and lots of impatient toe-tapping, he reached the cash machine. As he slipped eighty dollars and the withdrawal receipt into his wallet, a metallic trilling noise began to emanate from his pocket.

Wally West left the front of the cash machine so quickly that to those behind him in line, he seemed to have simply disappeared. The world around him blurred slightly and slowed. So great was his speed that to him it appeared as though everything else was standing still. Stashing his wallet in his back pocket, he ran to the street corner where the vendor was selling the cash-and-carry roses. The trilling noise continued to sound in his pocket but he wasn't ready to answer it just yet.

Emergency or not, he just needed a few seconds.

The flower seller—an olive-skinned man with sad

eyes and a drooping mustache—had propped himself up on the rear legs of the chair he had set out for himself. When Wally paused in front of him, a full-grown man who appeared to materialize out of thin air, the man nearly tipped himself over.

In the fraction of an instant when the flower man's balance could have gone either way, Wally slipped his JLA commlink—the one he carried when he was in his street clothes—out of his pocket and thumbed the button on its side. The moment he did so, a figure loomed into view on the comm's tiny screen with carefully mussed black hair and a dark green mask that covered only the area around his eyes. Apparently Green Lantern was on monitor duty at the Justice League's lunar base, the Watchtower.

"Kyle, hang on a sec," Wally said.

The flower man was staring at him, sad eyes now wide with curiosity. Wally smiled, pulled out a pair of twenties and asked for his roses. The bouquets were already prepared, wrapped up nice with baby's breath and ribbon.

"Okay," he said, glancing back into the commlink. "What's up?"

Green Lantern's expression was grim. "London. Some freak's out in front of Buckingham Palace threatening to banish the palace and everyone inside to some limbo world if the Queen doesn't knight him. Or something like that."

Wally handed the flower man the money and took the bouquet, waiting for his change.

"I don't get it," he told Kyle. "So some nut job's

running around in front of the palace. Isn't that what those stone-faced guards are for?"

"At least eight of the Palace Guard have already been sucked into the void this particular 'nut job' has opened in front of the palace. Not to mention an unknown number of civilians and half a block of prime London real estate."

For a second that seemed an eternity Wally stared into the tiny screen on the commlink. Then the flower man cleared his throat and Wally looked up, seeing recognition in the man's eyes. The world knew that Wally West was the Flash, but even here in his chosen hometown, people seemed surprised when they actually ran into him. This guy had finally figured it out. The vendor handed Wally his change.

"Thanks," he said, glancing back at the commlink. "Who's on it?"

"Me and you," Green Lantern replied. "Ready for transfer?"

Wally shook his head. "Give me half a minute."

He smiled at the flower vendor . . . and then he ran. In the time it took the man with the drooping mustache to blink in surprise at the way he had disappeared as abruptly as he had appeared, Wally was already halfway across town. His every heartbeat, his every breath, was in tandem with an energy field that existed within the fabric of all things. It was called the Speed Force, and over the years since he had first become the Flash, Wally had discovered a great many things he could accomplish by tapping into that energy. His uniform, for instance, was not made of cotton or

Lycra or any other fabric for that matter; rather it was a construct of his own will, fashioned from pure concentrated Speed Force.

Which was pretty cool, as far as Wally was concerned.

By the time the flower vendor, now miles behind him, had blinked a second time Wally had already gathered the Speed Force and clad himself in a version of the scarlet uniform that had first been made famous by his uncle, Barry Allen, the second man to bear the title of the Flash. Wally was the third, and though he had accomplished things neither of his predecessors had ever dreamt about, he still felt he had a long way to go to live up to the example Uncle Barry and Jay Garrick, the first Flash, had set for him.

He was nothing but a breeze, a blur, as he crossed Keystone City. As a red phantom, glimpsed out of the corner of the eye, he appeared inside the Dixie Kitchen and pencilled himself and Linda in for a seven P.M. reservation. The hostess had been in the midst of writing down another reservation and Wally snatched the pencil from her hand and returned it so quickly she barely missed a stroke.

Then he was off again, racing for home.

So much of the time he existed in a world apart from everyone else, on another plane of reality entirely. The population of the city seemed like department store mannequins to the Flash. There were times when it was disconcerting, but the legacy that he had inherited was a constant reminder of what he was fighting for; he would never let himself feel too apart from the rest of the world. And if he ever drifted, well, Linda was there to remind him.

She was hanging a new mirror in the bedroom when he raced into the house and up the stairs. He paused outside the room, not wanting to startle her into dropping the mirror. For a moment, as he slowed himself down, he simply relished looking at her. Her hair was like black silk, her features like those of a porcelain doll. Yet in her eyes was a fierce intelligence that made her all the more beautiful.

"Hey," he said.

Linda glanced over and smiled as she tried to get the mirror to hang straight. "Well, hey yourself," she replied. "Care to give me a hand with this?"

It was out of her hands and on the wall before she completed the sentence. Then the Flash stood in front of his wife, holding both of her hands in his and marveling as he always did at his great fortune.

"Gotta go to London," he told her. "I'll be back soon. We've got reservations at Dixie Kitchen at seven. And I left you something on the bed."

Linda frowned and turned around, a smile spreading across her features as she saw the bouquet of roses he had slipped in past her to place on the bedspread. When she turned back around to ask him what the occasion was, she discovered that he was already gone.

After standing in line at the ATM for twelve seemingly endless minutes of purgatory, Wally just wanted to run. The world warped around him and a smile spread across his lips as his legs pumped beneath him. He would have preferred to run from Keystone

City, across the Eastern seaboard of the United States and the Atlantic Ocean, all the way to London. But at that distance, even the fastest man alive could not beat teleportation.

"This is the Flash," he said, tapping the commlink in the right earpiece of his mask. "I'm a go."

He stopped short. The Watchtower's teleportation system—really a modified version of so-called "Boom Tube" technology—locked onto his unique energy signature, and then Flash felt his skin prickling. It was a bit like having a low-charge electrical current run through his body. His vision blurred into darkness and when he blinked and the world swam back into focus, he was on the other side of the world.

London, England.

With the time difference, it must have been about seven-thirty in the evening here. The late spring day was fading to night. There was a park nearby and a black wrought iron fence and, on the other side of a high wall, the spires of Buckingham Palace. Police cordons had been set up to keep people back, but there were still onlookers crowding forward, trying to get a glimpse of the chaos. Flash figured it was mostly tourists, that the locals would be smart enough to know that when some moron with superhuman abilities tore a black, sucking vacuum in the pavement in the middle of the street in front of the palace, it was time to go somewhere, anywhere, else.

In front of the palace gates there were dozens of guards, both the redcoated boys in their high, furry black hats that you saw in all the pictures and a contingent of men in the sort of dark suits usually associated with the American Secret Service. Special palace security, apparently. But what surprised Flash was that the high-hatted Palace Guard weren't all for pomp and circumstance.

Inside that police cordon and in full view of the gates, a sinkhole had appeared in the street. Yet there were no rough edges of broken pavement and nothing was crumbling. It was as if reality had been melted down in that place and someone had started to stir it, so that it swirled in a maelstrom of darkness, this abyss in the middle of the road. All of it was presided over by a thin, gray-haired man with wild eyes and an accountant's sense of style. He was about as ordinary looking a man as Flash had ever seen, yet the way he held his hands out—and the way the air between the maelstrom and the tips of his fingers wavered like July heat off blacktop—told Flash this was indeed the guy.

He took in all of this in a fraction of a second. In the next, the evening twilight took on a distinctly verdant hue. A green light bathed everything in sight. Flash glanced up as Kyle levitated above him, held aloft by the energy that emanated from inside the ring he wore. Once there had been a great many Green Lanterns in the universe. Now there was only Kyle.

"Right, listen you!" shouted the slender man in charge of the maelstrom. "Get 'er Majesty out 'ere now. I'll be a knight of the Order o' the British Empire by half seven or there won't be a British Empire left when I'm through."

Apparently the man was so caught up in his own lunacy he had not even noticed the arrival of two members of the Justice League. Flash stared at him a moment, wondering where his strange warping powers had come from and why the guy was so obsessed with becoming a knight, and hoping the people that had been swallowed by that weird maelstrom were somehow still alive.

"Excuse me, Sir Nut Job?" Green Lantern called to the man. "Maybe you want to think about this a little bit. You know, go on a quest for the Grail or something, prove you're worthy."

Lantern raised his hand and tendrils of green energy erupted from his ring and leaped at the man on the brink of the void. Without glancing backward the man raised a hand as if to ward off the attack and another wound tore into the fabric of the world, a swirling vortex of darkness that sucked the tendrils of power from the ring into its void.

In that moment it seemed to Flash that all of London held its breath. There was silence in front of the Palace as the police, guards and onlookers all turned to stare at Green Lantern. Kyle did not look pleased at all. A wave of menace radiated out from the gray-haired man in his charcoal trousers, bone-white shirt and black tie. He had looked ridiculous, there on the edge of that churning hole in reality, but all of that changed when he turned, slowly, to face Green Lantern and Flash.

His eyes were black maelstroms as well, sucking holes in the universe.

Flash swore, but the single syllable was left behind him as he raced at the man. His thoughts were awhirl as he gauged the probability that taking the lunatic down would close the abyss in the street, and what that might do to the people who had been sucked into it, if they were even still alive. He would have to distract the freak, get his attention, move his focus away from the maelstrom long enough for Green Lantern to probe the pit with his power ring and try to determine if the people could be retrieved.

He ran at the gray-haired man, his speed so great that the maniac could not possibly see him. But still, the man *looked* at him. A cloud of nothing burst from eyes, twin tornadoes that tore into the air between them, and yet another portal appeared, another window into the dark limbo he had threatened to swallow all of London with.

The Flash could not stop in time. One instant he was racing toward the man, thinking to spin a cyclone around him, trapping him there, perhaps sucking the oxygen from his lungs and driving him to unconsciousness. Then next instant he had plunged into that gray, formless, swirling abyss and he was tumbling in the dark, weightless in the void. He gazed about the shapeless, colorless limbo but he saw no sign of the portal through which he had entered.

No way back.

Daylight required stealth.

On the roof of an abandoned factory building in what had once been the garment district of Hub City, there were a dozen square columns that had acted as vents in the years when the Saxonville Hat Company had manufactured their products here. Also atop the building was an old water tower, a huge tin tub on stilts that sat on the roof collecting the rain. Once upon a time, before sprinkler systems were required by safety law, the water tower would have provided a good drenching in the event of a fire.

This day it provided only shade.

Shadows.

Within those shadows lurked the Batman.

He moved swiftly from the cover of the water tower to the two-foot wall that ran around the edges of the roof and ducked down beside one of the vent columns, blending as best he could. There weren't many cars on the street below. This section of Hub City had been left to rot over the decade by a succession of mayoral administrations. But he was aware of everything going on around him, as he kept his eyes on the windows of nearby buildings and on the street.

Batman disliked wearing the cape and cowl out in the open during the day. Unlike the other members of the League, he was only human. Trained to the peak of human capacity, true, but he had normal DNA and no special strength or power or weapon to give him an edge over the criminals and madmen he made it his business to bring to justice.

His edge was the myth, the darkness of the night, the fear that his presence brought out in people. In the years since the murder of his parents, and the vow he had made to himself to combat crime in Gotham City,

Bruce Wayne had crafted for himself an urban legend called the Batman. Those who believed Batman existed knew the vigilante as grim and merciless. But it was the uncertainty, the idea that Batman might well be a supernatural creature, that made them all hesitate.

In order to perpetuate that, he avoided being photographed whenever possible. And when circumstances demanded he be in costume during daylight hours, he did his best to move in secrecy.

He crouched now at the edge of the roof and studied the face of the building immediately across from Saxonville Hats. Like many of the old brick structures in the garment district it had been converted to apartments years ago. The fourth floor, third window from the left, was the bedroom of Zachary Graff, a thirty-three-year-old train conductor whose long runs often left him with layover days in Gotham City.

Graff had been killing people in Gotham, homeless men and women who'd found shelter in one of the city's train stations. The trainman would douse them with gasoline while they were sleeping and then set them on fire.

The first such murder had taken place while Batman was out of Gotham on League business. Circumstances conspired so that he was in the midst of containing a breakout from Arkham Asylum when the second killing had taken place. The night Graff took his third victim, Batman had been searching for him, patrolling Gotham with his usual vigilance but keeping an eye particularly on the train stations.

He had been in the eaves of North Square Station when it went down . . . all the way across the city in River Station.

People had been murdered. Innocents burned to death. By the time of the second killing Batman had eliminated as suspects any of the known arsonists in Gotham. He had trawled the homeless shelters trying to determine if there was anyone with motive, if the deceased had any enemies. Subsequent to the second burning he had established that there was no word of a stalker on the streets of Gotham. He had scoured the crime scenes several times, but even with the police cordon a busy train station was not going to hold onto evidence for very long.

What ate at him the most, this man who had turned himself into one of the world's foremost detectives, is that it had taken him so long to see that the real connection was not the homelessness of the victims, but the location of their murders, the comings and goings of the trains. The evening of the third murder he had already begun to examine digital video from security cameras and employee work schedules from those days.

The morning after the third murder, Batman had identified Zachary Graff as his primary suspect. It weighed heavily upon him that it had been too late to save that third victim—Henry Louis Bottoms, fifty-seven years of age, ironically a former train conductor himself before alcoholism cost him his job and his family—but Batman was determined that Bottoms would be the last.

Hub City. Far from home in Gotham. Out in the daylight in costume, the cape settled around him like a shroud as he crouched there on the edge of the building. Nothing moved in the window of Zachary Graff's apartment. Nothing at all. Batman settled in and waited, gaze taking in every detail, every car that passed, every kid that went by on a skateboard. School would have just gotten out, but there had been kids on the street earlier, kids who had not bothered to go to school.

His head turned only slightly as he scanned the street and the faces of the buildings. Left. Right. Left. On the next sweep, Batman froze. In the doorway of a smaller, better restored apartment building next to Graff's there stood a man in a dark suit, set back in the shadow of that doorway, out of the sun. Lingering. Watching.

Batman's eyes narrowed. Who else was keeping an eye out for Graff? Or was this mere coincidence, and not someone looking for the killer at all? He studied the overall build of the man in the shadows and thought of Vic Sage. Sage was a reporter in Hub City, but he moonlighted as a vigilante himself. Batman did a quick visual calculation of height and weight and then frowned heavily. Not Sage.

A moving van rumbled down the street, hydraulic brakes shrieking as it reached a stop sign. A small group of teenagers moved through the neighborhood, smoking cigarettes and hanging on one another, strolling and laughing and looking tough. All attitude, but Batman read no real trouble in their body language.

The man in the doorway stepped out into the light. Even from this distance Batman knew him immediately. The face belonged to a private detective named John Jones. Of course, the face was not real. It was, in its way, as much a mask as the cowl Batman wore to disguise his own features. John Jones did not exist; not really. Though he had been a police detective, and now continued to take certain cases in private, Jones was just one of dozens of identities used by J'onn J'onzz, one of the few survivors of an ancient Martian civilization.

Once upon a time Batman would have had a difficult time believing such a thing, but in the years since he had first dedicated himself to his cause he had seen things far more extraordinary. Extraterrestrial life seemed almost commonplace to him now.

On his homeworld, J'onn had been the equivalent of a policeman.

On Earth, the Martian Manhunter was a founding member of the Justice League and the only individual to have been numbered among its ranks during the entirety of the League's decade-long history. Though he never seemed to garner the kind of attention Superman or Wonder Woman did, J'onn was in many ways the heart and soul of the League. He was also a powerhouse in his own right.

The power of the Martian Manhunter's mind was extraordinary. He was a telepath, a shapeshifter, and able to control his molecular structure to the point where he could alter his physical density and even become invisible. He could fly. He could channel blasts of destructive energy through his eyes. Yet there was more to J'onn than power. He was a gentle being, a philosopher and scientist.

Not to mention a skilled detective.

Under normal circumstances Batman preferred to work alone whenever possible. And when it was not possible, he preferred to run the game, to call the plays. This was not an issue of ego, but of survival. If he understood and manipulated all of the variables in a given event, he could control the outcome. He could stay alive.

Batman did not like variables.

Still, J'onn—or John Jones—had obviously been hired either to investigate the burnings in Gotham or to look into Zachary Graff without being aware Graff was a serial killer. It was possible there was another reason for the Martian Manhunter to be on that particular street in Hub City on that very day, but the odds were infinitesimal.

With a glance around the roof and then across the street, Batman mentally calculated the distance and the wind speed, working out what it would take for him to get across to the other building and down into the street with J'onn without being too conspicuous. He reached for his belt and unclipped the grapple-gun, already eyeing the ledge he would have to target to swing out over the street, and the parked SUV whose roof he would land on, breaking some of his momentum before somersaulting to the ground only feet from where J'onn stood. There was a chance he'd seen, but very little that Graff would witness this move.

And it would be better if he and J'onn worked together on this.

The circumstances needed to be controlled.

Batman rose up from his place beside the vent column and extended his hand, thumb on the trigger of the grapple-gun.

Zachary Graff's bedroom window exploded outward in the blast from a shotgun, the report from the weapon echoing off the faces of buildings up and down the street.

Batman was in motion before the echo died.

The Princess Diana relished the feeling of the wind in her hair and the beauty of the city of Paris sprawled far below her, the many lanterns and streetlamps along the boulevards and the banks of the River Seine more than earning the nickname "City of Lights." Side by side she hovered in the air with Superman, the two of them scanning the city, with particular attention paid to the river.

The Notre Dame cathedral stood on the river's edge, its majesty undeniable. The Louvre called to Diana, as did so many other, smaller museums—Musée d'Orsay, the Rodin Museum—and she gazed across the city to the stark white steeple of Sacré-Coeur, high atop Montmarte, spotlights like beacons calling to her.

"You know, Kal," she said, "this is not the way I'd prefer to pass time in Paris."

Superman looked up, focusing on her for the first time in several minutes. His expression was grim, the frustration showing on his face even in profile. In the dark he seemed to be clad in shadow, save for the red cape, and even that seemed too dark now.

"I know, Diana. But the French ambassador specifically asked for Superman and Wonder Woman. And if these monster tales are true, there's good reason for us to be here."

He put the weight on the word *if* and Diana knew why. There had been dozens of attacks in Paris in the previous week, seven of them ending in death. According to eyewitnesses and survivors, the perpetrators of this violence were not human, but rather horrible monstrosities that reportedly had emerged from and later retreated into the Seine. But Superman and Wonder Woman had spent more than two hours flying low over the river and seen no trace of anything out of the ordinary.

Now dusk had come and gone.

"True," she admitted. "But it would have made much more sense for Arthur to come along."

Superman nodded. "But the French government doesn't like Atlantean politics, so there was no way they were going to ask Aquaman for help."

There was no arguing the truth of that, but Diana still could not help but think Arthur would have been helpful here. If there was anything in the Seine, they had not found it. They would likely stay another hour or so, make another pass over the river in case the creatures had suddenly decided they were solely nocturnal. And then they would return to the Watchtower before finally going home.

"Another pass?" she suggested.

Superman nodded. "One more. I hate the idea of leaving without having resolved this."

"If we don't find any monsters, there's not a lot we can do."

They set off again, flying slowly, two figures silhouetted against the night sky, following the river as it flowed through Paris. After several minutes of silent introspection, Superman glanced at her.

"It really is a beautiful city. When we're done, if you want, we could have dinner before we go back to the Watchtower."

Wonder Woman smiled. "You don't want to ruin your dinner, *Clark*. I don't need Lois mad at me."

Superman raised an eyebrow but returned his attention to the river below. Most of the time Diana called him Kal, which was short for his birth name, Kal-El. Though he looked completely human, Superman was the last son of Krypton, the only survivor from a planet that had destroyed itself years ago. As a baby, his parents had sent him to Earth so that he might escape the destruction of Krypton. He had been discovered by a kind, childless couple, the Kents, who had raised him on their Kansas farm.

To the world, Kal-El was Clark Kent, a reporter for Metropolis's major newspaper, the *Daily Planet*. His wife, Lois Lane, was also a reporter there. Though Lois knew, of course, that her husband was Superman, somehow they managed to rise above the pressures of the journalistic profession and the chaos that his heroism inevitably brought them, and to live a comparatively normal life.

Diana thought it was sort of precious, but only in the best possible way. Kal was her best friend in the world, and other than Lois, she was his. She was glad they were happy. Most of the time she called him Kal because to her, that was who he was. Superman never complained, never asked her to call him Clark. And when she did, it was always to tease him, to remind him of the irony that the individual the world called Superman was also Clark Kent, farmboy from Kansas, who liked to make pancakes for his wife on Sunday mornings.

Now Superman smiled at her. "Dinner in Metropolis isn't for many hours yet, Diana. And Lois is working on a story that's driving her crazy, so more than likely it will be me bringing home pizza. I don't think she'll mind. Of course, she'll be jealous that I was in Paris without her, but I can always bring her over when she's done with the piece she's working on."

Wonder Woman shifted in the air, turning slightly and descending toward the water. Something had caught her eye. Not a boat and not litter carelessly tossed away by a tourist. Something under the water, dark and moving swiftly beneath the surface.

"Kal," she began.

"I see it," he replied.

A scream tore through the darkness above the City of Lights.

CHAPTER TWO

That first single, horrifying scream was followed almost immediately by another. The same voice, yet laden with even greater horror. This was not a cry for help but the plaintive wail of a woman who in her mind had already surrendered her life to whatever terror she now faced.

Superman glanced once at Wonder Woman, who nodded. Without J'onn there was no telepathic connection between them. And yet in cases like this, these two old friends did not need telepathy.

"I'll take the river," Diana told him. "You get the screamer." Then she was off, diving toward the water almost too quickly even for his eyes to follow.

He reversed direction with scarcely a thought and propelled himself through the Paris night, back along the river. The scream lingered in the air as it did in his ears. He was able instantly to pinpoint her location. He saw her, heard her, even from this distance. A slender, petite woman of perhaps twenty, she wore a light spring dress and her dark hair was cut stylishly short.

Her fine features were contorted into a mask of fear as she ran across the Pont Neuf, the oldest bridge spanning the Seine. Her hands flailed wildly as though she was batting at a cloud of mosquitoes and she kicked off her shoes as she ran. The things that pursued her were humanoid in shape but in every other way they were monstrous. Their flesh was covered in red-black scales. Each had a single fin that began at the tip of its nose and ran up over its skull and down its back, where it thinned into a flat tail that must have aided its propulsion in the water. Their mouths were filled with needle fangs like a moray eel's. Their hands were long and thin, webbed between the fingers and tipped with vicious looking talons.

Three of the monsters chased her across the bridge but they were not alone; others were crawling up the sides of the bridge from the water. Now a chorus of other voices chimed in. People on the far side of the river began to point and cry out and scatter, wanting to help but unwilling to face the creatures themselves.

In a single instant, Superman took it all in. Before she could take another step, he was there. The lights along the bridge threw a warm yellow glow upon him as he descended, hovering in the air between the river monsters and their prey.

"No more," he said, his voice carrying to both sides of the river.

The creatures paused and glared at him. Several

others scrabbled up over the sides of the bridge and landed on the stone beside their kin. The woman they had been chasing let out a cry of relief and spoke his name. Superman kept his back to the woman and the other people who had massed on that side of the bridge.

The reptilian river monsters crouched and began to approach him, hissing, long tongues darting from their mouths. Their tails scraped against the stone of the bridge with a sound like sandpaper. There were seven of them now. If there had been anyone walking on the other side of the bridge, they had taken cover. But there was a Metro station behind the creatures, perhaps thirty feet away, and at any moment people were going to get off a subway train and come up the steps to find the bridge overrun by these things.

"Stop where you are and surrender yourselves," he told the creatures, and then he repeated it in French. There was no way to tell if they understood human language at all, but he had to try.

The creatures hissed and the air filled with the sound as though he had fallen into a nest of vipers. Then, as one, they lunged at him. He had been flying a few feet in the air the entire time but now he let his feet touch the ground, alighting upon the bridge and simply waiting for the creatures to attack him. Better to have them all in one place, to be the bait, than let one of them pass by and attack the spectators who were gathering.

Lights flashed and he realized that tourists were taking pictures.

Superman sighed. These things were savage killers, but with him there the people felt safe. Suddenly it had become a show to them. Didn't they understand how foolish that was? What would happen if just one of them got away? That was always the case, however. The very faith the people of the world put in him made it that much harder to do his job.

Yellow reptile eyes flashed in the night. Talons sliced the air as the things reached out for him, ready to tear him open.

He dodged the first swipe and ignored the others. Claws broke on his dense skin. Superman hit the first one in the temple and clutched the throat of a second. When the first one did not immediately crumble to the ground he knew they were more powerful than he had guessed, but he could not afford to assume. If he assumed, he might kill them, and that was never his first recourse.

With a barrage of lightning fast blows he lashed out at them, carefully modulating his strength. One by one they fell, unconscious but alive, to the stone floor of the bridge.

People began to emerge from the Metro station. A grizzled, white-haired man with a cigarette dangling from his mouth stepped out, eyes wide, and swore loudly.

The thing nearest the train station spun toward the sound and then lunged after the white-haired man, who staggered backward, cigarette dropping out of his mouth. Superman had time to knock another of the creatures unconscious and then he zipped across the bridge and grabbed the thing by its tail. It came up short just a few inches from the man, its jaws snapping and gnashing at the air in frustration.

He struck its temple, knocking it out.

Police sirens wailed in the distance. That was good. They would be able to cage these things before anything else—

Sandpaper on stone.

Superman turned and saw that one of the things he had knocked down had gotten back up. It sprang to the stone rail of the bridge and leaped down into the river, barely making a splash as it knifed into the water. Superman looked at the old man.

"Make sure the police gather the rest," he said in French.

The man still looked stunned but he was not about to let the monster go. There was no way to tell how many of these things were living in the river, but even one of them put the people of Paris in peril. Superman dove over the side of the bridge, propelling himself into the water. It was dark beneath the surface of the river, but his vision was superhuman. He spotted the thing swimming away—its speed in the water was extraordinary—and held his breath as he went after it.

His hands clasped it by the tail. The thing flailed, bent backward and tried to claw him.

Superman flew upward, bursting from the Seine with the thing dangling by its tail beneath him. It was kicking and trying to free itself, but at the moment it was the least of his concerns. He had seen others down there. Drainage grates were broken and yellow eyes had glowed inside those pipes.

How many? he thought, a sick feeling growing in the pit of his stomach. Even if they scoured the river, how could they be sure they had gotten them all? Where else did those pipes lead?

He glanced back at the Pont Neuf. The other six he had knocked unconscious remained so. Lights spun on top of Paris police vehicles. But none of those people who massed now on either side of the river were safe.

The thing in his grasp continued to kick and hiss.

Superman peered up the river, searching for Wonder Woman. Diana had gone into the water after things they had seen swimming under the surface, but now that he realized what kind of odds they were dealing with, he was concerned. Diana was one of the strongest, never mind most intelligent and capable, individuals in the world, but even she could not breathe underwater.

Still trailing the monster beneath him he flew back to the spot where he had parted from Wonder Woman. There was no sign of her and he began to worry. He stared at the river, able to see beneath the surface if he focused. When they had scoured the Seine earlier there had been no sign of anything unusual. Now there were dozens of *things* in the water.

Diana.

They were dragging her along the river bottom. Superman shot toward the water, still towing the creature behind him. That same moment, the surface

of the river erupted as Wonder Woman threw off her
attackers, one of them tumbling through the air to
slam into the riverbank with a crack of bone. Diana
thrashed them, shouting in fury, raven hair plastered
wetly across her face. She was a warrior born, the
Princess of the Amazons, and these abominations had
attacked her at their peril.

Superman paused in the air, thoughts awhirl. Wonder Woman could protect herself, but there were far
too many of these things. Again he wondered how
they could rid Paris of this infestation. Diana was
above the rushing river. The monsters leaped from the
river, slashing at her with their talons, and she kicked
them away, jaws and fangs shattering.

"Hello there!" a voice carried across the river. "You
look as if you could use a hand."

Startled, Superman spun to see where the voice
had originated. The woman who stood at the railing by
the riverbank was tall and powerfully built. Her chest-
nut brown hair was swept back in a ponytail, her eyes
were a crystal blue, and her accent identified her as
British . . . or more accurately Welsh. She had kind,
open features. He would have guessed her age at perhaps twenty-five.

She raised her hands and pointed at the water. The
smile disappeared from her face and she frowned in
concentration, twitched as though she was in pain.

The river started to boil.

The savage, reptilian horrors that lurked in that
water began to shriek in agony, to blister, and to die.

*   *   *

The shotgun blast echoed off the old Saxonville Hat building. Pigeons fluttered off of the roof, wings beating the air in a panic. Detective John Jones ran along the sidewalk toward the converted apartment building he had been watching and as he ran, he turned invisible.

Unseen by anyone who might have peered out a window at the noise of the shotgun blast or passing by in a car, J'onn J'onzz shapeshifted, his flesh and clothing transforming completely as he once more took on the familiar form of the Martian Manhunter. He took flight, then, rising quickly to the shattered window from which the gunshot had come.

Batman beat him to it.

J'onn sensed his comrade's presence the moment before Batman would have collided with his invisible form. He shunted himself aside and glanced around even as Batman retracted the cable upon which he had swung across the street, tucked his head and knees to his body, and somersaulted through the jagged-edged window.

It was always jarring, seeing him out during the day.

J'onn followed him in silently, floating through the window and willing himself to become visible again. The bedroom was empty save for the Batman, who leaped across the bed to the door and stood listening a moment. When the Martian Manhunter's boots touched the grimy carpet, Batman hesitated.

"Hello, J'onn," he said.

The Martian Manhunter smiled. "I thought I was the telepath."

Batman did not respond. A door banged open and shouts came from the corridor outside the apartment. The two Justice Leaguers ran through the apartment to find its door wide open. The stairs shook with pounding footsteps, two men, heading up.

Another shotgun blast resounded through the building, punctuated by the sound of shot tearing through wood and a grunt, but no cry of pain. Batman hit the stairs, heading up, and J'onn was right behind him. The two men had a significant head start on them.

The one fleeing will attempt to reach the roof, J'onn thought, telepathically projecting his words to Batman. *I will cut him off there.*

Batman neither spoke nor formed mental words to respond, but J'onn sensed his assent. The Martian Manhunter had complete control over his physical form and now he altered his density, changed his body on a molecular level to the point where he was intangible. Like a ghost he floated upward through the ceiling. As he passed through the building he saw that the two men were further ahead of Batman than he had imagined.

On the top floor he caught up with them. In any circumstance he would have expected to find an unarmed man running from the man with the shotgun. That was not the case. Rather, Zachary Graff carried the shotgun in front of him as he raced along the top floor corridor to the short stairwell that led up to the roof. As J'onn passed through that floor he saw Graff stumble up those few stairs, pump the shotgun, and blow out the lock on the door to the roof.

The door flew open and Graff burst out into the daylight that streamed in.

J'onn paused a moment to watch Graff's pursuer curiously. His jacket and the cotton shirt beneath had been shredded by the shotgun, but his skin was unmarred. The weapon had had as little effect upon this man as it would have had upon Superman. J'onn took this in with fascination, for it had been this man he had been following.

John Jones had been hired by the daughter of one of the homeless men murdered in Gotham City. Her father had disappeared years ago and she had only learned of his death from the authorities in Gotham; she had never known he was homeless, always believing he had simply lost interest in his family. The blow had broken her heart. J'onn had been incapable of turning the case down.

It also gave him an opportunity to put Bryan Francis to the test. Mr. Francis had put the word out on the street, let the private investigation community know that he was available as a consultant. His talent, according to the man himself, was psychometry . . . the ability to locate anyone or anything by simply touching something that has come into contact with the missing person or thing. He *read* objects. Or so he had said.

As Bryan stalked along the corridor now, pursuing Zachary Graff to the roof, J'onn nodded to himself. Using a crucifix found on the dead man's body, Bryan had tracked the serial killer to his lair. J'onn had read both Graff's name and his guilt in the murderer's mind. Bryan had obviously been telling the truth. But not all of it.

He had not mentioned invulnerability.

J'onn passed through the ceiling above him. On the roof he saw Graff swing the shotgun barrel toward the open door. The blue-black metal glinted in the sunlight of that spring day and a breeze blew the murderer's thinning hair back from his wide, terrified eyes.

Bryan came through the door.

Graff fired on an empty barrel. The shotgun was out of shells. The murderer dropped it and in one fluid motion retrieved a jagged knife that had been in a sheath strapped to his ankle.

Bryan laughed. "Look, mate, give it up already," the Englishman said. "You tried the bloody shotgun, you silly git. You think a blade's gonna do any more damage than that?"

Graff spat, and then laughed, more than a little lunacy in his voice. "Which one are you? Where's your costume?"

Bryan shrugged. "Don't need one. Not a soddin' superhero, am I?"

J'onn was about to make himself tangible and visible again, but in that moment Batman appeared in the shadows of the stairwell that led back down into the building. With the brightness of the sunlight on the roof, Batman seemed little more than a wraith cloaked in the darkness within.

"No," Batman said, his voice a rasp of gravel. "You're not."

The Martian Manhunter saw Graff's eyes widen in fear. The killer shuddered and took a step backward. Bryan Francis reacted somewhat differently. The psychometrist spun at the sound of that threatening voice, saw Batman in the shadows, and began to laugh.

"Excellent," Bryan said. "Well now, what've we here? Read about you in the papers, I did. Batman, yeah? Can't say I'm surprised to see you. Figured it was only a matter of time before one of you blokes in spandex came sniffing about." He tapped his chest where the clothes were torn but the flesh was intact. "Bit of a stupid power, innit? Invulnerability. Nice if you're a clumsy oaf like myself, keeps me from breaking my nose when I trip down the stairs. But it's the psychometry that's useful, I must tell you."

The dark wraith in cape and cowl growled. "Who the hell are you?"

Bryan was about to respond. But Zachary Graff had not spent the previous moments in terror. His initial fear after Batman's appearance had evaporated the moment he saw Bryan turn his back. Then Graff flexed his fingers around the hilt of the knife and rushed at Bryan, intending to stab him from behind.

The Martian Manhunter shrugged off his invisibility, his green skin the bright hue of maple leaves in the sunshine. Graff spun as J'onn reached for him, brought the knife down toward the Martian Manhunter's chest. J'onn grabbed the man's wrist, arresting the descent of the blade, and squeezed until the killer released his weapon.

The Martian Manhunter effortlessly turned Graff's arm behind his back and drove him to the roof, holding him there.

J'onn glanced up to find Bryan staring at him.

"Oi, I know you," the psychometrist said. "The Manhunter from Mars. From the Justice League, like. Look, nice to meet you an' all, but really, I had this under control, and I'm not lookin' to put on a mask, right?"

The Martian glared down at Graff. "Remain where you are. Lace your hands behind your head."

The serial killer did as he had been instructed. J'onn stood and crossed his arms, regarding Bryan sternly.

"The Justice League is not recruiting, Mr. Francis. And even were we, rest assured you are not under consideration for membership at this time."

The man looked miffed. He scratched at the back of his neck, where his close-cropped blond hair was the shortest, barely peach fuzz. "Why not? What's wrong with me? Not good enough for you? Or not weird enough? League's got no problem with aliens, that's plain. Fish-men. Freaks. M'I too normal, then? Or do I have to practice my lurking and the scary voice?"

Bryan hooked a thumb toward the doorway leading down into the building, but when he and J'onn glanced over there were only shadows there now.

Batman was gone.

Not that J'onn was surprised. It was daytime. The police would be coming, neighbors would be poking their heads out of apartments. Batman would want to disappear as quickly and completely as possible. It was part of who he was.

Bryan stared for a moment, unnerved by Batman's disappearance.

When he turned back, for the first time he seemed uncomfortable under the severe gaze of the Martian Manhunter.

"Your employer in this case instructed you to locate the perpetrator, not to confront him. Not to act as a vigilante and attempt to capture him. You also did not reveal your invulnerability. Despite your protestations, clearly you desire a certain amount of attention for your behavior and your gifts. But maverick antics such as this are only going to get you killed."

"Yeah, thanks for the advice," Bryan said. Then he paused, narrowing his eyes. "How do you know what I did and didn't tell my employer on this? How the hell'd you even get involved in this thing?"

"I know a great many things," J'onn replied. He doubted anyone would make a connection between John Jones, private detective, and the Martian Manhunter, but he was not about to spell it out either.

"You will stay and wait for the authorities to arrive and give a statement when they take Mr. Graff into custody?" J'onn asked.

Bryan sighed. "Yeah. All right. 'Course I'll stay." Then he shot a quizzical glance at J'onn. "Not even on the JLA's list, then?"

J'onn thought about that a moment. Then he raised an eyebrow. "We are . . . aware of you, Mr. Francis." He added just enough weight to his words so that

Bryan would never be certain if this awareness held promise or warning.

Bryan nodded once. "Good enough."

Green Lantern wasn't having fun anymore. From the start this had looked like a simple gig. Nut job with powers of spatial displacement—maybe even dimensional displacement—opens up a sinkhole in the street in front of Buckingham Palace, people fall in. Should've been a cakewalk. He was Green Lantern, after all. The energy that sprang from that ring was limited only by the boundaries of his imagination and Kyle Rayner, illustrator, was a pretty damned imaginative guy.

He wasn't alone, either. When he had seen the report come up while doing monitor duty in the Womb on the Watchtower, he had called in the Flash. They were members of the Justice League, two of the most powerful heroes in the world, against a skinny, white-haired old gent with glasses and an obsession with getting the Queen to knight him.

Not that he'd bothered to mention exactly what he had done to earn a knighthood.

It should have been simple. But now everything had gone wrong. The nut job had projected a maelstrom like the one on the ground into the air right in front of Flash. Wally had not been able to avoid running into it, and now he had disappeared into that swirling gray nothing.

Green Lantern was using his ring to try to grab hold of the old Scottish dude responsible for all of this, but he had torn open another portal that had drawn in the tendrils of green power Kyle had sent lunging for him and now it seemed to be pulling on the ring. The whirlpool that hung there in the air above the street was like a sucking chest wound in reality, bending light and vision at its edges, and it drew on the power of the ring, leeching at it, and Green Lantern was being drawn toward the maelstrom as well.

Three of them. The guy had opened three of them. The one in the ground had begun to expand again. People shouted and scrambled away in panic. Behind the gates of Buckingham the Palace Guard raised their guns and began to shoot.

"No!" Kyle snapped.

He willed a shield of green energy into existence. It stopped the bullets, stealing their velocity so they fell to the ground instead of ricocheting, which might have endangered the onlookers. There had to be a better way to end this than anybody dying . . . assuming the people inside the maelstrom weren't dead already.

But he wasn't going to think about that. Wally was in there.

A bicycle that had been abandoned by its rider lay on the pavement at the edge of the widening maelstrom. The blur of reality, that abyss that swirled around in the middle of the street, ate away more of the road and the bicycle tumbled away into the void.

"Ten seconds more! I'll be a knight, or there'll be no Queen!" the old man shouted madly.

With a grunt, Green Lantern shook himself, took

control of his will once more. He snapped his wrist, cutting off the drain on his ring. The maelstrom that the old man had created to sap it closed with the abruptness of a bubble bursting.

Kyle's eyes widened. They were that fragile? He could not allow the others to close like that, not until he retrieved the people that had been swallowed by the hole in the street.

"Look, just cut it out!" he called to the old man. "Let's talk about this, okay? I'm with the Justice League. We can sit down with the Prime Minister, maybe get a dialogue going, see if we can—"

With a dismissive flick of his wrist the old man opened yet another maelstrom. This one began small but blossomed wider, and stretched out toward Green Lantern as though intending to swallow him alive. Kyle was through holding back. The guy might look frail, but he was too dangerous to be careful with anymore.

All it took was a mental picture in his mind. Instinctively, the ring obeyed. A flash of green light burst across the evening twilight and a stream of energy flowed from the ring. Kyle used the power of the ring to form a spherical cage around the old man and the abyss he had torn in the world and sent buzzing voraciously toward him.

The new maelstrom, this slip in reality, collided with the ring's power and tried to siphon it again, tried to swallow it, but could not. The swirling abyss only slipped along the inside of the sphere, trying to spread and grow but contained within.

A bead of sweat ran down Kyle's forehead and he grunted with exertion. If the thing really was a rip in reality, it was like a black hole or something. It was sucking at the ring's energy, trying to make a hole in the sphere to slip through, trying to draw that green power into whatever horrid limbo world lay on the other side.

I can hold him, Kyle thought. It took him a moment to believe it, but then the difficulty of keeping the sphere intact lessened. The old man glared at him through the globe of green light and Kyle knew that he had won. He had captured the creator of these bizarre portals.

Now what? He could probe the maelstroms with his ring for those who were missing, but if he lost his focus the old man might escape and start trouble all over again. And if he kept him captive too long, there was no guarantee the maelstroms wouldn't just collapse, after which there might not be any way to—

"You just going to look at him? Thinking about pulling his wings off?"

Green Lantern glanced down and saw the Flash below him. Wally's red uniform was dark but the yellow lightning bolt on his chest stood out even in the early evening light.

"Wally?" Kyle's eyes widened. "How did you get out?"

"Ian."

The old man inside the sphere began to pound on it with his fists, losing control completely. He shouted and pointed in a rage, but Green Lantern could not hear him and he was still trying to register the fact that Flash was still alive.

"Who's Ian?" Kyle asked.

The Flash pointed toward the dark, swirling abyss in the street. On the edge of the maelstrom a man hung several inches off the ground, his body swathed in what appeared to be a web of electricity. He had his hands in the air as though he were an orchestra conductor. As Green Lantern watched, a grim-faced member of the Palace Guard appeared from out of the maelstrom carrying a pretty Middle Eastern girl in his arms, her eyes squinted shut, squeezing out tears. Both of them had that same static electricity crackling all over their bodies.

Next was a well-dressed older woman who had her hand clamped over her mouth as if to keep from screaming. Others followed. Kyle watched in fascination as this good-looking young guy with the spiky, just-cut hair, dressed as well as any store window mannequin, continued to pluck people from the abyss into which they had fallen.

For a long moment, Green Lantern only watched. In a blur of red, Flash zipped amongst those Ian had rescued, checking on them, making sure they were all right. Their rescuer looked relaxed, laid back even. He had a grin on his face as he withdrew the lost bicycle, a silent signal that no one else remained in that limbo world.

Green Lantern felt the pressure inside his energy sphere change.

Alarmed, snapped back to the danger of the situation, he whipped around to find that the old man was at it again. The white-haired would-be knight drew a circle in the air inside that emerald cage. Kyle watched in horror, really paying attention for the first time as reality crumbled inside the circle the old man had drawn. It fell in upon itself and began to wash outward.

This newest maelstrom grew and grew and began to force itself against the sphere. The power of the ring contained it, but not without effort on Green Lantern's part.

Inside the energy sphere, the old man gazed up at Green Lantern and sneered, then walked right into the maelstrom of his own creation, disappearing inside the abyss.

The pressure in the air itself seemed to flex upward and abruptly all of the voids the madman had created stopped swirling. The one inside the green sphere blinked out. The pavement in front of Buckingham Palace became solid again, but there Kyle could actually *see* reality taking shape once more. It was more than a little disconcerting.

He withdrew the sphere's energy into the ring and lowered himself to the ground. The maelstrom was gone but the police cordon was still in place and even if it weren't, Kyle had a feeling nobody would be interested in testing out the ground's apparent new solidity.

Green Lantern alighted in the precise center of what had seconds before been utter nothingness. Flash came out to greet him, along with the guy who had saved all of those people. For a moment Kyle felt almost put out at the idea that this guy had just stepped into the situation and made himself a hero. Then he realized how ridiculous that was. The man had saved lives and the moment Flash introduced them, Kyle could not help but like him.

"Green Lantern, meet Ian Partington. Our unexpected backup tonight," the Flash said. "Ian. The Green Lantern."

"Nice going," Kyle said. "Thanks for the assist."

Ian waved the words away. "Nah. Just glad we got it sorted," he said with an easy chuckle. "Look, you lads fancy a pint? They'll never believe this down at the pub otherwise."

CHAPTER THREE

It would have been easy to think of the conference room as the heart of the Justice League Watchtower and, in truth, J'onn thought it was likely many of the others thought of it that way. It was where the League met, after all, where decisions were made and new members inducted, where debates were settled and tragedies mourned. But the Martian Manhunter always believed that the Monitor Womb was the heart of the place, for it represented everything that the League stood for. This was where these individuals—gifted with power that could change the world—watched over the planet they had sworn to protect.

Green Lantern served Monitor duty more often than anyone else. It seemed that Kyle had more time on his hands or was more willing, though much of his time on duty was spent pilfering J'onn's secret cache of Oreos and watching reruns of *The Sopranos*. Still, J'onn sensed that Green Lantern felt it, too, this sense

of purpose that was stronger in the Womb than anywhere else in the Watchtower.

The chamber was small by comparison to the rest
of the Watchtower, the high walls lined with screens
showing news reports worldwide, not merely CNN
and MSNBC, but signals broadcast from Moscow,
Paris, Baghdad, and Rio, among hundreds of others.
The Monitor Womb had direct links to the United Nations, Interpol, the FBI, and other national and worldwide law enforcement agencies.

When J'onn was not on a mission or on Monitor
duty he spent most of his time in one of the myriad
identities he had established around the world, studying the human race he had come to love and admire
so much, discovering something new about them
with every passing day. He had seen the worst horrors the species had to offer but that did not erase the
extraordinary beauty he found in their diversity and
imagination. His passion for his adopted homeworld
made his time on Monitor duty all the more precious
to him. When he was in the Womb he was the care-
taker of the world and he approached this charge
with grim sincerity.

The days and weeks were a string of crises, from a
single life in jeopardy to threats on a galactic scale.
The Justice League faced them all. Yet the individual
members of the League had lives of their own. Arthur
was the King of Atlantis, an entire nation beneath the
ocean surface, and Wonder Woman was Princess of
Themyscira. Superman and Flash had wives and
Green Lantern a girlfriend. Both Clark and Kyle had

jobs. Batman left the running of his corporation to others for the most part, but he bore the weight of an entire city upon his shoulders. Everything that transpired in Gotham was his business, every crime that went unhindered a failure in his mind. The burden of that was extraordinary, and yet still he found time to serve the goals of the League.

J'onn had many lives and yet all of them were, more or less, disguises. He had been there at the beginning, at the founding of the League, and through all of the various changes in its roster over the years since. They relied upon him to maintain focus, and he did so. As part of that focus, he did not merely serve duty in the Monitor Womb, but searched constantly for patterns of events, for early warning that small crises might develop into larger ones.

Such a pattern was emerging now. He was simply not certain what to make of it as yet.

J'onn sensed Aquaman's arrival even before the Atlantean cleared his throat. The Martian Manhunter turned the Monitor chair around to face the entrance to the womb and saw him there, silhouetted in the light from beyond the doorway. Whenever a new metahuman being appeared in public for the first time the media seemed in a race to craft an appropriate new appellation . . . at least, when the metahuman had not already coined one for him or herself. In the case of "Aquaman," this tradition had produced unfortunate results. Yet Arthur Curry never seemed to be bothered by the name. In truth, for the most part, he ignored it.

"Hello, J'onn," Arthur said, stepping into the Womb, his footfall heavy with the extreme body density necessary for him to survive in the ocean depths.

"Arthur?" J'onn replied, raising a curious brow.

The two had been part of the quintet that had founded the League—along with Barry Allen, Hal Jordan, and Black Canary—but they had never understood one another. Arthur's relationship with humanity was fundamentally antagonistic and J'onn's was anything but. Arthur was a king, J'onn a willing servant to his own ideals. Over the course of a decade they had rarely spoken beyond the scope of their duties with the League.

"I am taking the next shift in the Womb," Aquaman explained.

J'onn almost smiled. Arthur's long blond hair and full beard gave him the air of an ancient Viking. His Atlantean clothing was appropriately regal and his severed left hand had been replaced by a cybernetic substitute. In his way, Arthur could be even more imposing than Batman. J'onn was the tallest member of the League and by appearances the most inhuman, yet it was Arthur who seemed the most out of place performing a duty as seemingly tedious as manning the Monitor Womb.

"I see," J'onn replied, for lack of any better response. "It has been quiet. Hopefully it shall continue to be so."

Arthur made no move toward the chair to relieve him of duty so J'onn did not rise from his position yet. There was something odd in Aquaman's bearing and the way his brows knitted. The Atlantean monarch was troubled. J'onn could have sifted the upper levels of his consciousness to determine what was bothering his comrade, but he tried to allow other beings as much privacy as a telepath was capable of providing.

"Quiet today," Aquaman noted. "But anything would seem quiet in comparison to yesterday."

J'onn nodded. "You've read the reports, then?"

For a long moment, Arthur did not respond. At length he nodded.

"What is troubling you, Arthur?"

Aquaman's eyes narrowed and he scratched at his beard. When he spoke, as always, it was with the strangest, most indefinable accent. That was the one thing they had in common, J'onn knew. Their voices were very different, but each had a strangely lyrical accent, no matter what language they spoke. Of course, Arthur still had Atlanteans with whom to speak his native tongue. There were no Martians left for J'onn to speak with.

"Did Flash and Green Lantern really go out for drinks with this Ian Partington?" Aquaman asked.

J'onn gazed at him, wary of the judgmental tone in Arthur's voice. "They went to a café. For coffee. In civilian clothes."

Arthur seemed to consider that a moment. J'onn wondered why he had focused on that element rather than the more extraordinary facets of the previous day's events. Superman and Wonder Woman had provided as much information as they could about Julia Williams, the Welsh woman who had boiled the monsters that had been plaguing Paris in the River Seine. The French government seemed pleased with the outcome, but Kal-El and Diana had been careful to distance the League from such a radical solution. Likewise, J'onn and Batman had left the psychometrist, Bryan Francis, to turn the killer, Graff, in to the authorities.

"They'll all bear watching," Arthur said. "These new metahumans."

"Of course," J'onn agreed.

But Aquaman's troubled expression only deepened. "I assume you noted the connection. Francis. Williams. Partington. Even the one at Buckingham Palace, the one the papers are calling Maelstrom."

J'onn nodded. "They are all from the United Kingdom. How could I fail to notice?"

For a long moment the two merely stared at one another. Then Arthur took a step deeper into the Womb and J'onn rose from the Monitor chair. After Arthur had settled into it he turned away, beginning to scan the hundreds of screens in the Womb, apparently finished with the conversation and uninterested in something so trivial as a courteous goodbye.

Another day J'onn would have left without comment, neither expecting courtesy from Arthur nor offended by its absence. But this day he remained, watching Aquaman closely. At length Arthur turned around in the chair to regard him again.

"J'onn?"

"What is it that's troubling you, Arthur?"

Aquaman thought for a moment and then let out a

long breath he had been holding. "I'm not certain. I had occasion to be in the Gulf of Mexico last week. Something there was frightening the dolphin population. I encountered it. I believe I drove it off. A monster of some kind, with rough plating covering its hide. It was nothing I had ever seen before . . . and yet . . . "

"And yet?" J'onn asked.

Grimly, Arthur ran a hand across his bearded chin and his gaze became distant. "And yet there *was* something familiar about it."

There were police snipers on the roof of the building across from Five Hundred Park Place, the offices of the law firm of Lyons & Winter. Blue and white lights spun on top of police and emergency vehicles, throwing that city canyon into a flickering, eerie zoetrope of unfolding tension and danger. Beyond the limits of those flashing lights the shadows had grown deeper, darker. The eyes of spectators and police alike were on the windows of the five-story structure that houses Lyons & Winter and so no one noticed the figure slipping silently through the shadows.

In the midst of the chaos, Detective Renee Montoya turned her considerable fury on a bystander who was getting a little too eager with his camcorder. Montoya backed the man up, letting him know in no uncertain terms that if he tried to move beyond the cordon again he would regret it for all eternity. Disgust rippling across her features, Montoya began to turn back toward the negotiation team, the officers in charge of the scene.

Batman allowed her to see him.

Montoya paused, glanced around to see if she were being observed, and then casually moved through the crowd and made her way over to him. Batman had arrived on the scene only moments before, insinuating himself into the chaos without anyone noticing. The building across from Lyons & Winter had an underground parking garage and he observed the scene from the darkness of the ramp that ran beneath the building.

Now he waited as Montoya came to him.

"Glad you're here," the detective said quietly as she joined him in those shadows. Only someone who was expecting to see someone in the darkness of that garage ramp would have noticed them.

Batman gazed steadily at her. "Tell me."

Montoya looked back at the law offices. "Greg Rao. Didn't make partner. Apparently he thought he should have. Shots fired, which is how we got the call, but no confirmed DOA's. Office manager confirms at least three attorneys and four paralegals were still at work when it started."

"How do we know it's Rao?"

"Hostage negotiator's got him on the phone but he won't confirm anyone's dead or put any of the hostages on the line."

"What does he want?" Batman asked.

Montoya sighed and turned back to him. "He wants to be partner."

Batman nodded once, solemnly. If Rao had asked for money, transport out of the country, or anything that seemed logical, he might have allowed the police to continue to run the scene their way, holding back in case things got out of hand. But the man was so far gone, psychologically, that he believed that even after all this he could force the firm to make him partner. He had lost it.

"Keep him talking," Batman told her.

"Of course," Montoya replied, glancing at the law offices again.

By the time she turned to look back at him, Batman was gone and Detective Montoya was left alone in the shadows. He had slipped over the wall of the garage ramp and off into the night, and as he moved away he heard the detective mutter softly to herself about how much she hated it when he disappeared like that.

In less than two minutes, Batman was inside the law offices. Neither the police nor the shooter had seen him enter. He had established from watching the eyes of the officers in charge and the angle of the barrels of the snipers' rifles that the hostages were being kept on the third floor. But that was not his immediate destination. Instead he headed down, swiftly descending the stairs to the basement.

This was Gotham City, and the Batman knew its every street and building intimately. There were video cameras in the lobby but nowhere else. Once you passed the guards at the front desk, that was it. But Greg Rao was an employee. There would have been no reason for the guards to stop him. Lyons & Winter was an old, venerable law firm whose board had constructed this building in the late 1940s. The security and sprinkler systems had been added decades later and their controls were likely accessible from a security area on the first floor.

But the main power switch was in the basement.

Batman planted a tiny explosive on the power main, retrieving the miniature detonator from a compartment in his belt, and then he raced back up the stairs. The clock was ticking. Every second was another moment closer to Greg Rao becoming tired of negotiating with the police, another moment closer to him snapping completely.

In a case of assault or murder or robbery—and often when dealing with metahuman criminals—Batman could resort to a frontal assault. But he had no way of knowing what the situation was in the offices upstairs, where the hostages were on the third floor, where Rao was and what weapons he carried. He had heat-sensitive night vision goggles that would have allowed him to see all of those things from across the street, but had he attempted a frontal assault on the building it was possible the snipers would have taken a shot at him. By virtue of their job, snipers were on edge. A stray bullet meant for Batman could kill a hostage. No, he wanted to keep the snipers from having to fire at all.

He stood on the landing outside the door to the third floor and slipped the night vision goggles on. The detonator was the size and weight of a plastic domino in his hand. With his left, he reached out and grabbed hold of the doorknob.

His thumb touched the detonator. Soundlessly, the

power blew and the entire building was swallowed by darkness. There were shouts beyond the door and he slipped silently onto the third floor. The corridors were not completely dark, however. Where doors were open the lights of the city and the splash of blue from the police vehicles threw a dim illumination through office windows, spilling a kind of mist of light into the hall. Not that he needed it. With his night vision goggles he could have seen perfectly in complete darkness.

The shouts came from further along the corridor. Batman heard a whimper and heard the angry snap of a voice commanding the others to silence. That had to be Rao. He spotted the edge of the man's shoulder as Rao began to shuffle from one of the offices.

"Any of you try anything stupid and Bev's dead. I mean it, Terry. Move and you'll be killing her," Rao said, voice cracking in panic.

Batman slid quietly sideways into an open office and waited. Rao had made a serious mistake by gathering his hostages in the rear of the building. It meant that for him to figure out what was going on he had to move to the front, to look out through a window on the street side. Batman listened carefully. The awkward footfalls told him that Rao was dragging a hostage with him—likely "Bev"—and coming down the corridor. Chances were the snipers would not take a shot if Rao appeared in one of the windows with a human shield, particularly when they had no idea if anyone had been hurt, but Batman did not rely on chance.

"Bev, I'm sorry," he heard the broken man whisper

as he marched his hostage along the hall. "You know I never wanted this. I . . . we're friends, right? They screwed me. I couldn't just let it go."

Batman was completely still as Rao muscled the woman past the open door as though she were a marionette, a heavy Colt Python revolver pressed against her skull. He heard Bev whimper again. Through the night vision lenses Batman could see Rao's eyes, lost and frantic.

One fluid movement carried him into the corridor. Rao heard the rustling of his cape and began to turn, but Batman was already upon him. He tore the gun from the lawyer's fist with one hand even as the other closed around Rao's throat. Batman slammed him against the wall with a hollow thud and the plaster cracked. The hostage, Bev, whispered a prayer to God and held the back of her hand over her mouth like Fay Wray in *King Kong*. She staggered away and crumbled to the floor in relief and shock, blinking as she tried to see through the gloom, staring in astonishment as Batman hustled Rao down the hall to the stairs.

He left her there. The police would get to her soon enough.

Batman took the stairs. It was always better to have the freedom of movement they offered than to be boxed in on an elevator. Rao had been silently weeping as they descended to the first floor, not asking for mercy or forgiveness. In the lobby Batman emptied the shells from the Colt Python to make sure it would not fire accidentally, and then he propped the front door open. Spotlights hit the door instantly, lighting up most of the lobby. Batman tossed the Colt out and it skittered and scraped across the pavement.

He hid himself from the light as best he could behind Rao and in the dark cloud of his cape and cowl.

"Lace your fingers behind your head. Walk slowly. Don't give them a reason to shoot you." Batman waited until Rao had complied and then gave the man a shove through the door, propelling him toward the police barricades.

When he spotted Montoya moving in on Rao, her gun drawn, aim not wavering even an inch, he knew it was over.

It was early yet.

In the ensuing hours of Gotham City's night he prevented two rapes, a convenience store robbery, a domestic murder, and a two-man breakout from Blackgate Prison, and took down a couple of gang-bangers responsible for the previous evening's drive-by shooting and a ring of heroin importers he had been tracking for weeks.

All in all, a quiet night.

The eastern horizon was already beginning to flirt with dawn when he returned to the vast cave beneath his family estate. Methodically, he stored away all of the equipment he had used over the course of the night's work. He never felt as comfortable anywhere else as he did in the cave, not even upstairs in the house in which he had grown up. This was *his* place, far more than the drafty halls of Wayne Manor or the boardroom of WayneTech.

Billions of dollars bore fruit down in that hole in

the Earth. The vehicles accounted for only a fraction of that. The lion's share had been expended upon research that he had either done himself or caused to be done by scientists working for WayneTech under some pretense or another. The cave was sparse, of course. What would be the point of decorating it? Echoes of nothing seemed to drift through like the mutterings of ghosts or the shifting of the earth. Often the flutter of bats' wings and their high-pitched cries would whisper off the stone walls.

There were a great many bats in that cave.

Not far from the staircase that wound up through the hewn stone to the Manor above was the nerve center of Batman's operations. The computer and audio-visual array on the platform above the floor of the cave provided him with instant access to his records and contact-on-demand with the handful of operatives whom he had authorized to function in Gotham. Not that there was any official capacity to this authorization, but it was widely understood that Batman would not allow vigilantes to operate in the city without his approval.

He knew he ought to sleep, at least for a few hours, but there was an item of interest that had been in the back of his mind throughout the night and he could not rest until he had checked on it. As he walked up the short flight of metal stairs to the platform, he pulled his gloves off and then slid his fingers under his cowl, stretching it upward and drawing it back over his head to settle around his neck.

Bruce Wayne pushed his fingers through his hair

and then settled into the high-backed chair in front of his computer array. He laid his hand upon the palm scanner, which lit up immediately. The computer recognized him and the huge main screen flickered to life. The monitoring program he had set up before going out on patrol this evening had been running the entire time he had been gone.

The screen showed a map of the world dotted with red and green lights, some of which were blinking. When he had set up the program, he had placed a single red dot on London, England, and green ones on Paris and Hub City. He had programmed a worldwide search of all reports within the preceding twelve weeks of the appearance of previously unknown metahumans, and he had set up the system to monitor worldwide broadcasts and news services as well as encoded government and law enforcement channels while he was on patrol.

Green represented metahumans who were apparently benevolent. Red marked those who were malevolent. There was one other condition he had programmed into the search and the monitoring system.

Recently discovered metahumans who had been reported to have originated from or speak with an accent from the United Kingdom were represented by blinking lights. The red and green dots were scattered, though most of them appeared in the U.S. and Western Europe. But the highest concentration of both colors was in the U.K. itself, specifically in London. Overall the program had recorded twenty-seven new metahumans reported in the past three months—a startling statistic—and all but four of them were blinking.

The British Isles had produced twenty-three new metahumans in three months; most of them within the past two weeks.

The early morning light streamed in through the bedroom window, throwing a distorted square of sunshine across the bed and casting the room in a warm golden glow. Clark Kent stretched beneath the sheets and yawned luxuriously, enjoying these moments just after waking. He had grown up on a Kansas farm and he still loved his hometown of Smallville, but he was equally passionate about and equally at home in Metropolis, one of the largest and most advanced urban centers in America. The early morning hours were just as precious here as they were back on the farm.

Clark climbed out of bed and stretched again, but already his senses were taking in not only the activity in the apartment he shared with his wife, Lois Lane, but the sounds in the city itself. He heard sirens wailing in three locations in the city, but no gunshots, no screams, nothing that would disturb the morning. Of the sirens, two were police cars and one an ambulance. He would know if he was needed, but for the most part he let the heroes on the street do their work. He could not respond to every domestic disturbance or heart attack. Not even Superman could withstand that sort of pressure. Over the years he had learned to rely upon the police and firefighters and EMTs and doctors, and even ordinary citizens, to handle most of the day-to-day problems that came up.

When Superman was truly needed, he was there. Not just in Metropolis, but all over the world.

But even Superman could not be everywhere.

Clark listened a moment longer and then, satisfied that there was nothing in Metropolis that required his immediate attention, he padded from the bedroom in his white T-shirt and red cotton pajama pants. Lois was seated on the sofa in the living room, clad in a navy blue shirt that had once belonged to her husband but now passed as her nightgown. Her legs were tucked up beneath her and she wore white socks—her feet were always cold in the morning. Her ebony hair was mussed and she wore no makeup, yet it was at times like this, when he caught her early in the morning with her nose in a book, curled up on the couch, that Clark thought she was more radiantly beautiful than at any other time. And when she turned her gaze upon him and her face lit up with that knowing smile, she was illuminated with the same warm, golden glow that slipped through the windows early in the morning.

"Hey there, sleepyhead," Lois teased. "I was thinking about crawling back under the sheets and waking you up, but you looked so cute and comfortable I couldn't bring myself to disturb you."

Clark grinned. "Like that's ever stopped you before?" He went into the kitchen and poured himself a glass of orange juice. It was sweet and pulpy and it made him feel instantly more alert. "How long have you been up?" he asked as he returned to the living room.

This time Lois did not look up from her book. "About an hour," she said, as though the boredom of that hour had been near fatal. "Just sitting here waiting for blueberry pancakes."

With a single motion he drained the rest of the orange juice. Then he arched an eyebrow and gazed at her. "If you wanted them so desperately—"

Lois chuckled softly. "But they taste so much better when you make them."

He knew she meant they tasted better because she had not had to do the actual work of preparing them. But Clark smiled mischievously and said: "I know."

"Hey!" Lois cried.

She picked up a pillow from the sofa and hurled it at him, but faster than her eyes could have seen he moved out of the way of her missile and rushed up behind the sofa. With a smile he bent to kiss her on the forehead.

"Blueberry pancakes, coming right up."

He started toward the kitchen, bent and snatched up the pillow she had lobbed at him, and tossed it back at her. It struck her in the back of the head and she spun around, lowering her book, trying to glare at him without laughing.

Clark pretended he had done nothing and stepped into the kitchen. A moment later the morning calm was interrupted by a trilling noise from the bedroom. He paused, the glow suddenly banished from the morning like a mist burned off the surface of a lake by the rising sun. With a sigh he passed through the living room. Lois was watching him somberly but Clark did not meet her gaze.

On the bureau was his JLA commlink. He tapped it and a three-dimensional holo-image of Wonder Woman fountained into being above the bureau.

"Good morning, Diana," he said.

"Sorry to disturb you," Wonder Woman replied, "but something's come up. Batman's asked that everyone gather at the Watchtower within the hour."

Clark heard a rustle of cotton by the bedroom door and glanced over to see Lois leaning against the doorframe. She could not hide the disappointment in her eyes, but he read other things in her expression as well. She understood. That was the thing that had made their relationship possible, that held it all together. He was both Superman and Clark Kent. As Clark, he was a reporter for the *Daily Planet*. So was Lois. Lois might not have metahuman abilities, but the battle he waged every day was her fight just as much as it was his. Husband and wife, they were a team. She did not want him to go any more than he wanted to. But she would back him one hundred percent.

Clark smiled at her, then turned back to the holo-image of Wonder Woman. If there were lives in the balance that very moment, the Justice League would have been called to immediate action. Within the hour gave him forty-five minutes. If Batman could wait that long, another thirty or so wouldn't bother anyone but Bruce himself. Between his wife and Batman, Clark did not have to even think about it.

"I'll be there as soon as I can. I've got to make blueberry pancakes first."

Ten years ago . . .

Hal Jordan stood on the tarmac at Swinderby Air Base surrounded by Royal Air Force jets and squinted against the sunshine. In his limited experience, and according to everything he had been told, it was rare for the United Kingdom to get this kind of perfect blue sky day.

It was an excellent day to fly.

A pair of R.A.F. fighters had taken off twenty minutes earlier, apparently on routine patrol. At the moment the airfield was completely empty of personnel save for the trio of officers who surrounded Hal's employer, Carol Ferris. As he watched her now, he could not help smiling. Carol had strong, beautiful features and an elegance in her manner that made every man who met her stand up a little straighter in her presence. She was not a woman to be underestimated, and today was the perfect example.

The R.A.F. was interested in having Ferris Aircraft modify its Kestrel A-12 jet, which had yet to get out of the experimental stage, to make it a fighter. Hal knew they must have someone who knew what they were looking for, because the Kestrel was the fastest, most maneuverable bird he had ever flown. Under normal circumstances, the client would have had to send someone to Ferris Aircraft to see a demonstration of the Kestrel. But Carol had wanted to make an impression, to cement the deal. So instead of forcing the R.A.F. to send someone to her, she had cleared a flight plan with the U.S.A.F. and the R.A.F. and had Hal fly her to England in the very plane she hoped to sell them.

The woman was used to getting what she wanted.

Hal slid a hand into his jacket pocket and fished out his sunglasses. He popped them on and took another look at Carol. Where the officers' faces had once been etched with doubt as she began her sales pitch, the men had now obviously been charmed by her. Carol did not play upon this at all. Her face was all business, her manner professional.

She turned toward Hal, beckoning to the officers to follow as she started toward him. Carol did not bother to introduce Hal to the men, but he took no offense. She was on the job, trying to close the deal.

"Hal. Would you mind showing these gentlemen what Ferris Aircraft has to offer them?"

"Not at all." He smiled genially and then turned toward the Kestrel, which gleamed in the sunshine. The jet had been fueled almost immediately after they landed and it was ready to go. The journey to the U.K. had been a milk run, taking it easy. Now he had a chance to play, to get the adrenaline rushing, put the Kestrel through her paces.

Hal was about to climb into the cockpit when a young airman came running across the tarmac shouting to the officers.

"What is it, Goss?" barked Air Marshal Simkins, the senior R.A.F. man.

Flight Lieutenant Goss was panting as he drew up to them. Goss did not even glance at the Kestrel, or at Carol, so he certainly didn't notice Hal perched on the side of the plane above him.

"Radar's picked up an atmospheric incursion, sir. In our air space."

Hal frowned. *Atmospheric incursion.* From the look on Goss's face whatever had entered Earth's atmosphere above the United Kingdom was not a meteor.

"Ms. Ferris, I'm afraid we're going to have to postpone your demonstration for the moment. Flight Lieutenant Goss here will show you to a canteen where you can relax and have something to eat if you like."

The only sign of her pique was the way Carol smiled then, her lips pressed just a little too tightly together. "Of course, Air Marshal. We're happy to wait. You certainly have more vital duties than this."

But Simkins wasn't really listening. He and the other two officers were hurrying back toward the main building, leaving Goss to escort their American visitors. Carol sighed and glanced up at Hal.

"You coming, hotshot?" she asked.

He smiled. "In a minute. I just want to lock her down. No way to know how long a delay we're looking at." Hal glanced at Goss. "If that's all right with you? Better safe than sorry."

Goss debated a moment, obviously reluctant to leave him there. At length he nodded. "You stay put, then. I'll escort Miss Ferris to the canteen and come back for you. Visitors are not allowed to wander the base without an escort."

"Not a problem. I'll be right here," Hal lied.

The moment they had walked into the midst of the fighters that were out on the tarmac and he knew he was hidden from view, Hal *changed*. He raised his hand and emerald energy erupted from his ring, sheathing him in shimmering green power. His clothing altered, becoming a uniform, and a mask covered his face around his eyes.

Hal Jordan was a member of the Green Lantern Corps, assigned to Sector 2814, which just happened to contain his home planet, Earth. If there was an atmospheric incursion of any kind—but particularly the kind that would alarm military men—he knew there was work for him to do.

In a brilliant flash that he hoped would not be noticed by anyone at the base, he sliced upward through the blue sky at top speed, rocketing into the stratosphere. He had known immediately that Goss's "atmospheric incursion" was some kind of UFO and had begun to go through his mental catalog of alien races capable of interstellar invasion. If invasion was indeed what this was.

His heart raced, adrenaline raging through his body with far more fervor than even if he had been in the cockpit of the Kestrel. The jade energy surged and crackled around him. Being a Green Lantern was the ultimate responsibility, but it was also the ultimate thrill.

Hal shook his head, clearing it of all distraction. He wouldn't know what he was facing until he found them. With the ring, he crafted a screen that hovered in the air in front of him and sent out energy pulses. It was his own sort of radar, and he spotted the incursion immediately, due north. With the speed of thought he propelled himself in that direction.

In less than a minute, he had a visual on them.

Not one object, but ten. Fire flickered around them, friction from their entry into the atmosphere igniting the air. Green Lantern froze in the sky, staring at the objects. They were not starships, as he had feared.

They were creatures. Gigantic, monstrous beings plummeting, burning, toward the Earth.

CHAPTER FOUR

Now . . .

"I never get used to the smoking," Kyle Rayner said, glancing around the smoky, gleaming steel-and-wood interior of All Bar One.

The place was on New Oxford Street in London, part of a chain according to Ian. There were loads of people on the first floor, eating lunch or just drinking coffee. A rounded metal staircase led to the second floor, but it was mostly deserted save for a large group of twentysomething women, many of whom were the source of the shroud of cigarette smoke that drifted along the ceiling of the place.

"This?" Ian asked, brows knitting as he gestured around them. "You're joking. Should've seen it here ten years ago. I grew up in Norwich but it didn't matter where you went. Cigarettes everywhere. Make a fella sick." Ian raised a mischievous eyebrow. "This, now, this is bloody fresh air in comparison."

Wally nodded appreciatively. "It is a lot better than it used to be. And much better than on the European continent, where it still seems like everyone smokes. But compared to the U.S.—"

"Yeah, well we're not keen on making it a crime here," Ian interrupted archly. "We figure you want to kill yourself, sort of a personal matter, isn't it?"

Kyle considered getting into the whole secondhand smoke debate, but thought better of it. Ian was playing with them, and getting serious would blow the whole laid-back atmosphere of the lunch they had scheduled together. It was a good time, too. Kyle had a deadline for the magazine he was working for, but he had been glad to use the JLA teleporter to hang out in London for a few hours. Ian was a nice guy, and probably was so freaked out by having "powers" that he could use the company of some other guys his age who knew what it was like.

Wally seemed to be enjoying himself as well. Kyle had glanced several times at the Flash and was surprised to find that Wally's fingers weren't drumming on the table, his feet weren't tapping beneath it. Kyle was drinking strong coffee, Ian had a pint of something dark and aromatic, but Wally had stuck to just English lemonade. Which was fine with Kyle. Caffeine was the Flash's enemy—and the enemy of anyone who wanted to spend any downtime with the guy and not want to have to anchor him like a runaway parade float.

It was nice, this. Just hanging. And kind of weird, too. Under normal circumstances, Kyle and Wally got on well enough. Sure, Wally was married and had been established in the metahuman community since childhood. Kyle had a girlfriend and, though the ring made him one of the most powerful beings on the planet, he was pretty much the new kid on the block. Sometimes the two youngest members of the Justice League knocked heads. But Ian complemented them nicely. With him around, any differences between Wally and Kyle seemed to dissipate.

"So, you've been asking about us this whole time," Wally put in, spearing a french fry into his mouth. "What about you, Ian?"

"What *about* me? Boring, really. Not much to tell. Got a job at an advertising firm. Been off and on with the same partner for years."

"Partner as in . . . ?" Kyle asked, before realizing that his curiosity could have been construed as rudeness.

Ian smiled and waved a hand in the air. "Nah. It's only my girl, Sara. We don't go in for precious words like boyfriend and girlfriend here. A bit silly. No offense. Anyway, we've a flat in Battersea, lovely area."

A silence fell amongst them then. A ripple of laughter came from the large group of women across the room. Kyle took the moment to study them and was fascinated. There was a simplicity to their mode of dress, nothing too flashy or too sexy, mostly earth tones and blacks, yet they were all elegant. The women wore very little makeup and most of them had their hair pulled back into ponytails. It was all about practicality for these young London working women, and Kyle admired that, but they still managed to catch his eye.

Kyle glanced back at Ian, at his generous smile and broad, strong features. Just a regular guy. He felt a kind of kinship with Ian that he had never found with any of the other members of the JLA.

"So how long have you been able to do it? The telekinesis?"

Ian's smiled disappeared. Not because he was angry, but because a kind of cloud passed over his features then. It was obvious he was not at all comfortable with the power he had.

"Been able to do a bit of it since I was, dunno, maybe eighteen? At first I thought it was just luck, right? Can of paint falls off a ladder, dropping right down at me, yeah? But it shoots off sideways like a feather on the wind and I don't get a drop of paint on me. Little glimmers like that. But I've only been able to really control it the last couple of months. Got it sorted pretty well, now."

"So we saw yesterday," Wally noted. "It's pretty impressive stuff, Ian. Have you thought about what's next for you?"

Ian took a long sip of his ale and then leaned back in his chair, away from the plate upon which sat the demolished remains of his lunch. He regarded Wally carefully as if wondering where the joke was and then glanced at Kyle. At length he slid his hand around the pint glass again and smiled.

"What, you mean the whole spandex bit? Super-heroes, that sort of thing?"

Kyle laughed softly but shrugged. "Why not? Is it as bad as all that, trying to use your talents to help people?"

"S'pose not," Ian allowed. "No insult to you, but doesn't it seem a bit theatrical? All the swagger, I mean. Not to mention the fetishistic element of the costumes and things. Really creepy in a way, isn't it?"

Kyle stared at him, then slowly turned to look at Wally only to find that he too was gawking at Ian. It was that expression, mouth hanging open as though he might begin to drool, that struck Kyle as hysteri-cally funny. He began to laugh loudly enough that the women across the room stopped their own chatter to glance over at him. His eyes watered as he continued to laugh, covering his mouth and forcing himself not to continue, though at any moment he knew he might be reduced to a fit of giggling.

He glanced at Wally, who seemed annoyed.

"I'm sorry," Kyle said, struggling to catch his breath. "You just . . . you had to see your face."

Wally tried to maintain that straight face but it crumbled and then his face split into a wide grin and he chuckled softly.

"Creepy's probably not the word I would have chosen," the Flash told Ian Partington, who had the good sense to look chagrined and apologetic.

"No offense," Ian ventured.

Kyle waved the pseudo-apology away. "No, you're right. We can see how you'd look at it that way. Thing is, for the most part you'll find that anyone in this line of work who dresses up in uniform or costume does so for a good reason. Sometimes it's because the outfit has uses of its own, or to honor a tradition. Sometimes it's the urge for secrecy run amok. Sometimes it's to convey a message to criminals, or whoever it is you're up against."

"And sometimes," Wally added with a smirk, "it's because they like it."

"But there's no rule says 'you want to save the world you've gotta dress like a wanker'?" Ian asked, deadpan.

"No," Kyle assured him. "No rule."

"Right, then. I'll give it some thought."

Any replies that might have been forthcoming from Kyle or Wally were derailed by the simultaneously abrupt, grating beeping of their Justice League commlinks. They glanced at one another and Kyle reached into his jeans to pull out the flat card version of the commlink. Ian was watching him closely, as was the waitress, who had just come up the metal steps from the main section of All Bar One and winced at the tinny beeping noise.

When the holo-image of Wonder Woman blossomed into full-color, three-dimensional life above the card on the table, the waitress dropped the tray she was carrying.

"Very subtle," Wally muttered under his breath.

"Kyle. J'onn tells me Wally's with you. You're both needed at the Watchtower."

"You've got us," Kyle replied.

"Hang on just a sec," Wally said. He stood and leaned over to Ian and the two shook hands. "It was good seeing you. We'll have to do this again."

"Oh, absolutely," Ian said, attempting to be nonchalant as he stared at the holo-image of Wonder Woman. "She's a goddess," Ian whispered.

"Actually, she is," Kyle agreed as he stood up beside Wally and leaned over to shake Ian's hand. "See you soon, amigo. Stay out of trouble." He picked up the flat commlink card from the table.

"We're good to go, Diana," Wally announced.

As the Watchtower's teleport equipment retrieved them from All Bar One—transporting them to the League's moon-based headquarters—Kyle caught a final glimpse of the amazed look on Ian's face.

"Now what was that about spandex?" he said, but most of the sentence was lost in the ether between London and the moon.

The Flash loved the Watchtower. For the most part it was a cold, sterile environment; only the trophy room and the individual members' quarters added much personality to the place. But he was not bothered by that. The Watchtower was the physical manifestation of everything the Justice League stood for. Certainly there were those who would portray this as a negative thing, an Orwellian "Big Brother-ness" orbiting the Earth so that the League could keep order on the planet below. Wally had never seen it that way.

The members of the Justice League were not shepherds watching over the human flock, but servants to the needs of the planet and its people.

It was the greatest gig in the world.

With the abilities he had been gifted with, Wally could do so much good. His life was lived not in the eye of a hurricane, but in its midst. Even when he slowed down long enough to kick back a bit as he had done with Kyle and Ian in London, or simply to spend some downtime with his wife, Linda, he rarely had the presence of mind to really think about his life. He had dedicated himself to the ideals of his uncle, Barry Allen, who had been the Flash before him and a founding member of the Justice League. He was always aware of that, of Uncle Barry's noble and courageous example. But his life moved so fast that he rarely had time to savor it.

And yet . . .

Every time Wally West 'ported into the Watchtower, this enormous structure on the *moon*, he took a moment to pause and consider what it was he was a part of, and what brought all of them there, together.

The moment after he and Kyle arrived at the Watchtower after Wonder Woman's summons, the Flash manipulated the Speed Force, fashioning from it the scarlet uniform that was modeled after the one his Uncle Barry had worn. It was appropriate. There had been times he had been in his civilian clothes at the Watchtower, but it was rare. Here he wasn't Wally West anymore. He was the Flash.

"Business attire, huh?" Kyle noted as he observed the costume change. "Works for me."

Emerald light flashed from the ring that was ever present on Kyle's finger, throwing strange shadows upon the walls, and the energy from the ring refashioned Kyle's clothing into the uniform of Green Lantern. It was subtle, but the Flash was always cognizant of a change in Kyle when he wore the mask and the uniform. Green Lantern had a history to live up to as well, and his was even more daunting in its way. Once upon a time there had been thousands of Green Lanterns policing the universe.

They were all gone now, and nearly all of them dead.

Kyle Rayner was the last Green Lantern.

No one was there to meet them when they teleported into the Watchtower, but that was not unusual. The League was likely gathering already in the conference room. The Flash ran ahead—knowing Green Lantern would be flying along the corridors right behind him—moving through the vast facility in an instant and arriving at the conference room.

At the speed he was moving, the gathered members of the Justice League seemed a frozen tableau of power. Aquaman and Wonder Woman stood on the far side of the room where viewports allowed an extraordinary panorama of the moonscape and, across the gulf of space, the Earth spinning below. Superman and the Martian Manhunter were engaged in grim conversation. The only member of the League who was already seated was Batman, who sat with his gloved fingers steepled beneath his chin, grimly silent, as if he had retreated into himself to await the arrival of the League's full complement.

Flash stood still and the room caught up to him. He could hear the low voices of J'onn and Superman, see the impatience in Aquaman's every gesture, but his arrival was so sudden—as though he had stepped out of thin air—that it took a moment for them to realize he had arrived.

Batman was the first to notice him.

"Good," he said. "Now we can get started."

Green Lantern entered the room a moment later, but already the members of the Justice League had begun to take their places around the conference table. This was another tradition that the Flash took quite seriously. It was no accident that the table was round, nor that each of the chairs set around it bore a symbol representative of the person to whom it belonged. These were purposeful allusions to the Round Table of Arthurian legend and the knights who gathered there.

The Flash took his seat. Difficult as it was for him to remain still, he did so. For a long moment, none of them spoke. He studied the others and saw a strange exchange between Batman and Superman—a hard look from Batman, which Superman chose to pretend he had not seen.

"Get on with it, Batman," Aquaman said curtly, imperiously. "I dislike being summoned on your whim, particularly when as far as I know there's no great planetary threat that should require this meeting."

"Yes, Batman," Wonder Woman agreed. "We've been very patient."

The Flash glanced around at the members of the League—his friends, his heroes—and he tried to stifle the smile that teased the edges of his lips. However grave they all behaved, no matter how much they might protest, Wonder Woman obviously had not balked at Batman's request that she leave off her Monitor duty to gather the others, and none of them had ignored the summons. That was because, like Flash himself, they all knew that if Batman thought there was something going on that required the League's attention, it had to be seriously nasty.

"There *is* a planetary threat," Batman said at length, sitting back in his chair and regarding the rest of the League. "But my hope is that we will have caught it in its infancy."

Batman touched a key on the arm of his chair and light blossomed from the center of the table, forming instantly into a large spherical rotating hologram; the Earth itself. At various points on the globe were glowing dots of red and green. The members of the Justice League looked to Batman for an explanation—all save J'onn, who had either already figured out what this was about or had picked up the information telepathically from Batman.

"In the past few days we have all come into contact with previously unknown metahumans," Batman said. Though he was speaking to all of them, his gaze most often fell upon Superman. This came as no surprise to Flash. J'onn might be the heart and soul of the

League, but Batman and Superman were the North and South poles that created the axis upon which debates so often turned.

"Superman and Wonder Woman encountered the pyrokinetic, Julia Williams, in Paris. J'onn and I had contact with Bryan Francis, whose talents include psychometry and invulnerability, at the very least."

Batman glanced over at Green Lantern and Flash, narrowing his eyes. The cowl crinkled soundlessly, making him look even more menacing, and Flash held his breath. Batman had touched upon primal human fear in weaving his vigilante persona, but it had very little to do with the outfit. Most anyone else in that cape and cowl would have seemed ridiculous. But Batman had tapped into something, some ancestral memory, the kind of thing that had made early humans huddle in their caves. Amidst this group of individuals, he was the only one without metahuman abilities, and yet of all of them, he was the only one whose presence unnerved the Flash. More than once, Green Lantern had commented that he wouldn't want to run into Batman in a dark alley.

Flash's response was always the same: *Who would?*

"Green Lantern and the Flash dealt with not one but two new metas in London. The one the media is calling Maelstrom has disappeared. And Wally and Kyle have just come from lunch with the telekinetic, Ian Partington."

"Someone's been peeking at my appointment book," Green Lantern muttered.

Batman ignored him, glanced around once and

then continued. "They aren't the only ones. There has been a dramatic spike in the number of new metahumans in the past two months. I'm sure some of you are aware of this. J'onn, you especially. You've always taken a special interest in new talent, so I'm certain this has not escaped your notice."

The Martian Manhunter nodded once, urging him to continue.

"This holo-image represents my mapping of fresh metahuman activity. Green for benevolent. Red for malevolent. You'll note that they are scattered, but that the highest concentration, an extraordinary majority, are located in the United Kingdom."

Flash studied the spinning holo-sphere. Batman was understating it. Nearly all of the green and red blips were in the U.K., with only a handful in the U.S. and continental Europe, and one or two elsewhere.

"My research shows that most of those new metas outside of the U.K., including Julia Williams and Bryan Francis, are *from* the United Kingdom. Obviously something happened there that has spurred an entire new wave of metas, altering the landscape of this world. Today a woman in Los Angeles robbed a bank simply by asking the tellers nicely to give her the money. They did so, happily. Obviously there are mental abilities at work there.

"More of them are appearing, with no obvious end in sight. The question is, what are we going to do about it?"

For several moments, silence reigned. J'onn and Superman looked troubled, but Aquaman and Wonder Woman seemed only curious. The Flash glanced at Green Lantern, but Kyle's expression was partially hidden by the mask that covered his eyes.

"Well," Green Lantern began, "it can only be good to have more heroes, right? I mean, I'm looking at the big hologram and I'm seeing a lot more green dots than red ones."

"Yes. So far," Superman said.

Batman lifted his chin ever so slightly, but right then Flash felt that the decision had been made. He had never doubted a moment that the League would take seriously any issue that Batman would bring before them, but now, with two words, Superman had shifted it from an issue for discussion to an issue for action.

"I agree it bears looking into," Wonder Woman began, "but I'm not certain there's cause for great alarm. We can continue to monitor these new metas the way we always have. It's possible that this spike in meta development is a natural evolution rather than the result of anything sinister."

"Possible, yes," Aquaman noted. "But that is the question, isn't it? Not what is happening here, but why?"

"Could be that freaky English diet," Green Lantern suggested. They all stared at him, but he persisted, leaning back in his chair with an innocent grin. "Seriously. Bangers and mash. Blood sausage. Eat enough of that stuff, who knows what it'll do to you?"

Batman ignored him. He leaned forward and the cape seemed to swallow him like a living shadow, though the room was brightly lit. "Something has triggered these developments. They're too concentrated in both geography and chronology. With every single new meta there is a new threat."

Says the one without powers, Flash thought, even though he knew Batman was right.

J'onn sat up a bit straighter in his chair. His thick brow was knit in contemplation and the white pupils at the centers of his black eyes seemed oddly large. It always seemed to Flash as though the Martian Manhunter could see inside of him, but that had more to do with those penetrating eyes than with J'onn's telepathy. When J'onn J'onzz spoke, in that low, gravelly voice, even the most powerful members of the Justice League deferred to him.

"The Monitor Womb will be programmed to collate reports that match with this pattern. The League should begin to check up on these new metas personally. If there is no objection I will generate assignments for each of us. All save Batman, of course."

Green Lantern straightened up in his chair, a spark of energy off his ring revealing his pique. "Huh? No offense, but Batman's obviously more spooked about this than anyone. Why isn't he making house calls along with the rest of us?"

The Martian Manhunter's grim expression lightened somewhat then. J'onn raised an eyebrow and glanced at Batman. "If I'm not mistaken, Batman will already be far too busy investigating the apparent source of this wave of meta-evolution."

The Flash stared at the spinning holo-image of the

Earth, watching as Europe came around again, noting the cluster of red and green blips in the United Kingdom.

"You're going to England," he said.

Batman's only response was a single, barely perceptible nod.

Ian Partington whistled tunelessly as he strode along the sidewalk toward the Holborn tube station. It was the weekend, and he had about a dozen errands planned for the afternoon. The weather was pleasant, hardly a cloud in the sky, and that was unusual enough for London that it lifted his spirits. He still was not used to the idea that he was knocking about with the Flash and Green Lantern. As regular as Wally and Kyle seemed, there was no getting around the fact that they were members of the Justice League. These blokes were heavy hitters, had saved the world a dozen times over. Maybe more. Wally'd been in the superhero business since he was a kid.

Sure, it was a bit silly, all that marching about in tight clothes. Ian could not imagine spending his days doing that sort of thing. But ever since the telekinesis had really kicked in a couple of months back, a kind of instinct had been niggling at the back of his brain. All his life he had been fond of saying that if anyone ever gave him a billion pounds he'd probably give away most of it. What was the use of having all that money if you couldn't use it to do some good?

Well, this wasn't a billion pounds, but didn't the

same rules apply? What was the use of having this ability if he didn't use it to do some good?

On the other hand, he was not about to move to America, and you just did not get the kind of metahuman crime and such in England that they had in the States. Ian was not cut out to be a superhero, and he sure as hell was not going to dress up in bloody tights and prance around like a prat, come up with some code name.

As he passed by an uptight fellow with a cell phone clapped to the side of his face, Ian snickered to himself. *Yeah, I can see that. Look, up in the sky, it's Super-Git!*

Down a narrow alley there was a merchant selling fresh fruit to the office workers who slipped out to take advantage of his wares. An enormous blond man and his diminutive wife herded their four children along the sidewalk across the street, the husband clutching a map in his hand. Tourists, though their clothes did not immediately give them away as Americans.

Ian slipped into a Boots Pharmacy on the corner to get himself a Coke. He was inside for less than a minute, but when he emerged once more onto the street, chaos had erupted. Shouts and cries of terror filled the air. People pointed. The huge blond man and his family were still there, across the street, the man trying to corral his offspring and drag them away.

In the middle of the street a rough-looking middle-aged man with a crooked pugilist's nose was holding a black, bulbous taxi over his head. The vehicle appeared to weigh next to nothing as the man hefted it with both hands, tipping it so that the gray-haired driver fell forward against the inside of the windshield, his face splayed against the glass.

"Bloody thief!" roared the man with the crooked nose. He shook the cab and the windshield splintered under the weight of the driver bouncing against the glass from the inside. In a moment it would shatter.

"I've lived in this city all my life. Not some bleedin' tourist you can bugger. You don't take the long way 'round when I'm in yer cab. Not a chance!"

One more shake and the windshield would break, slashing the driver as he fell out of the taxi and tumbled to the pavement. If the broken glass did not kill him, the fall might.

Spectators were gathering at what they presumed was a safe distance, waiting to see how this would all play out. The papers had been full of insane things like this in recent weeks. Another metahuman shows up on the nation's radar. Just like Ian himself.

For long seconds he just stood there, a spectator himself, wondering what was going to happen next, wondering if anyone was going to try to talk to the man with the crooked nose, or stop him somehow. It took him several moments to realize the obvious.

He could help. He could step in.

Ian Partington shook his head in amazement and a small chuckle issued from his lips. Wasn't this what he had just been thinking about? It looked like fate was not going to give him a choice. *Here comes Super-*

Git, he thought in horror, wondering what Sara would think when he told her he'd played superhero today.

Focusing his thoughts, Ian reached out with his mind, and a cable of golden energy shimmered in the air and grabbed hold of the taxi. He was stepping in. He was helping.

But no bloody tights, he thought. *One must draw the line somewhere.*

CHAPTER FIVE

The city of Belfast was under siege.

Northern Ireland had been torn apart for generations by struggles between Catholics and Protestants—between those who longed for an Irish Republic and those who supported the union with England. Bloodshed and carnage were the order of the day for so very long, and a bomb blast or a sniper's bullet were familiar even to the city's children. The world was gray and red. In recent years the troubles had calmed somewhat.

Today, there was only chaos, and not the familiar kind.

Gray skies hung menacingly low over the city's spires and chimneys and rain poured down, running in the gutters as if to scour Belfast clean. People ran screaming from Donegall Square; a young man slipped on the rain-slicked curb and the back of his head struck the ground hard. Gunshots rang out in

the square and the police in front of Belfast City Hall
shouted instructions to the people who were even
now running for cover. They were used to taking
cover, these people.

But not from this.

A flash of red and blue, Superman emerged from
the thunderclouds above Belfast accompanied by tendrils of lightning that hung for an eyeblink like spider-
webs spun between heaven and earth. The storm
lashed at the city with cold fury, but it was not the
storm that had wrought chaos of Donegall Square.

The road had erupted in the middle of the square
and from it had crawled a monstrosity, a kind of
golem constructed of earth and pavement and granite, as if the city itself had risen up to terrorize its resi-
dents. It was a towering behemoth, twenty feet in
height when the first report hit the JLA Monitor
Womb, but as Superman flew down toward Donegall
Square he gauged that it was near thirty now. It was
growing. With every massive footfall that cracked the
pavement, it picked up some of the debris of its destruction and it grew.

Fire flickered from its eyes and from cracks between the earth and stone that made up its body. Its
arms were much too long and it lumbered with an
apelike stoop. Its face was crude, as though a child
had sculpted it from clay, but its jaws were jagged
stone, and when it opened them and roared it was the
sound of a landslide.

From this height, Superman's extraordinary vision
caught sight of tanks rumbling across the city of

Belfast, heading for Donegall Square. Instantaneously he gauged the distance and the time and he knew that far too much damage would be done before they arrived. Even if they made haste, the police in front of City Hall had already proven that guns were going to be useless. Even now Superman heard gunshots, saw bullets lodge in the soil that was the creature's flesh and others ricochet off its stone parts.

Not everyone was smart enough to run. In the twelve minutes since the thing's obscene birth had begun several journalists and camera operators had set up on a rooftop on the far side of the square. Even now a van with a news logo on the side rolled along a street near City Hall. Spectators had massed in front of one of the buildings, gaping in horror at the thing that had torn itself from the ground. It moved slowly, and Superman thought that perhaps these people believed they could escape if it came for them.

A foolish presumption. All this thing needed to do was bump into a building and it would likely crumble around the thing's knees. Several cars had been crushed beneath its heavy tread and smoke rose from the crater it had been born of—ruptured sewer pipes pouring into the hole—but the earth-beast had yet to attack any of the buildings surrounding it.

That was only a matter of time. Already Superman could see that it was moving more quickly, that the fire burning in its eyes seemed to focus more on the architecture around Donegall Square. It stumbled forward another giant step, collapsing the sidewalk under its bulk. Then its huge head swung around and with that crude face it stared at City Hall.

It raised its hands to the sky in an unnervingly human expression, as if pleading to the heavens for their intervention. Those massive, three-fingered hands of stone and earth then came down to cover its eyes. Liquid fire leaked like tears from behind those hands and slipped down its oddly sculpted features. When the hands came down its stone lips ground together in an expression that could only be hatred, and it began to march toward City Hall, long arms reaching out with malicious intent.

All of this took place in seconds. Superman had taken in the situation, trying to figure out the best way to stop the thing. No matter how unnatural it was, it had not killed anyone yet and mindless destruction of an apparently living being was never his first choice.

He flew at the monster with such speed that the friction of the air upon his skin and his uniform dried the rain before it touched him. His cape whipped in the winds of the storm and he knifed down through the gray afternoon light, then pulled up short, hanging in the air above Donegall Square, face to face with this thing that had crawled from its belly.

"Stop!" he shouted, raising a hand, trying to determine if those burning eyes even saw him. "If you can understand me, you're destroying the square. I can't let you continue."

The ground shook as the behemoth took another step. It had ignored him, or not understood. Now he threw himself at it, slamming into the earth-beast's chest and forcing it backward a step. A bicycle that had been abandoned in the street was obliterated beneath its foot. The thing tried to continue forward. Superman pushed against it, unwilling to allow it any further progress. He just needed to buy himself a few seconds to figure out how to handle this. He would have to carry the thing out of there, just haul it out of Belfast and deal with it in the countryside. Or drop it in the ocean. If he could extinguish the flames that jetted from the cracks in its earth flesh, that might stop it.

The plan was formulated in an instant.

But the thing was faster than it looked. One of those massive hands swept down and batted him away, pavement and broken water piping cracking as it collided with his chest and head. With a grunt of pain and surprise Superman was thrown across Donegall Square. He crashed through the wall of the building atop which the journalists had begun to gather, plaster and brick and glass crumbling around him.

No, he thought frantically. Fast as he was able he flew back out through the hole in the building, the air roaring in his ears as he thrust out into the stormy afternoon sky. Below him, Superman saw a cluster of spectators. Several of them were tending to the man who had struck his skull on the curb earlier—the man appeared to be all right—but they still seemed not to recognize the danger they were in. In one of the windows above them, a man with a rifle thrust the barrel of his weapon into the rain and fired at the monstrosity.

The crack of rifle fire echoed across the square. The shots thunked uselessly into the earth-beast but its blazing eyes turned toward the sniper. Its stone lips ground together and then it stomped across the square, gouts of flame spilling from its joints like blood pouring from open wounds. It was coming for the gunman, but the spectators in the street were in the way.

Faster than one of the sniper's bullets, Superman shot toward the ground. He hung several feet off the pavement, rain and wind whipping at him, soaking his hair, furling his cape. The people stared at him with wide eyes, yet without fear. They had lived under the shadow of a constant threat of danger their entire lives. This monster was real, not a threat, and they were fascinated by it.

"Get out of here!" Superman told them. "Go, now."

His tone would brook no argument. A couple of the men turned hardened faces up to him and seemed as though they might debate the command, but he left them no room to do so. He was Superman.

At last they began to retreat. A camera crew out in the street even left their equipment and clambered toward their van. Many of the people glanced back at him, then up at the monster slowly thundering across the square. Its foot stomped at the center of Donegall Square and set off a chain reaction, shaking the surrounding buildings so badly that windows shattered and masonry crumbled.

In the midst of the departing crowd Superman caught sight of a lone, fortyish woman whose brown hair had been plastered to her face by the rain. Water ran across her cheeks but he did not think all of it was from the sky. Her features were etched with such profound despair that looking at her caused him to catch his breath. She stared not at him but at the monstrous golem that was even now coming for them. The woman shook her head, lower lip trembling, and pressed the heels of her hands against her eyes. Then a man grabbed her by the arm and dragged her along with the retreating crowd.

Superman was baffled, but the earth-beast gave him no time to wonder about the woman. Fire dripped onto the pavement, melting the road in places. One of its long arms shot out. The sniper had not abandoned his perch. Bullets from his rifle struck the monstrosity without any effect at all.

The golem was going to tear the building apart to destroy the sniper.

Superman knifed through the air, collided a second time with its chest, and drove it back a step. He flew upward and shot out his fist in a blow that shattered the beast's stone jaw into three pieces. Granite blocks fell like broken teeth from its lips and crashed into the pavement below, but instantly its earth and rock flesh began to reform.

It opened its mouth and vomited a torrent of fire at him. Superman turned away, shielding his eyes, and the force of the blast slammed him to the ground, his body cracking the road. The fire scorched him, blackened his cape, singed his hair. But it did not harm him.

Back to the plan, he thought. *I've got to get rid of this thing.* He had no idea how he would defeat it, but he could at least remove it until he figured it out.

A Centrelink bus rumbled into the square, the driver unaware until it was too late that he had never faced a more perilous obstacle. The brakes squealed and the tires began to slip on the rain-soaked street. There would be no stopping. The bus was aimed directly at the monster's legs but the driver accelerated again and cranked the steering wheel over to angle away from it, toward the front of City Hall. The thing howled its earthquake cry once more and reached down to grasp the bus in both hands.

In that moment Superman saw it all illustrated on the canvas of his mind, what was to come. The people in the bus would die. The earth-beast would hurl the bus at the ornate dome of one of the finest Classical Renaissance buildings in Europe, likely killing many others inside in the building.

More than anything, it wanted to destroy Belfast City Hall.

Another bolt of lightning flashed across the sky. Before it had dimmed, Superman had raced at the golem and torn the bus from its grip. He flew across the square and set it down, the passengers all apparently safe, but when he turned back toward the monster it was slowly, inexorably, lumbering toward City Hall.

Why? he thought. *What does it want with this place, with the City Council?*

Images flickered through his mind. Upon his arrival he had seen the thing gaze toward the heavens and then cover its eyes as if in grief. But the monster was not alone in its grief. *The woman*, he thought, and in his memory he could still see her, sodden hair plastered across her face, tears lost in the rain, covering her eyes.

He was torn. He had to get the thing out of Belfast. But if he did not stop the woman now he might never find her. And he knew there was a connection. He could feel it.

Superman whipped around, his remarkable vision pinpointing the woman instantly a block away, being hustled along by the fleeing crowd. She was trying to hold back, pausing to get glimpses of the chaos and impending destruction in Donnegal Square.

In a heartbeat he was there, buffeted by the wind as he flew across the square to land right in front of her. He gazed at her, searching her eyes, trying to understand. The woman covered her mouth and stared at him.

"You're doing this, aren't you?" he asked gently.

She collapsed on the street in a puddle, her skirt instantly soaked through, and she wrapped her arms around herself. Superman glanced over his shoulder and he saw that the golem had paused as if uncertain. It wavered on its feet.

"You have to stop," he said, crouching by her and reaching out to place a comforting hand on her arm. "People are going to die. Please."

The pain in her eyes seared him. "They killed my

Jamie, my little boy," she said, biting off every word. "The bastards were shooting at each other and he was in the way."

Once more she pressed the heels of her hands against her eyes and now she gazed up at the heavens, though for succor or forgiveness Superman did not know.

"Dunno who it was, IRA or Unionists, but it doesn't matter. I'm not going to let them do it anymore. Never again."

But her tears belied the firmness of her words. She searched Superman's eyes as though she might find some answers there. His heart broke as he understood he could never give her what she sought, he could not take the pain away.

"Not like this," he told the woman. "You can't do it like this. Don't let Jamie's death make you less than who you were. Let it make you more."

The woman bit her lower lip and for the first time Superman noticed that she was beautiful. She shuddered and fell forward, letting him wrap his arms around her, weeping silently against his chest as the rain battered down upon them and the last of the light drained from the storm-gray sky, afternoon slipping on toward night.

In the middle of Donegall Square, the giant golem crumbled, stone and earth, pavement and pipe falling in a barrage of debris that tumbled and spilled across the square, crushing abandoned camera equipment and three cars that were parked on the side of the road.

It was over.

For now.

J'onn was surprised at how well it was going. Though Batman was understandably troubled by the sudden spike in new meta activity, thus far the League's investigation had unearthed very little unexpected difficulty. Wonder Woman had captured a shapeshifting thief in Hong Kong and a venomous, serpentine serial killer in Bangkok. But the others had in general had better luck, turning up individuals who had recently, and quite abruptly, found themselves with abilities ranging from telepathy to elemental weather control. Some of them needed psychological evaluation, but others were dealing with these new abilities with surprising alacrity.

Yes, this part of the plan—the part that required the cataloguing and observation of new metas—was going well. But J'onn had heard curiously little from Batman about his investigations in England, and that was what concerned him more. Whether they wanted to use their abilities to aid people or to burn down the world, the Justice League could handle any new metas that came along. For now. But the more of them there were, the bigger the problem would become. Simply because they had been fortunate thus far did not mean things would remain quiet.

Maelstrom was still out there, undoubtedly likely to appear again. The woman from Belfast, Ella Devlin—who wielded enough power over the earth to craft monsters from it and control them—was in custody, under constant supervision and sedation. But Batman had been correct that there were more of them, perhaps not with every passing day, but certainly with each week that went by.

J'onn had determined that they would have to begin biological testing on some of the new metas to see if any clues could be found about their origins. For now, he continued to follow up on reports of new ones. He had just come from Bal Harbor, Florida, where an eighty-two-year-old Scottish woman had proven herself suddenly clairvoyant. Most such claims J'onn would have discounted almost out of hand. There were thousands of hustlers posing as psychics of one kind or another. But not all of them were from the United Kingdom, and not all of them had suddenly developed these talents at the age of eighty-two.

The woman, Mrs. Agnes Holligan, was delighted, and entertained her many friends in the condominium complex where she and her husband had retired nine years before. But when J'onn had spoken to her—as John Jones—she had confessed that she had found rather quickly that her ability had proven less welcome among those older folks than among their vacationing children and grandchildren. Elderly people did not really want to know the future.

"There are so few surprises left," Mrs. Holligan had told him in her heavy Scottish burr. "Nobody wants to spoil them."

But that had been two days ago. Now J'onn was in Decatur, Georgia, striding down a hospital corridor, the soles of his shoes squeaking on the tile floor. Though he loved so much about humanity and the Earth, there were many things that disturbed the Martian Manhunter as well. One of them was this, the odor that permeated the air of any human hospital, the acrid aroma of sickness and death.

The role of John Jones was one he had adopted a very long time ago, and he wore the appearance and clothing of the man quite comfortably. Even now he loosened his tie and slipped off his jacket, throwing it over his shoulder as he walked toward the nurses' station outside the Intensive Care Unit. Though the patients on that ward were fighting for their lives, all seemed quiet within at the moment.

A nurse with features like carved ebony glanced up at him as he approached.

"Can I help you?" she asked, her tone letting him know she did not think he belonged there.

J'onn nodded. "I hope you can. I'm looking for one of your doctors, Felix Nutman?"

The woman pursed her lips and shot him an acerbic glance. "Join the club."

A tremor of concern rippled through J'onn. He had had high hopes for Dr. Nutman. Several weeks earlier, if the local news was supposed to be believed, he had begun healing ICU patients with nothing more than his touch. There was nothing at all evangelistic about the man, and he had apparently avoided any opportunity at the celebrity his healing hands might have offered him. The doctor—a British man whose resemblance to the quirky actor John Malkovich had been

played up by the media—had given a single inter-
view, reluctantly, and then had hospital spokespeople
handle things from that point on.

"Could you possibly elaborate on that a bit?" J'onn
asked.

The nurse had gone back to her computer terminal
and was tapping in notes from a clipboard. Now she
glanced around to see that no one was near enough to
overhear their exchange and fixed him with a suspi-
cious stare again.

"Who wants to know, honey? If you're a reporter,
it's gonna cost your bosses plenty."

He slipped out his wallet and showed her his identification. A small laugh eased from her lips as she
glanced at it.

"Private investigator, huh? Nice work if you can
get it, finding lost people and tracking down cheating
husbands."

"That's not the sort of work I usually do," J'onn
replied with as much dignity as he could summon
without seeming to dismiss the woman.

"It is this time," the nurse told him. Then she
smiled brightly. "You find Dr. Nutman, you let him
know that he's missed two shifts already. Lot of people losing sleep to cover for him and keep these patients alive. We could use those magic hands about
now."

J'onn frowned deeply. "He's missing? But there
have been no reports on the news. Where has he
gone?"

She sat back in her chair and stared at him as

though he were the stupidest being on the planet. "If I knew that, darlin', he wouldn't be missing. Doc Nutman hasn't showed up here for a couple of days, and his wife says he hasn't been home either. Maybe he just got tired of all the people wanting him to touch them. He's sort of quiet, Dr. Nutman. Didn't like the spotlight. Maybe he just took off."

Perhaps, J'onn thought. But there was something in the woman's tone that told him she did not believe that.

"Is Dr. Nutman the type of man who would leave his duties unattended, who would impose upon his colleagues and ignore the needs of his patients?" J'onn asked.

The woman's eyes narrowed. "No. Not when you put it that way."

J'onn turned his back on the nurse, leaving her to go back to her computer. As he strode from the hospital he was relieved to be escaping that sick smell, but he was troubled by the disappearance of Felix Nutman. A winged man in Montreal, Canada, had also gone missing, and the League had lost track of Julia Williams, the metahuman who had come to the aid of Superman and Wonder Woman in Paris.

Whatever the reason behind these disappearances, they did not bode well at all.

The building on Tottenham Court Road was a lovely example of early Victorian architecture, but in the city of London it was entirely unremarkable. It was neither rundown nor recently renovated and it had no markings on the front door save the street number. There was no doorman, nor any visible security, but anyone attempting to enter uninvited and without the proper authorization would be dead before they crossed the lobby.

This nine-story structure was but one of the offices utilized by M.I.5, Britain's domestic intelligence agency.

Peter Joyce had worked for M.I.5 for seventeen years. His dedication to the job and the ways in which it had changed him—made him paranoid and secretive—had cost him his marriage. But he still loved the job.

Most days.

Tonight he only wanted to go home, nestle up beneath a blanket and watch something mindless on the telly, even a bad American film on Sky would be sufficient. It had been a very long day. Long week. Long couple of months.

Peter zipped his fly as he exited the restroom, unmindful of being seen. Other than security, there were very few people left in the building. He yawned and twisted his neck round, satisfied with the cracking noise it made, and then he hurried back to his office at the far end of the corridor.

The entire floor was secure, so there was no reason for him to close his own office door, but he did so regularly. That extra dash of paranoia had served him well more than once, and even saved his life when M.I.5 had dealt with some homegrown terrorists during the millennium celebration.

He pushed the door open and stepped inside, so

tired it took him a moment to realize that the lights were off. The room was dark, illuminated only by the light seeping in through the windows from the street.

Peter froze. Then his hand darted out to the switch on the wall. Its click echoed uselessly in the dark.

"Close the door, Peter," a deep voice instructed from the far corner of the room.

A tremor of fear passed through him. It was impossible. No one could have gotten into the building, never mind this room, unobserved. The windows were still locked, they were . . .

Not locked. One of them, in fact, was open just a crack. A cool breeze whispered through the darkness. The window was open, but no alarms had gone off.

Peter was about to go for his gun when a figure unfurled from the shadows and stepped forward, the pointed ears of his cowl silhouetted in the glow from outside the windows.

Batman.

Heart trip-hammering in his chest, Peter let out a short breath of anger. "You nearly gave me a stroke," he said, relieved and yet not completely. The presence of the Batman was not at all comforting.

"You can guess why I'm here," Batman said, his strong voice insinuating and filled with general disapproval.

Peter Joyce did not venture any further into the darkened room. He waited for his eyes to adjust, but Batman remained a silhouette, a flowing shadow, and though he knew the detective was a human being, he could not shake the impression of the supernatural that seemed to cloak the man.

"Why not give me a clue," Peter suggested.

"Metahuman activity. The League's been monitoring it, charting it out. You and your people here have been doing the same. It's a matter of national security for you, but it's bigger than that. I need to know where they're coming from."

For a long moment Peter only stared at him. Years of secrecy were ingrained in him. The hell with the Justice League; his job at M.I.5 did not give him leave to discuss operations with anyone who was not cleared. But that was the thing about Batman. He had been instrumental in aiding M.I.5 in over a dozen cases in half that many years. Peter owed him, though Batman would not find it necessary to mention that debt.

"You're usually ten steps ahead of us," the man admitted. "What don't you already know?"

A dry rasp came from the shadows. "Try me."

"Whatever jumpstarted the abilities these people are manifesting happened no fewer than nine years ago, and no more than twelve. The Instigator, we're calling it. The Instigator is pinpointed within those time parameters because it was the only period during which all of the new metas were living in the U.K. We're trying to narrow it down further. Also, the Instigator was widespread, covering most of the country, including Scotland and Wales. The woman in Belfast was in London visiting relatives at the time."

"They're starting to disappear," Batman said. "Where are they going?"

Peter glanced at the floor, taking a deep breath. There were some truths he wanted to keep secret from Batman more than others—in this case, the fact that M.I.5 was at a loss—but he had to respond.

"We don't know yet."

When Peter glanced back up he expected Batman to be gone. The detective had an uncanny ability to silently disappear with just a moment's distraction. But no, he was still there, cape rustling slightly in the darkness.

"That's it," Peter replied with a shrug.

"No."

That single word, uttered by the Batman, chilled him to the bone. Peter wished desperately that the lights would come back on, but he had never believed in magic.

"No?" he asked.

Batman moved forward. For a moment his silhouette grew in the light from the nighttime street, but then he loomed so large that his cape seemed to blot out all of the light from outside.

"Three members of Parliament have developed metahuman abilities."

Peter shook his head. "How can you know that? No one knows—"

"Sir Ian Rackham is missing. Was he one of the metas in Parliament?"

For a long moment Peter stared at him. He knew Batman could help, knew the Justice League might

well be a necessity in this crisis, but it galled him that
M.I.5 had not been able to keep its secrets.

"You'll be pleased to know I have confirmed the
abilities these three metas are alleged to have, but not
their identities. It upsets me," Batman admitted.

Peter Joyce allowed himself a small smile of satisfaction.

"Was Sir Ian one of them?" Batman asked again.

Slowly, Peter nodded, gaze once more dropping to
the floor. A moment later he blinked as the light from
the street reached him once more. When he glanced
up the window was wide open, and he was alone in
the darkness.

CHAPTER SIX

The entire city of Leicester trembled. It was not an earthquake, merely a kind of rumble that thrummed underground, but neither did it roll through and then subside. By the time the Flash ran through the city it had been going on for more than five hours. He could feel it rattling up through the soles of his boots, a low trembling of the earth that he could feel in his bones.

"You'd think it wouldn't have taken so long to ask for help," he said into his commlink.

"You'd think," Green Lantern replied, Kyle's familiar voice almost inside the Flash's own head. "But people like to think they can deal with things on their own. And there hasn't been much damage. They were probably just waiting for it to subside—"

"And called us when they realized it wasn't going to," Flash replied.

"My thought," Green Lantern confirmed.

The Flash raced into the center of the city, amazed

to see that now that the rumbling had been going on so long, many people were just going about their business. Cars rolled by, men were unloading stock from a truck in front of a grocer's, and there was even a woman strolling along the sidewalk with a baby in a pram.

When he stood still, Wally's teeth rattled in his mouth. His fillings felt strange, as though he had been chewing on aluminum foil. He closed his eyes and focused on the trembling of the ground. After a moment he looked around again, his gaze focusing off to the left.

"Lantern, I think I can track it back to its source." The Flash looked up into the gray sky above Leicester. A light rain was falling. Above the city he saw two spheres of glowing light making their way toward him, high in the air. Green Lantern was carried along by a streak of bright green energy, but beside him there was a slash of golden illumination that cut a swath across the cityscape. They had been searching for a former R.A.F. pilot named Simon Ewell, the man who had been identified as a visual match for photographs of Maelstrom that had been taken at Buckingham Palace weeks earlier, when Lantern and the Flash had first met Ian Partington.

Ian had been helping them search, and the Flash was more than a little impressed with how far the guy had come in a short time. No costume, of course, but Ian had become very adept at using his telekinesis in a variety of ways. The second the identification on Maelstrom had come in, Wally and Kyle had agreed that Ian ought to be in on the search for him. Neither one of them mentioned to their new friend that part of their motivation was that they were supposed to be keeping an eye on Ian in the first place.

"Go for it," Green Lantern said, his voice clear on the commlink.

The Flash ran. He could feel the vibrations from the ground traveling up his legs and he followed them, knowing by their intensity when he was nearer to their source or further away. As he raced through the streets a high-pitched noise reached him, but at his speed it took him a moment to mentally slow it down enough to know what it was. Car alarms. Several of them had been set off by the trembling earth. As he moved past cars that to him seemed to be standing still, he noticed more than one window whose glass had been broken.

Then the city seemed to give way and there was grass beneath his feet. The Flash stopped short and looked around. The style and layout of the buildings told him he had just stumbled onto the campus of the University of Leicester. His deduction might also have had something to do with the dozens of young people milling about who were so very obviously students. Some of them were gathered under umbrellas— though there was hardly enough rain to deter the average British citizen—but others had clustered under the eaves of buildings. The largest number had abandoned all pretense of shelter and were milling around a grand old structure even as administration and faculty members seemed to be trying to drive them back.

"I'm at the University," Flash said into the comm-link.

"We can see you, Wally," Green Lantern replied with a chuckle. "You run fast, but you didn't go that far."

Kyle's words were amusing, but a bone-deep dread had settled into Wally now, and he did not even crack a smile. Instead he rushed across the campus and through the clustered students in the space between heartbeats. There was a ruggedly handsome middle-aged man in a suit and tie barking orders to the other university faculty, so the Flash zeroed in on him. The man was shouting and waving at security officers who had just arrived.

When Flash stopped short in front of him the man let out a shout of alarm and took a step backward, bringing up his hands as though to ward off an attack. Wally had become used to this reaction. At best, when he was moving slowly, people without superhuman speed saw him as a blur of red. To them it would seem as though he had appeared out of thin air.

"Good God!" the man shouted, but the fear was gone from his eyes in an instant, to be replaced by more than a little pique. "One day you're going to kill someone doing that," he said.

"Sorry. I just don't like to waste time. I'm the Flash, representing the Justice League."

The man frowned, knitting thick eyebrows together. "I know who you are. Do I look like an idiot to you?"

Wally swallowed hard. For a moment he felt as

though he were at school here and this man was his own intimidating headmaster. He forced himself not to respond to the man's comment. Instead he glanced at the large building that seemed to have everyone's attention—and which, if the quivering ground was any indication, was also the source of the nonstop tremor.

"What's going on here?"

The stern expression on the man's face seemed to crumble, revealing the trepidation beneath. The man glanced away. "We really don't know."

Before the Flash could follow up on his initial question there was a ripple of astonished sounds from the crowd. His own arrival had startled them, but when Green Lantern and Ian appeared above them, swathed in the crackling green and golden energy of their respective powers, there was a sense of spectacle around them. The two men hung there in the air above the crowd, Kyle in his Green Lantern costume, Ian in expensive trousers and a black greatcoat, his face unmasked.

"What's up?" Green Lantern called down to him.

"Why don't you two start by moving this crowd back from the building," Flash replied.

Even as emerald energy began to extrude from Green Lantern's ring, Ian turned his attention to the crowd. With a gesture, golden light surrounded the gathered students and they were forced half a dozen steps backward as though each of them had been gently propelled. Several of them stumbled and fell, but for the most part they just looked incredulous.

"He's getting pretty good," Flash said quietly into his commlink.

"He is. We might just have to nominate him for the League if he keeps up with this," Kyle replied.

Even from the ground Flash could see Ian grin and poke a finger at Green Lantern. "I'm finding I quite like this job. But no spandex."

"You'd look so cute, though," Kyle teased.

The Flash rolled his eyes. "That's enough, you two. We've got a situation here."

With a frown he turned his attention back to the intimidating official he had first approached. The man had been watching Ian and Kyle in amazement, but now his gaze snapped back to meet Wally's.

"What, precisely, is the situation, Mr. . . ."

"Claprood," the man replied, eyes narrowing, face pinched with the gravity of the circumstances. "When the earth began to shake, there was panic. Some students remained in the dorms and classrooms, others chose to gather on the lawns in case it grew worse and buildings collapsed. In the anarchy that ensued, it was hours before anyone realized that no one had emerged from the library. Not staff. Not students. It was then that we began to realize that the tremors were worse the closer one stood to this building.

"We attempted to see through the windows but there is only darkness inside. Eventually I sent an instructor and a security officer into the library to investigate. That was nearly an hour ago. They have not returned."

The Flash stared at him. "And at what point were

you planning to let the rest of the world know about this?"

The man stiffened and glared at him. "You are here now, Mr. West. We would appreciate any aid you can offer us."

"Lantern, did you get that?" Flash asked in his commlink.

"Every word," Kyle replied, his voice low and grave in Wally's ear. "We going in?"

The Flash turned to gaze up at him, levitating in a haze of green above the campus beside Ian. "We're the Justice League," the Flash replied.

In a sliver of a heartbeat he crossed the distance to the heavy double doors of the library. The light rain had continued to fall and the stone steps were slick. Ian and Green Lantern alighted upon the stairs just behind him.

"Ian, I'm going to want you to hang back," Wally said.

The man raised his hands, golden energy crackling around each finger and leaking out his eyes. "I'm fully capable of taking care of myself."

Green Lantern put a heavy, insistent hand upon his shoulder. "It's not you Wally's worried about." He hooked a thumb toward the crowd. "If anything happens to us in there, someone's got to protect these people, make sure no one else goes inside until we know more. If we didn't think you could handle it, Flash would be bringing you in there and leaving me out here."

For a long moment Ian seemed to consider his words, but then he only nodded. "Right."

Side by side, the Flash and Green Lantern slowly entered the library. Kyle manifested a shield in front of them in case there was some kind of ambush waiting. But what they discovered upon pushing through the heavy wooden doors was another kind of attack entirely, an assault on the senses.

It was impossible.

The library was almost completely empty, though perhaps empty was the wrong word. The Flash stared around in anger and horror. Ten feet inside the door the floor fell away into nothingness. From what must have been the basement all the way up through three stories to just beneath the roof of the building there was only a void, a gray, swirling abyss whose edges seemed to pull at reality, to bend color and matter and the very air itself. The building shook with the rumbling in the ground where the horrid dimensional tear wore away at the bedrock, a cyclone scouring the foundations beneath the building.

"Maelstrom," Green Lantern said, forced to speak up to be heard over the roar of the churning air and the rumbling ground. He lit up the whole place with green light emanating from his ring.

In an instant Wally ran recon around the edges of the maelstrom that had consumed most of the library. When he returned to Green Lantern's side only a moment later, Kyle had already raised his hand and sent tendrils of green energy into the gray abyss, searching for the students and faculty who had been lost within that terrible limbo.

"No sign of Maelstrom, or of anyone else for that matter."

For perhaps fifteen seconds, a time that seemed an eternity to the Flash, Green Lantern probed that maelstrom with his power ring. Eventually those tendrils of energy withdrew from the abyss and dissipated and Kyle turned to him.

"Nothing. I have no idea how big it is over there, how much room, but if there are any survivors we're not getting them back without a full-scale rescue mission. Let's get J'onn on the commlink and—"

His words were interrupted by a loud hiss that supplanted all the other noises in the room. The two of them snapped around to stare in horror at the maelstrom as it collapsed in upon itself. Flash barely heard Green Lantern shouting in frustration. He reached out his arm and started a cyclone of his own, whipping the air into a tornado of activity in hopes that he could prevent the maelstrom from closing. Even as he did so, new tendrils of power reached from Kyle's ring and tried to force the gray, swirling portal to stay open.

They could do nothing. Despite their efforts the maelstrom collapsed like the ash from the tip of a cigarette. A moment later all that remained of it was the destruction it had left in its wake, the enormous library that was now little more than a man-made cavern.

"Damn it!" Green Lantern snapped. He grunted in

frustration and looked at the Flash. "Do you think I caused that? That by searching in there, I—"

"I don't know. Maybe," Flash admitted. He was not going to lie to Kyle. "There's no way to know if there were any survivors. You were trying to save them. You can't beat yourself up."

Green Lantern shot him a hard look. "Why? Wouldn't you?" Once again he shook his head. "We've got to find Maelstrom. That's the only shot we've got at finding out if any of those people are alive, and of getting them out of there if they are."

Flash watched him carefully, then he nodded. "Come over here. When I was searching the place, I saw something . . . weird."

He ran around the circumference of the ravaged interior of the building, careful not to tumble into the chasm that had been torn in the floor. Sheathed in electric green, Kyle flew across that massive pit to join him on the other side. Once there, Wally pointed to a place near the far wall, not far from a bathroom door, where there were still the remains of several toppled bookshelves. Amidst the mess there was a spot perhaps four feet wide where the wooden floor had been torn apart as if something had bored right through it. This portion of the building had no basement. Beneath the wood had been stone foundation, but that too had been broken apart. They could see through the wood and stone and into the dark soil beneath.

The Flash knelt by the hole and touched the corner of a hardcover book that had been churned under and now jutted from the mix of stone and earth in that hole.

"It's like something . . . tunneled out of here," Kyle said, clearly mystified.

"Something," Wally agreed. Then he glanced up at Green Lantern. "Or someone."

The Martian Manhunter was deeply troubled. Over the past several days his efforts to track the missing metahumans had been nearly fruitless. He had found one man—a British-born carpenter working in Greece—who had apparently developed the ability to shapeshift. J'onn had located him in a Greek village not far from the city he had vacated, only to discover that his abilities were apparently magical in nature and that he had left the city because his fiancée's parents had threatened to kill him if he did not. The woman's mother and father thought he was a witch.

Aside from this unfortunate—who preferred not to discuss how he had come by these magical abilities—J'onn had failed to locate a single one of the new metas on his list. Nine missing people, all with metahuman powers, gone without a trace.

Or is there a trace? he thought now.

For each of those who had gone missing he had been able to pinpoint the last place and time at which they had been seen. But there was no way to be certain if they had disappeared an hour or a day later. Most of their residences had turned up no clues.

Yesterday, however, that had changed. At the home of a British musician who made his living as a studio guitarist in Nashville, J'onn had discovered an odd phenomenon. In the man's backyard was an area perhaps five feet in diameter where the earth had been churned up, freshly turned as though it had been dug up and then replaced. At first J'onn had wondered if this was a grave, but upon further investigation it had proven to be a tunnel of some sort . . . a tunnel in which the tunneler had removed the soil from in front of it and replaced it as it passed by, just the way an earthworm did.

This was curious and warranted further investigation, but J'onn's priority at the moment was tracking the missing metas. He promised himself he would return in a day or two to look into it further.

But then this morning he had gone to investigate the last name on his list, a Scottish barrister whose employers had sent him to Minneapolis to handle a case for one of their clients who did business on both sides of the Atlantic. His firm had apparently been unaware that he had recently begun to manifest the ability to speak to and even control animals. The man's wife had only revealed this after his disappearance. Apparently the barrister had felt he would be sacked if he spoke up about what had been happening to him, that no one would believe him.

As it turned out, no one had believed his wife, either.

That day in Minneapolis, the barrister had gone to the bathroom in the basement of the courthouse and never returned. J'onn had spoken to the investigators on the case and discovered that—though it had since been repaired—the tiled floor of the men's room had

looked as though someone had taken a jackhammer
to it.

Now, as he flew across the skyline of Hub City, invisible to anyone who might have chanced to look up
as he went by, a single thought echoed in his mind.

Meta-thieves.

It seemed incredible, but the missing metahumans
and the evidence that something had emerged from
the ground to abduct them pointed in that direction.
As John Jones he had been a detective for years, and
he was not prone to drawing conclusions based upon
partial evidence, so J'onn would withhold judgment
until he knew more. But for the moment it certainly
seemed as though someone or something was either
attacking or abducting these metas from under the
ground.

He still could not make sense of the connection or
of the source of the powers manifested by the new
metas. However, given that no established metas were
being abducted, it seemed to follow that whatever
was happening to them now was also related to the
source of their meta-evolution.

Frustrated by the lack of tangible results from his
investigation, he focused instead on the business at
hand. Bryan Francis, the powerful new meta he had
employed in the matter of the serial killer Zachary
Graff, had phoned John Jones in pursuit of the final
payment for his services. But when J'onn had attempted to contact him in return, the psychometrist
was nowhere to be found. When repeated calls only
ended up with the man's voice-mailbox full, J'onn

grew concerned that he was yet another name to add to the list of the missing.

He had come to Hub City to find out for certain.

It was a clear, cool day but the sky seemed to grow somehow dingy as he flew past the fringes of the recently redeveloped section around City Hall. Sparkling office towers gave way abruptly to decrepit brownstones and neighborhoods that looked as though they had changed little—and only for the worse—in a century.

Bryan had no office, but his apartment was the top floor of Two Hundred Eleven Magyar Street, easy enough to find.

J'onn located it without difficulty and alighted upon the roof, allowing himself to become visible again but morphing his body into the guise of John Jones, in case he should be seen. Or on the off chance that Bryan Francis was home and simply not returning his calls, a possibility that seemed less likely with every moment that passed.

There was something in the air here, something that was indefinable and yet unnerved him. Not a taste or a smell, but perhaps a strange frisson of dread in the atmosphere around this place. He had sensed it before. In the basement of a Minneapolis courthouse. On the Nashville property of a transplanted English guitar player. And other places as well. But only now was he able to recognize it, to connect this feeling to those other places.

A psychic static seemed to fill his head. Something terrible happened here.

Without waiting, J'onn made himself intangible and passed ghostlike down through the roof of Two Hundred Eleven Magyar Street. As little more than a specter he slipped down through the ceiling of Bryan Francis's apartment. As he solidified once more the stench hit him immediately. There was an open jug of milk on the kitchen counter and it had gone badly sour. The garbage can was full and had obviously not been emptied in days.

He made his way down the corridor past the bathroom and a spare bedroom that had been converted to an office. At the end of the hall was another door, partially open, that he presumed must be the man's bedroom.

The Martian Manhunter pushed open the door.

"By H'ronmeer's hands," he whispered, flinching at the scene before him. A ripple of revulsion crossed his features and he felt bile rising up in the back of his throat.

Pillars of black smoke streaked the sky above the television studio lot, flames leaping high from three fires that were already burning. There were emergency crews on the lot—security procedures would demand it—but nobody dared go near the source of the blazes. One of the burning structures was the hastily constructed set for a series pilot, the second was a commissary, and the third was a bungalow type structure where the producers of *Monkey Business* had once had their offices.

Wonder Woman had collected that much information from the Monitor Womb before she and Aquaman had teleported to Los Angeles.

"I hate this town," Arthur muttered now, as the shroud of energy from their teleport dispersed.

Diana silently echoed his sentiment. Los Angeles—Hollywood—was a hollow place, filled almost exclusively with people who hungered for attention the way a heroin addict yearned for his next fix. It was a city of oddities. But this day L.A. was bearing witness to oddities it was ill prepared for.

They had teleported onto the street inside the gates of the studio. People could be seen huddled behind parked cars and at the windows of some of the two-story buildings with their faces pressed to the glass. Some of the windows were shattered. The security booth at the front gate was vacant and even now a car rolled up to the gate and the driver laid on the horn, the sound of it tearing across the lot.

"Is the man blind or merely an idiot?" Aquaman snarled as he glared at the car.

"Neither, I'd wager," Wonder Woman replied. "They make film and television here, Arthur. It's likely he thinks the fires are controlled. An effect."

Aquaman grunted. He did not have to express his thoughts about such foolishness; his expression said it all. He looked around at the damage that had been done—at the fissures that had opened up in the pavement, some wide enough that they had swallowed cars entirely—and started moving swiftly toward the fires.

"We must stop this before the one with seismic powers starts up again," he said.

Diana caught up with him, but her attention was diverted. She was studying the buildings. From the look of them she determined that the permanent structures would likely withstand the seismic activity, but that the temporary sets would collapse. Her real concern, however, was the fire. The wind coming down from the east had picked up and the flames were spreading.

"Arthur, the blaze—"

He shot her a hard look. Aquaman was far more interested in stopping the metahumans who were rampaging across the studio lot than in saving the property of a multibillion dollar corporation. But Wonder Woman regarded him evenly and after a moment he nodded. He glanced around and then pointed skyward.

"I'm not sure that tower will contain enough water, but I should be able to douse the two nearest fires with its contents."

Wonder Woman looked at the structure he had indicated. She frowned. The water tower bore the studio's logo and she had no idea if it was purely decorative or if it actually had water in it. There was only one way to find out, however.

"You'll catch up?" She glanced at Aquaman.

He nodded once and then set off running toward the tower.

Diana took two running steps and launched herself into the air. She flew quickly over the pavement, past the burning commissary and the bungalow that was on fire. There were trees below at the edges of the

parking lot and golf carts that were apparently used
by studio personnel to traverse the vast lot. A single
security vehicle was parked sideways in front of the
burning bungalow and a guard was on his mobile
shouting for the firefighters to hurry.

The lines of bungalows gave way just ahead to a
long five-story structure of glass and steel. The
metahumans were ridiculously easy to spot. The two
large men marched shoulder to shoulder across the
lot toward that long office building, unmindful of
the gawkers at the windows and the trio of people
who cowered behind an SUV. The one on the left
was more than six and a half feet tall and bald, and
his hands were on fire. His companion was shorter,
dark complexioned, but still had the build of a
weightlifter.

As she glided silently toward them, forty feet in the
air, Diana took their measure. The one with the dark
complexion must be the seismic meta, thus she had to
take him out first. The flames would be easier to deal
with. They approached a road that separated the line
of bungalows from the office structure and she
waited, wanting them to be in the center of the road,
as far from the buildings as possible.

Determined, they strode on toward the five-story
building.

Abruptly, with a sound like a thousand crickets,
there came a flash of light and a figure appeared to
block their path. A teenaged girl with wild red hair
appeared in front of them in a burst of static that
could be both seen and heard. *Teleporter,* Wonder

Woman thought, and not like the one on the Watch-tower. This girl's power was innate, not artificial.

From this distance she could not hear if the girl said anything, but she rushed the two metas and leaped up into a high kick. Her boot caught the seismic meta in the face and the weightlifter staggered backward and collapsed. He rose to his knees, clearly disoriented, but by then the new arrival was going for Firehands.

She was fast, this lithe little redheaded girl. Had the pyrokinetic meta only had fire hands, she would have been fast enough. But the man opened his mouth as though to roar and vomited a stream of liquid flame at the girl.

Wonder Woman clenched her fists and flew down toward the melee, knowing she would be too late. She need not have worried. With another screech of static noise, the girl teleported away from the attack, appeared behind the fire-breather, and rabbit-punched him in the kidneys with such force that it sent him sprawling half a dozen feet.

Teleportation and enhanced strength, Wonder Woman observed with great interest. If there had not been lives at stake, she might have hung back to observe the girl further. That was part of what they were doing, after all, observing the new metas.

As the fire-breather started to rise, the redhead knocked him down again. Then she started to move in, ready to kick him.

Wonder Woman saw it about to happen. She sped toward the battle, coming down out of the sky so fast that the wind whistled in her ears. The seismic meta had recovered and was kneeling. He put his hands on the pavement and the ground began to rumble. With an ear-splitting crack, a fissure opened up in the road, snaking toward the teenage girl. The earth opened up beneath her and she cried out, taken by surprise, as she tumbled into the chasm, her red hair flying upward as she fell.

Wonder Woman reached the kneeling meta an eyeblink later, her mind awhirl as she hoped the girl would be all right. All of the righteous fury of the ancient Amazons rose up within her as she reached out and grasped the meta by the throat and lifted him bodily from the ground.

She cocked her fist back.

The blow fell.

Yet even as it did, he began to change before her eyes. The meta's flesh grew darker and began to crack in places. Instead of skin, he had armor plating the color of brick.

Wonder Woman's fist struck the meta, and he stumbled backward, but she had felt her knuckle break on his armor plating. That was not supposed to happen. *What are you made of?* she thought as she stared at him.

And the meta continued to change.

CHAPTER SEVEN

The water tower came down with a shriek of tearing metal. Aquaman had carefully gauged the angle of its fall. The bungalow was too distant for the water to reach, but the commissary was near enough, as was the false façade of a brownstone building on a larger set that was obviously meant to be Keystone City. The tank on top of the tower struck the ground and exploded outward. A massive wave of water washed out across the lot. Far too much of it was wasted, but there was enough to douse the commissary fire completely. The faux brownstone was a different story. The flames had spread to the top of the structure, so though the fire on the lower portions was doused—helping to keep it from spreading—the top continued to burn.

Aquaman took it all in, and then chose to ignore it.

He was Arthur, King of Atlantis, part of the Justice League. He had not come here to fight fires. Already he could hear the scream of sirens. The humans would arrive momentarily to complete the work he had begun. But now there were other things he had to attend to.

Aquaman ran across the parking lot. A wide fissure blocked his way but he leaped over to the rear fender of a car that jutted from the chasm, then jumped the rest of the distance to the other side. He sprinted along the lane that ran between two rows of bungalows, following the path Wonder Woman had flown. The burning bungalow was just ahead and there was a security guard standing just outside his vehicle, glancing around helplessly as he watched the small office structure go up in flames. When the man spotted Arthur rushing toward him his eyes went wide and his jaw fell slack.

"Aquaman?" the security officer said, awe in his voice. "What can I do? How can I help?"

On another day Arthur would simply have instructed him to stay out of the way. But as he raced toward the man, boots slapping the pavement, black smoke billowing from the bungalow and choking his lungs, Aquaman shot the man a grim look.

"Get that fire out," he instructed.

A fire truck had started up the lane behind him, siren screaming.

"We will," the officer replied gravely.

But Aquaman was not listening. He had already run past the security guard. Far ahead he saw a lone figure in the air above the studio—Wonder Woman.

Without warning the ground began to rumble and

shudder beneath his feet. Aquaman gritted his teeth and stumbled once before regaining his balance and running on. He picked up speed, wishing in that moment that he was as swift out of the water as he was beneath the waves. Seconds later he raced around the corner of the last bungalow, into the shadow of a five-story office building.

In the street that separated him from the building, Wonder Woman traded blows with a monster. The creature was humanoid, and if the reports they had received were correct it might once have been a man. It was entirely covered in a copper-brown plating.

Aquaman paused, eyes narrowed. Something about that plating, the way the tiles were arranged across its body, the shape and color of them, brought back an echo from his memory.

The armored creature struck Wonder Woman with an open hand, its plating clacking against her skull with a terrible dull thunk. Princess Diana reeled backward, then took flight to escape the monstrosity, gaining precious seconds to recover. As she did so, she spotted Aquaman.

"In the fissure!" Diana shouted to him. "The girl!"

Girl? Aquaman frowned. *What girl?*

But he did not pause to inquire. Even as he watched Wonder Woman fly down at her assailant again, pummeling him with a rain of blows that might have driven even Arthur himself to his knees, Aquaman raced toward the edge of the fissure.

Which was when he saw the other combatant on this field of battle. Across the wide chasm that had been torn in the road was a large bald man with burning eyes and flaming hands. He was climbing to his feet, his fiery gaze locked on Aquaman. Arthur's first instinct was to leap the fissure and beat him into submission. This was obviously the meta who had started the fires, which meant the other was the one with seismic abilities.

But the urgency in Diana's voice echoed in his mind and so he ignored the flaming man. Aquaman ran to the edge of the fissure and looked down. Even with the shadow of the building blotting out the direct sunlight, the day was bright enough that the entire interior of that chasm was illuminated.

In a crevasse a short way down was the unconscious form of a red-haired teenage girl. Her limbs were splayed wide but as far as he could tell she was not badly injured.

"You! Aquaman!" shouted the hulking man with the blazing hands.

Arthur glanced up. The man was fifteen feet away, on the opposite side of the fissure, staring furiously at him. In the heat of the moment it took him time to realize that the man had an English accent, something they had come to expect in recent days.

"Yeah, your Highness, I know who you are. This is none of your business, mate. None at all. These ignorant wankers, they took off me favorite program. Canceled it, they did. Well maybe once upon a time there wasn't anything I could do about it, but now there is. Me and Andrew, we're not going to take this one lying down."

A chill went through Aquaman. As ridiculous as the man's comments seemed on their surface, they brought to mind Wally and Kyle's report about their first contact with Maelstrom at Buckingham Palace. That day, the meta had been demanding that the Queen of England knight him. This crusade seemed equally absurd, but Aquaman had to wonder if there was a connection, if the powers these new metas were manifesting were also warping their minds in some way.

These idiots had come down to the studio to burn it down in punishment for the cancellation of their favorite television show. Aquaman was going to enjoy thrashing them soundly.

In a moment.

Right now, he had the girl to think about. He stepped over the edge of the fissure and dropped down inside it. Even as he did so, the pyrokinetic meta roared in fury and flame gouted from his mouth, shooting in an arc across the fissure to melt the pavement where Aquaman had been standing a moment before.

Aquaman landed on a small ledge near the unconscious girl, but now he was wary. He was a target, down there in the fissure. The King of Atlantis snatched up the girl from the ground and cradled her against his chest, which rose and fell rapidly, his lungs trying to process the smoky air.

In his arms, she groaned. He glanced down at her as her eyes fluttered open.

"Are you all right?" he asked.

The pyrokinetic shouted angrily and raised his hands, pointing down at them. Arthur knew he had to get out of the way, find cover, but the only way he could see to do that would have been to go deeper into the fissure. He prepared to drop further into the chasm, clutching the girl against him.

Then the pyrokinetic shouted again, but this time in pain.

"What?" Arthur grunted, and his head snapped up. He stared in astonishment as the pyrokinetic cried out in agony, slapping at his arms, tongues of flame licking up from his fingers. His skin had started to split all over in a grid pattern, as though invisible knives were slicing into his flesh. Then it began to change, to harden and darken.

In seconds, the meta had armor plating similar to that of his companion, but with a more crimson tint that reminded Aquaman of brick.

"What . . . Aquaman?" muttered the redheaded girl as she came around.

Arthur looked down at the girl in his arms, shot another glance at the evolving, fire-handed meta, and began to climb back up the side of the fissure toward the street. In seconds he emerged from that chasm in the pavement, and now the girl was fully awake and aware.

"Thank you," she said, shaking her head and blowing out a long breath, blinking her eyes to reorient herself. "I could've teleported, but I guess I was just . . . too scared. And then I hit my head, and—"

The ground shook again. Another split appeared,

snaking off from the first. The pavement tore open. Arthur and the girl backed up to avoid falling into it. Aquaman turned around and saw Wonder Woman still trading blows with the seismic meta. Her face was bleeding now and there was a long gash on one of her arms.

"Diana!" Aquaman shouted. He shot the girl a sideways glance. "I don't know what you're doing here, but you said you can teleport. Get out of here, then. I can't protect you and take these things on at the same time."

Things. Not men, things. Where are you going with this, Arthur? he thought. But he knew the answer to that question. He remembered where he had seen plating like this before.

But it had not been on human beings. That much was certain.

The pyrokinetic had been completely altered. Though larger, it looked almost identical to the other meta. It ran to the edge of the fissure—its heavy feet shaking the ground—and lunged across the gap. Its thick, plated hands caught the edge of the crumbling pavement and it began to pull itself up.

Aquaman was just grateful it could not fly. If the other one could do so much damage to Wonder Woman, the two of them together were a serious threat. He ran toward Diana, blond hair flying in his face. There would be no hesitation now, no quarter given. These things had to be dealt with before the situation got even further out of hand.

As he approached her, Wonder Woman grabbed

the seismic meta and took flight, holding its head between her hands. Her muscles rippled as she used her
extraordinary strength to lift the heavy monstrosity
off the ground. Then she hurled it back at the street,
shattering the pavement. For a moment, the thing lay
still.

It began to stir just as Aquaman reached it.

As it rose, he hauled back his fist and struck the
thing. Armor plating cracked and it staggered. Pain
shot up Aquaman's arm but he hit the thing again
and again. With a glance out of the corner of his eye
he saw the pyrokinetic climb up out of the fissure and
start toward him.

Wonder Woman cut off its attack. In mid-flight she
dropped down and kicked it in the head. The thing
stumbled three steps but did not fall. Though he
would never have admitted it, a certain trepidation
filled the heart of the King of Atlantis then. These
things were fantastically powerful, not to mention
durable. If what he suspected was true, there might
be many more where these two came from.

"What are you?" Aquaman demanded. He stared
into the eyes of the seismic meta, buried as they were
amongst the armor plates. Its gaze burned yellow, but
in that moment Aquaman realized that as far as he
knew neither of the metas had spoken since their
transformation.

He launched a kick at the thing's abdomen. He felt
the blow in his bones, and wondered if it had hurt
him more than it had his target.

The seismic thing reached for him with its huge

hands and Arthur wondered what its powers would do if they were turned on a person instead of the earth. He did not want to find out. Aquaman blocked the attack, preparing to launch another blow at the thing, but then the monstrosity began to jitter as if it were having some kind of seizure.

Its torso cracked and stretched, elongating, and its mouth gaped wide, tearing at the edges of its plated lips, so that its maw now split its head nearly in half.

Aquaman cursed under his breath, calling on the gods of Atlantis.

A heavy hand clamped upon his shoulder and he spun, prepared to defend himself, presuming that the pyrokinetic had momentarily gotten the better of Wonder Woman. But Diana was still battering at her opponent. The hand that had spun him around belonged, instead, to the red-haired meta girl.

Whose hair was gone.

She, too, had evolved. Her entire body was now covered with that same plating and even as he looked at her, Aquaman saw her mouth growing wider, lips splitting. Her torso stretched and she lashed out at him. Aquaman's fist hammered down toward her face.

With a static hiss she disappeared, blinking out of existence. He had barely had time to register her presence behind him and begin to turn when she brought both armored fists down upon his back. A grunt of pain escaped him and Aquaman went down.

But the transformed metas—these nightmare creatures who had been normal humans only weeks ago,

and at least humanoid metas only minutes earlier—
were not attacking him any longer.

The one with seismic powers, its torso now so long
it seemed almost serpentine, dove face first at the
ground. Its maw gaped wide and its thick, plated fist
ripped at the pavement, and in the matter of a few
seconds it had tunneled and gnawed its way into a
hole in the ground, and disappeared beneath the
earth. The other, the female that had been his ally only
moments before, followed suit.

Slowly, gaping in amazement, Aquaman stood and
stared at the two round holes that had been bored in
the street. He wondered for a moment if they were
going to come back, if this was some feint, but he
knew that was ridiculous. They had had him down,
vulnerable, and they had simply left him there.

"Arthur?"

He glanced over to see that Wonder Woman's battle with the pyrokinetic had somehow taken her to the
other side of the fissure. Still streaked with her own
blood, she held a hand over her wounded arm and
stared at him, then glanced down at a hole in the
pavement at her feet that was identical to the two
near Aquaman.

"What in Hera's name is going on here?"

In the Hub City apartment of Bryan Francis, J'onn
J'onzz stood just inside the bedroom and stared at the
corpse splayed across the bed. His position as a member of the Justice League had brought him into contact
with a parade of abominable things over the years,

but these experiences had not inured him to the hideous. He shuddered in revulsion, and yet beneath that was a creeping dread that lingered in his mind like the ever-present whispers of the thoughts of those around him. Such was the lot of a high level telepath.

If only he had sifted more deeply through Bryan Francis's thoughts.

More clinical now, he narrowed his eyes. It was difficult to be certain if the thing on the bed even *was* Bryan Francis. Or had been. Portions of its body still seemed human, the throat and the left arm, to be exact. The rest of its exposed flesh simply was not flesh any longer. The skin had been replaced or covered by a reddish-brown plating that made J'onn think, first, of an armadillo, and a moment later, of the Qifftu, a desert animal native to ancient Mars.

The hands of the corpse clutched a shotgun.

The face and skull had been obliterated.

The suicide of Bryan Francis—or the thing in Bryan's apartment—had sprayed blood and brain tissue across the wall in an arc, an artist's interpretation of sunrise in Hell. But the blood was bright orange like the skin of a pumpkin. Not human at all.

That dread came surging up within him again, and he stared at the plating on the dead man. He remembered his conversation with Aquaman some time back in the Monitor Womb, how Arthur had come into conflict with something beneath the waves that had seemed familiar to him. That thing, too, had had armor plating.

J'onn stared at those plates.

They were familiar to him as well, but he could not figure out why. A memory niggled at the back of his mind, trying to surface, but it would not come.

In time, he thought. *In time, it will come to me.*

Green Lantern stared across the table at Superman. The entire Justice League was gathered in that room, and yet for a long moment the Watchtower was eerily silent save for the thrumming of the electrical and life support systems.

"So, you're saying Ian is going to turn into one of those things?" he demanded.

Superman's expression was grim. But it was J'onn who replied.

"It is regrettable, Kyle," the Martian Manhunter said, the kindness in his eyes belying the almost emotionless tone of his voice. "But given my discovery in Hub City and what Aquaman and Wonder Woman experienced in Los Angeles, we have to proceed under the assumption that all of those who meet this criteria will transform, just as Bryan Francis did.

"We had been baffled by the disappearances of some of these new metas, and now, it seems, we have the answer we were seeking. It is not at all what we had hoped for, yet there is a preponderance of evidence to support this new theory, not the least of which are the remains of Mr. Francis himself."

When Green Lantern glanced over toward Wally, he discovered that the Flash was no longer in his seat. This was not unusual—with Wally's speed he might go anywhere without anyone noticing him slipping away. Kyle glanced around the room and located the Flash standing in front of the long viewport on its outer hull, his sleek red uniform silhouetted against the dark vastness of space beyond.

The Flash turned to face them. "Just because some of them have . . . evolved, that doesn't mean they all will."

"Wally, we all wish this wasn't happening," Superman said.

Batman had been perfectly still during the conversation thus far but now he leaned forward, his elbows on the table. This simple movement drew the attention of the entire League. The lighting was so bright in the conference room that Green Lantern had always figured it must be extremely uncomfortable for Batman to be that exposed. Even amongst his comrades-in-arms. Whenever he wasn't participating, Batman was as still as a statue.

Now all eyes were upon him.

"But it *is* happening," Batman said, that voice more ominous than ever. "This isn't all guesswork, Kyle. A lot of this we know. The rest is hypothesis based upon that knowledge. J'onn found parasitic organisms inside Bryan Francis's remains, some of which were on a cellular level. They were changing his genetic structure.

"At some point within the last decade or so—we're still narrowing the time frame—some catalyst struck the United Kingdom and infected a portion of the population. Whatever this viral mutagen is, it's caused at least some of those afflicted to develop metahuman abilities. The effects are so widespread that the weather is the only factor likely to have touched all of these new metas. A simple storm front might have spread the virus, but that means the majority of the population is resistant to it, otherwise the infection would have been far more widespread. What that mutagen is or how it got here, we do not know."

Superman gazed around the table at the members of the League. When the Kryptonian's focus settled upon him, Green Lantern shifted uncomfortably in his seat.

"It's possible, Kyle," Superman said. He glanced at the Flash. "Wally. It's possible that Ian's metahuman abilities are unrelated to this phenomenon."

Green Lantern sighed. "But not likely."

"Highly *un*likely," Wonder Woman added. "The question then, becomes, how can we help him, and all of the others who haven't transformed further."

Now Batman sat back in his chair and steepled his gloved fingers under his chin, his eyes narrowing beneath his cowl.

"From the data we've collected, a few hypotheses can be advanced. One, that the wave of new metahumans has either reached its conclusion or slowed dramatically. We have identified eighty-seven new metahumans. At last count three are confirmed dead and forty-one have disappeared. Of those who have disappeared, it is possible that some of them have abandoned their former lives due to their metahuman development.

"Most—or even all—of them must be presumed to have undergone the same further metamorphosis Diana and Arthur encountered in Los Angeles, and which Bryan Francis killed himself to halt. I've done a chronological examination and it appears that those metas who developed their abilities earliest also disappeared earliest. There are exceptions, however. Logic dictates that some will take longer than others to further evolve, but it would be premature to believe or even hope that any of them will be able to avoid the secondary metamorphosis without help."

A shiver went through Kyle. Ian had developed at least the first vestiges of his telekinesis even before many of the other new metas had first evidenced their abilities. He shot a glance at the Flash, but Wally only stared at Aquaman, clearly troubled deeply.

Batman looked closely at Kyle before turning his attention at last to Superman. "There are going to be some cases that we haven't heard about yet. There may be some we never hear about. Some of the people who have developed metahuman abilities are going to hide them."

He paused, but there had been a weight to his voice that told the rest of the League that he had not finished, that his explanation was leading somewhere unpleasant.

"Contacts in British Intelligence have helped me to confirm that at least two members of Parliament have developed meta powers that the British government is doing its best to keep quiet. This is growing more difficult because their behavior has become erratic and volatile, just as we've seen with some of the others."

Aquaman leaned forward, his metallic hand thumping on the table. "Flow charts and observation aren't going to stop these things."

The Martian Manhunter regarded him coolly. "Batman's investigation must continue. It is imperative that we have as complete a list as possible of those infected so that we can help them if that is feasible, or stop them if it is not."

"Wonder Woman and I saw what these people are becoming," Aquaman said grimly. "As far as we know there are dozens of them burrowing underground in the U.K., mainland Europe, and the United States. These are monsters with a massive capacity for destruction. We have to—"

"What?" Flash asked sharply. "Destroy them? Track them down and kill them? They were people first. Before we do anything, we've got to figure out what caused this and if there's a way to fix it, to turn them back."

"That is precisely what we are doing," J'onn noted, his thick brow furrowing, his green skin somehow pale. "Further examination of Bryan Francis's remains should tell us a great deal, possibly including the answer to whether or not this process is reversible. However, there will be a limit as to what can be ascertained from the deceased. We will also need to study the physiology of one of the new metas who has not yet undergone that secondary metamorphosis to compare the two."

Green Lantern took a deep breath and let it out. He stared down at the gleaming table. At length he glanced up, first at Flash, then at Superman, and finally at J'onn.

"You want us to bring Ian to the Watchtower."

"To S.T.A.R. Laboratories, actually," Superman noted.

"So what are we supposed to tell him?" Flash demanded. "I don't guess you want it to be the truth."

"That might be very dangerous," Batman noted. "We don't know what triggers the secondary evolution, but if there's a chemical catalyst, stress might do it."

Green Lantern looked around the table. "So what *do* we say, then?"

Superman frowned. "Tell him the Justice League wants to see him."

Ten years ago . . .

The single headlamp on her motorcycle made eerie shadows on the striated stone walls of the tunnel as the Black Canary sped through the hidden passage that led to the headquarters of the recently formed Justice League of America. It was almost surreal to her still. Dinah Lance had grown up around members of the Justice Society, the original team of heroes back in the day when people still used the term superhero. Her mother had been a member of the Justice Society in its later days.

Now here she was, part of the new generation. *Me,*

Dinah Lance, and four cute guys. Well, all right, three cute guys and a Martian. Not that she was the kind of woman who was going to be caught up in any inter-office romance. Much as Hal and Barry might showboat for her, the Black Canary knew neither one of them was doing more than flirting. Barry was engaged, and Hal . . . well, Hal's life seemed too complicated for Dinah. She liked things simple.

Aquaman—Arthur—was something else entirely. He was still trying to become accustomed to the surface world, to dealing with human beings, and there was a standoffish quality about him that she hoped he would grow out of one day. He had a good and noble heart, but he was in serious need of a brush-up on his social skills.

The motorcycle hit a bump and the engine revved beneath her. Dinah's hair flew behind her and she grinned, rocketing through the tunnel. Up ahead was the cavern where she could park it, and the entrance to the HQ. Doing this—the entire Black Canary thing—meant everything to her. Her mother had been the first Black Canary, and it was cool to be carrying on a tradition. But it was more than that. This was her life now.

The work she had done on her own, solving crimes, tracking killers, stopping terrorists and lunatics from taking their hatred and madness out on the world . . . it was its own reward. But being a part of the Justice League, dealing with international conspiracies, metahuman criminals, and alien invasions, was something else entirely. On her own, she saved lives. With the Justice League, she had already saved the world more than once.

And it looked like today might offer her yet another opportunity.

The Black Canary parked her motorcycle, propped it on its kickstand, and raced toward the door that would let her into the interior of the HQ. She identified herself for the computer security system, let it take a voice-print, and then pressed her left eye to the peephole in the door so it could do a retinal scan.

"Welcome, Black Canary," the computer buzzed. There was a click and the door opened.

"Thanks," she replied, and then she went inside, the door clicking shut after her.

The place was quiet and gloomy, only a few lights on deeper inside the structure. Dinah clucked her tongue and flicked the switch that made the recessed lighting flash on, illuminating the entire room in a gentle white glow.

"Hello?" she called.

There was no response from inside the HQ, which was odd, since she had received a call from J'onn J'onzz on her commlink, asking her to come to the headquarters at once.

"Anybody home?"

There was a click and a whirr and then the electronic voice of the computer spoke to her again. "Hello, Black Canary. There is . . . one . . . other member of the Justice League here. Aquaman is in the . . . monitor room."

Dinah chuckled and shook her head. The computer

always cracked her up. All she could think about when it spoke to her was *2001: A Space Odyssey.* "I'm sorry, Dave," she whispered to herself now. "I can't *do* that."

She stretched, muscles popping in her neck and shoulders. It had taken her nearly three hours to get here, and that only because she happened to be in the area. Dinah had seen movies and television programs where they had teleporters and crazy things like that, and she wished that sort of technology were real and available. *Wouldn't that make life easier,* she thought.

Deep inside the headquarters, past the personal quarters and the conference chamber, she came to the monitor room. The door was open and inside, she could see Aquaman perched on the edge of a chair, staring at whatever was on the screens before him. The light from the monitors flickered on his face and for a moment Dinah was taken aback. He was a handsome man, with chiseled features and blond hair, yet usually there was a kind of alien grace about him. But seated there in the dim glow of the monitors, there was something grim and pugnacious about him, an edge to his bearing that she had not noticed before.

"Aquaman?"

Arthur glanced up at her and nodded in greeting. "Come in, Canary. Though I don't know why J'onn called us. There's little we can do for them from here."

Dinah frowned. *What on Earth did that mean?* But then she entered the room and upon the screens she saw the R.A.F. planes and the tanks and soldiers, saw the monstrosities with their brick-red, armored bodies stomping through a village on one screen, a green field on a second, and through London itself on a third.

"They're in England?" she asked.

Aquaman quickly filled her in on what little he knew, how Green Lantern had first encountered the things as they made planetfall, burning through the atmosphere and then crashing to Earth in various places around the United Kingdom. He explained that the Royal Air Force had attacked the giant creatures after the first one had begun thrashing through Ealing, and how the R.A.F. planes had been torn from the sky by the swift, brutal monsters.

"J'onn was in Spain when it began. He's only recently arrived in England to help. The Flash was at home, but obviously Barry is fast enough that he was there not long after Green Lantern contacted him."

Black Canary only nodded and continued to stare at the horror unfolding on the monitors. "So what do we do? Why are we here? There's no way we can get there in time to make a difference."

"True. But we don't know yet if this is an isolated incident. If it spreads, we need to be able to act on that, particularly if America is next. As for England . . . we'll just have to hope that the three of them can handle it without us."

Dinah nodded. Of course they could. Arthur was strong, certainly, and she was a formidable fighter, both hand to hand and with her Canary Cry, but Hal and J'onn were the real powerhouses, and Barry could hold his own. They'd figure something out.

She stared at one particular screen, live camera footage from a newsman in a helicopter above London. The monster's horns and its armor plating gave her chills, but what bothered her more were its many eyes. There was nothing remotely intelligent in them. They were simply cold and determined and emotionless.

"What do they want, do you think?"

"Does it matter?" Aquaman replied darkly.

The Black Canary turned to gaze at him. "Of course it matters. Where are they going? What are they doing here? Is it an invasion, or something else? Are they lost? Are they out to destroy humanity, or just visiting?"

The Atlantean glared at her. "Are we watching the same footage, Dinah? I don't care what their purpose is. Lives have already been lost. People trampled underfoot. Buildings collapsed on top of them. Both the British military and the League have attempted to communicate with the invaders and to reason with them, and those attempts have failed. This has been going on for three hours already and the yield so far has been death and destruction. The aliens are incredibly durable, their flesh apparently impenetrable. They're destroyers, Canary. And every minute that goes by until they are stopped is another one that costs us dearly.

"There's only one real option, here. They have to be stopped. No matter what it takes."

CHAPTER EIGHT

Now . . .

Far beneath the waves of the Gulf of Mexico, Aquaman swam for the surface, the ocean giving way before him as though even the water itself obeyed the whim of the King of Atlantis. He sensed the mood of the ocean in his every nerve ending—its temperature and undulating currents—and his mind stretched psychic tendrils out through the water and touched all of the living things around him in the Gulf.

He breached the surface with such speed that it catapulted him out of the water and he knifed back into the nearest swell. Then Aquaman raised his head from the water and pushed his long, sodden hair away from his face. *Yes*, he thought, *this is the place. Or near enough*.

Though he was several miles out, he could clearly see the ravaged shoreline of North Captiva Island, the hurricane-damaged trees that had been blown down, somehow sparing the few homes on the island. It was the same view he had had on that day when the Justice League had first become aware of all the new metahumans that had been popping up.

Among those places of the surface world he admired, the Gulf Coast of Florida was of particular note. The sky was such a bright, crystal blue here, and at dusk when the sun went down on the horizon there was a display of colors so rich they looked as though they had been painted with a palette of ancient Atlantean magic. If it had not been for the humans and their boats and waverunners, it might have rivaled some of the breathtaking undersea vistas he had witnessed. But on the surface it was impossible to escape the humans and their pollutants. There were only a handful of pristine places left on Earth.

At least, above the water.

And the number was diminishing beneath as well, but it was not the people of Atlantis and the other denizens of the seas who caused this tainting of the oceans. It was humanity, of course. A significant by-product of Arthur's tenure with the Justice League had been his attempts to draw the attention of humankind to what they were doing to the world's oceans. In general, however, the human race was an exceptionally bad neighbor.

Swayed by the waves, bobbing in the water, Aquaman closed his eyes and drifted a moment. Somewhere far off in the distance he could hear the thumping rhythm of a human radio and the ding of a buoy. He tuned these sounds out, just as he erased from his mind his awareness of the fishing tour boat that was chugging back toward Captiva and Sanibel, heading away from him.

His consciousness spread through the water itself and he touched everything. Tarpon and grouper, cobia and blacktip sharks, horseshoe crabs and shrimp, stingrays and sea horses, and a family of lazy manatee. A knot of anxiety formed in his gut, an undercurrent of dread that had been present the last time he was here, and remained now, though it was not quite as powerful as it had been. The ocean life was agitated the way it always was when there was a tropical storm or hurricane on the way. But there was no impending storm now, no natural cause for their agitation.

As his mind touched each of theirs, Aquaman soothed the creatures of the Gulf as best he could. Then, at last, his telepathic voice reached other intelligent minds. He had found what he had been searching for.

Aquaman submerged and began to swim due west. He was about to correct his course, but he did not need to. Already the pod of dolphins whose minds he had touched had begun to alter their own heading, turning toward him in the water. As he swam deeper he looked around, eyes automatically adjusting to the increasingly dim light beneath the surface. There were far fewer fish than he would have normally found in this part of the ocean, but he knew it was not due to overfishing. Something had scared them away a while ago, and he was unsettled by the fact that they had yet to return.

He swept through the water at great speed but then slowed so as not to alarm the dolphins. A moment later he was among them, the pod swimming past him and then circling, their squeaking cries traveling through the water to him. There were perhaps twenty-five of them, a decent-sized pod, but not large by the standards of the region.

Hello, my friends, he thought, putting the words in their minds with the marine telepathy that was his birthright. *It is good to see you again.*

A psychic barrage of greetings assaulted his mind as the dolphins responded to him, but Aquaman sifted through them, sensing that at least some of these creatures were familiar to him. One of them, the matriarch of the pod, swam closer to him and brushed against him. He ran his right hand over her body as she passed.

You are troubled, the dolphin replied, her thoughts so unlike those of a human and yet Aquaman understood her perfectly. *You come back because the monster is still here.*

An image flashed through his mind of the last time he had been here, of the savagely swift, hideous monstrosity that had attacked him. He had been responding to the anxiety among the sea creatures here and had been several fathoms down when it appeared from the darkness below. The thing had been covered in thick brown and red scales that he now realized were similar to the armor plating on the transformed metahumans. It had arms, but its lower half was all fish, a demonic mer-creature he had presumed to have been some sort of mutation.

Aquaman had gored the thing with the barbed harpoon attached to his left wrist. There had been no intelligence in its eyes and it had not occurred to him to think it might be—or might once have been—human. He had left it for dead.

It was not dead, was it? he thought now, as the dolphins circled him. He could feel the pressure of their passage through the water like caresses against his skin.

We thought it was dead. It drifted and it bled, the matriarchal dolphin thought. *But then it opened its eyes again.*

Where did it go?

She swam right at him. *Deep. It went deep. Come, we will show you.*

As one, the pod turned and began to swim further west, descending further beneath the waves. Aquaman joined them, swimming amongst them as though he were part of the pod, with the same respect and courtesy they afforded him. The ocean bottom was mostly sand and shells nearer to the islands, but out here the terrain was different. In places there were rocky shelves among the marine vegetation.

In the distance, through the murk, he saw an ancient wreck, its skeletal remains jutting up from the ocean bottom.

But then a whisper in his mind distracted him. His name. And the whisper resolved itself from a light touch to the rich, full mental voice of the Martian Manhunter.

Arthur, J'onn J'onzz said, his voice in Aquaman's mind, far clearer than the dolphins'. *I wondered where you had gone off to so quickly.*

J'onn's telepathy was far more powerful than Aquaman's. The Manhunter had searched the world for him and located him. Of the many things J'onn contributed to the League, his wisdom was the most valuable. Second only to that was his telepathy, which kept the members of the League in contact with one another, something that was vital in times of serious conflict. Yet J'onn never looked too deep, never pried if he could avoid it. Aquaman was always careful to use his own telepathy to make certain of that.

At times, however, a touch from J'onn's mind communicated elements of J'onn's own thoughts. For instance, Arthur could practically see the Justice League Monitor Womb around him now, though he was fathoms deep beneath the surface of the Gulf of Mexico, and J'onn sat in the Womb up on the moon.

And now you've found me, Aquaman replied, putting a stern tone to his thoughts. *What do you want, J'onn?*

I think you know. We spoke about it once before. You said you had come into conflict with a creature whose plated flesh reminded you of something but you could not remember what. I had a similar reaction to the armor plating on the corpse of Bryan Francis. You've seen it now, Arthur. I'm sure it raised the same questions in your mind as it did in mine. Perhaps we were both eager to brush off the similarities, and the unique elements here—the fact that the subjects in question are altered human beings rather than an interstellar threat—well, that made it easy to rationalize that the two were unrelated. But it's gone beyond that now, don't you think?

As he listened to J'onn's telepathic voice in his mind, Aquaman continued to swim with the pod. The wreckage of the ship ahead was clearly of some significant age—at least significant by human standards. A Spanish galleon, perhaps, lost in a storm with all hands and whatever wealth it was carrying to the New World. Of course salvage divers would have stripped it of treasure and secrets long ago. But time could create new secrets.

The dolphins shied away from the ship, yet they swam about to make certain he knew they were indicating that he should have a closer look.

Arthur? J'onn prodded.

People thought they were starships at first, do you remember? Aquaman thought. *When they first appeared on radar, people thought they were ships.* He could clearly recall the monstrosities that had landed in the United Kingdom, towering, hideous alien horrors whose bodies had been covered in a jagged kind of plating that was similar in coloring and texture to the thing Bryan Francis had been evolving into.

They were chaotic days, those first few months after the League formed, J'onn replied. *So many threats erupted all at once, it seemed, and we rose to the occasion as best we could. We have learned a great deal since then about how to deal with planetary crises.*

Aquaman did not respond. There was no need. They

both knew that the way the League had dealt with that particular situation had left a great deal to be desired. The dolphins held back, but Arthur did not. He swam down into the wreckage of that ship. Its hull had mostly rotted away, leaving a kind of rib cage behind.

I do remember, J'onn continued. *Those ten creatures caused great destruction. Surely, Arthur, you cannot have forgotten where they landed, where they first appeared on radar.*

Aquaman had just swum around the bow of the rotten shipwreck. Now he froze in the water, eyes widening to take in all available light as he stared at a hole that had been burrowed in the ocean floor beside the ship. Something had tunneled into the ground here, and the wound it had left behind on the ocean bottom looked very much like those that had been made by the creatures he and Wonder Woman had fought in Los Angeles.

It was while he stared at this hole in the ocean floor that J'onn's words began to filter into his mind. He had stopped listening for a moment, but now the words sunk in. The truth of it was that the connections were all there, and had been there. The armor plating. The United Kingdom.

But these are humans, J'onn.

He felt the ominous weight of the Manhunter's next thought. *Or, at least, they were. Perhaps it is time we speak of this to the rest of the League.*

The campus at Ivy U. was a large part of what drew the students there. Certainly the university had a great many other lures, not the least of which was its stellar faculty, but the tree-lined campus was beautiful and the buildings hearkened back to another, more elegant age.

Who wouldn't want to go to school here? Ray Palmer thought as he strode across the academic quad toward Yorkshire Hall, which currently held the offices of the university's physics department. As far as Ray was concerned, he had one up on the students. As a professor, he didn't have to leave after four years.

It was a pleasure to be in a place where he was appreciated both as a physicist and as a teacher. The administration supported his research, no matter how avant-garde it might seem to his colleagues, and he got on very well with most of his students. He was thirty-five years old, single, and though he spent most of his time in the lab or the classroom, he was having the time of his life.

The truth of the matter was, it seemed too good to last. Every time that thought crossed his mind he would knock on wood—even scientists have a little superstition in them—and so far, so good.

"Professor Palmer!"

Ray paused on the freshly cut grass and turned to see Candace Dunphy hurrying after him. She was a tall girl with bright red hair and a face that seemed always to be filled with mischief. As she hurried to join him, he reflected on the fact that though he thought of her that way, Candace was not really a girl anymore. She was twenty-one, a senior. He did not have her in any of his classes this time around, but she had been one of his star students in recent semesters.

"Hey, Professor Palmer," she said, smiling as she caught her breath. "Sorry. I saw you cutting across the quad and I keep wanting to talk to you but every time I come by your office you're at the lab, and vice versa."

Ray smiled at the girl with the sparkling eyes and shifted his briefcase to his left hand. "You've heard of this new device, the telephone?"

Candace arched an eyebrow. "I wanted to do this in person."

His interest piqued, Ray grew serious. "Do what?"

Abruptly Candace lowered her gaze. She seemed suddenly unsure of herself and hesitated. A flash of insight went through Ray and he wondered if the girl were going to ask him out for coffee or something. There had always been a flirtation with her, the way she talked to him during lab and in conferences, but he had done nothing to suggest to her that there was anything between them. *How do I handle something like this?* he thought.

Candace smiled sweetly, finally meeting his eyes. "Look, I know you're going to lose Jayne Belichek in the fall. I'll be a first-year grad student. I was hoping you'd be interested in having me T.A. for Quantum Physics. It's just about the only way I can keep my work-study money."

Feeling more than a little foolish, Ray couldn't help chuckling at himself. *Right, Ray. You stud you. She sooo wants you. All the girls do. They're all drawing little love-you's on their eyelids with mascara, like in* Raiders of the Lost Ark. *Hell, you're hotter than Indiana Jones.*

A pained look crossed Candace's features and her mouth opened in a little moue of despair. "Are you laughing at me?"

"No," Ray said hurriedly, shaking his head. "No, Candace, I'm sorry. I just . . . something struck me as funny, but it was just me." As the girl breathed a sigh of relief, he hurried on. "I think you'd make a perfect T.A. Of course the department requires that I take applications, but get yours in early. Given your GPA and your status on work-study, I doubt anyone will come in that deserves it more."

Now her face blossomed into a radiant smile. "Oh, Professor Palmer, that's . . . thank you so much. I know . . . I mean, I know you can't make any promises. But that's . . . that'd be great."

Candace wrapped her arms around him in an awkward hug made even more so by the thoughts that had been going through his mind moments before. Ray nearly dropped his briefcase.

"I think so too," he told her as she bounced away from him, full of excited energy. "You can get an application from the department secretary. So . . . I'll see you soon."

"Definitely," Candace promised. Her eyes still sparkled and if there was something slightly suggestive in them, Ray ignored it completely. No way was he going to make any assumptions. Not about anything.

As she strode away he set out again for Yorkshire Hall. It was quiet; most of the professors were teaching class or at the lab. He waved at Elaine as he passed the department secretary's open door, then went up the steps to the second floor. He fished his keys out of his pocket with his left hand, briefcase clutched in his right, and then switched hands to unlock the door. He turned the knob and pushed the door open with his knee.

Inside, he set his briefcase on one of the chairs that faced his desk and slid his keys back into his pocket. A tremor of alarm went up his spine and he paused. Light spilled in from the hallway but otherwise the office was dark. Someone had drawn the shades. Ray never drew the shades in here.

He made as if to turn on the light switch, but instead, he slammed the door shut, throwing the room into almost complete darkness. The instant he did so, he willed himself to shrink.

In the space of a single heartbeat, six-foot-tall Professor Ray Palmer *diminished*, growing smaller and smaller until he was barely three inches high. Once upon a time, the process had disoriented him horribly, for from his perspective it seemed that the world expanded around him, walls and furniture thrusting themselves up to extraordinary height. But those times had passed.

Ray Palmer was the Atom. He was in complete command of the science that gave him this ability.

The Atom ran beneath his desk. He was aware of something rustling in the office, someone breathing very softly. At this size he was always somehow more keenly aware of the world around him. Beneath the desk he paused to get his bearings. Whoever had attempted to get the drop on him was in for a surprise, for the Atom had powers beyond merely altering his size. He could change his density, could funnel atomic energy into his fist so that a blow from him had many times the impact of a normal human of average size.

In the darkness, he waited for his eyes to adjust.

Someone clicked on the lamp on top of his desk and wan yellow light spilled onto the carpet. Ray waited in the shadows beneath the desk.

Then the intruder spoke, and the voice was all too familiar.

"Professor Palmer, please come out. Time is short and the League needs you."

More than a little irritated, the Atom stepped out from beneath his desk and stared up at the towering form of the Batman, twenty-five times his current height. He was imposing enough when they stood eye to eye, but from down here . . .

"You spooked the hell out of me," Ray chided him as he willed himself to grow.

Batman ignored the comment. Instead he held out a Justice League commlink as if he had no doubt at all that Ray would take it, that he would jump at the chance to go back into action with the League, even if only temporarily.

He was right.

*   *   *

Ian was tired. He loved his work at the ad agency, but there were days when it simply exhausted him. The partners who ran the agency could be the sourest, most uptight men and women in all England. While the campaigns they devised were often amusing, one would never expect this from having met those who captained the efforts of the agency. After a day like today, most of which had been in unendurable meeting after insufferable conference call, all he wanted was to be home with Sara, curled up in front of the telly.

It was already growing dark as he stepped out onto the sidewalk and began walking toward the tube station among a platoon of other people marching for home. He was tempted to pop in somewhere and get a cup of coffee to warm him up. The air was chill and damp and it seeped down to his bones almost immediately.

I should just fly home, he thought. But he brushed the impulse away. The last thing he wanted to do was to draw attention to himself at the moment, so close to the office. More and more of late he had begun to think that a mask was not so terrible an idea.

Just ahead, the river of homeward-bound commuters parted to flow around a pair of men standing on the sidewalk. It was a strange phenomenon, the way the people parted and then came together once more, and for several seconds he was so busy observing the rush of that human river that he did not even look at the faces of the two men.

Then something caught his attention, a spark of

green from the eyes of the man on the right. In the gathering gloom of the early evening, Ian focused at last on their faces, and then his own expression blossomed into a smile. He laughed softly, feeling the release of the tension that had been nurtured all day by his pompous employers.

"Well, look what the cat's dragged in," he said, pausing to become a third obstacle in the flow of that exodus. People swore as they shoved past him, shoulders nudging his harder, perhaps, than necessary. He hung his briefcase in front of him to avoid having it torn from his grasp.

Kyle Rayner and Wally West barely seemed to notice the traffic problems they were causing on that sidewalk. Wally fidgeted as usual, and Ian had found that if he stared intently at the man's features, there was a kind of blur to them.

"Hey," Kyle said, flashing a smile that seemed somehow empty, a bit of melancholy beneath it. Ian wondered if he was all right. He was concerned, but was not sure how awkward it would be if he inquired.

"How are you doing, Ian?" Wally asked. There was no smile on his face, not even a game attempt such as Kyle had made. On the contrary, Wally's demeanor was grave.

"Better than you two, I'd say," he replied, frowning. "Had a long day, myself, but no more than usual. What's going on, lads? Should we go off in search of a pint, then?"

"Actually, we're here on business," Wally replied.

"Yeah?" Ian asked, pointedly glancing at their street clothes, jackets and jeans and sneakers. "Maybe you ought to've worn the fighting togs, then, eh? You need a hand with something?"

"Not that kind of business," Wally explained. His eyes darted around, never focusing on anything for more than an instant. "We need to talk to you."

Ian arched an eyebrow.

"Well, not us," Kyle added. It had begun to drizzle lightly and his dark hair was damp. He brushed a raindrop from his cheek. "Superman wants to see you."

For a long moment Ian only stared at them. He cocked his head slightly to one side, his gaze ticking back and forth between them. A kind of fiery rush had blossomed in his chest and reached his cheeks and he wondered if he was blushing. At length, he laughed nervously.

"I'm sorry. It sounded like you just said Superman wanted to see me."

Wally nodded. "That's about the size of it."

Now Ian laughed out loud, more from disbelief than amusement. He shook his head. "What in God's name for? I mean, all right, we've been having a bit of fun chasing down a handful of freaks and a few nasty-minded tossers here and there, but what could Superman want with me? It's not as if I'm a member of the—"

He froze. Wally and Kyle were staring at him, both with gazes heavy with knowledge they clearly wanted to impart but could not. An extraordinary thought had just occurred to Ian. It was absurd on the face of it, and yet as he turned it over in his mind it was the only thing that made any sense in light of his friends' behavior.

A shudder went through him and he scratched at the back of his neck, where the skin was dry and irritated. It had been bothering him for several days now, and other patches of rough skin had appeared on his arms. Ian attributed it to stress but Sara thought he'd rubbed against something he shouldn't have. He had joked that it might have been Martha, the redhead in accounting, but Sara never smiled at that one.

Again he scratched at that irritated skin and he studied Wally and Kyle carefully.

"Superman, eh?"

They nodded soberly.

Ian smiled broadly. "It's just, all right, he's Superman, if you see what I mean."

"Trust me," Kyle said. "We do."

"'S he want me to join the League?"

Ian would have liked to hide the excitement that tinged his voice, but it was impossible. On the face of it, it seemed amazing to him that he could be so thrilled by the idea of gallivanting about the world with a crew of spandex Samaritans. But if he scraped away the cynical crust that had formed around his heart since childhood, he could admit to himself that this was the sort of thing every kid dreamed of.

He was so lost in this fantasy that at first he did not notice the reaction his question received from Kyle and Wally. Both of them averted their eyes. Wally anxiously tapped his fingers against his leg.

"Oh, now bloody Hell, boys. Enough of this. What's the problem?"

"It isn't about joining the League," Kyle said.

They had been there on the sidewalk for a couple of minutes now and the flow of pedestrians had thinned out some. The three of them drew closer to one another and Ian watched their eyes.

"Yes, I can see that, Kyle. Momentary flash of wishful thinking on my part, yeah? But obviously there's quite a bit here you're not telling me."

Wally put a hand up, glanced around to make sure no one was close enough to hear him, and then patted Ian on the arm. "Kyle's right. It isn't about joining the League. But we do need your help. There's a crisis brewing. It's huge. Planetary. That's what Superman wants to talk to you about."

Ian let his briefcase dangle from his left hand as he studied their grim expressions. Something about their manner unnerved him, but then how were they supposed to act if there really was some horrible threat to the Earth at the moment? Idly he scratched the back of his neck again.

"I'll need to phone Sara. Don't want her to be alarmed if I'm late home."

"You can call her from the lab," Kyle suggested.

"Lab?"

"S.T.A.R. Laboratories. That's where Superman is at the moment. We'll teleport you there with the Watchtower's equipment."

"And you can get me home the same way, yeah? A quick jaunt to America, nice as you please, as if there's nothing at all remarkable about it." His thoughts swirled in amazement.

They stared at him expectantly. Of course to them teleportation *was* unremarkable.

"Right, then," he said, waving his free hand. "Let's go."

Kyle let out a long breath as if he had been holding it, then tapped something on his wrist. "J'onn, we're good to go."

"Wait, now? Give me a second to—" Ian began, but his words were cut off. There was a loud rushing sound in his ears, and the world seemed to turn to static around him. The buildings and the people, the home-rushing throng, became washed out ghosts passing by.

He had not wanted to fly so close to the office, and he wondered now if anyone from the agency would see him disappearing with two American strangers in a flash of light. It was too late to think of such things now, however.

His skin prickled and his stomach lurched. The roar of static in his ears seemed to drive into his skull, rushing all around him. He squeezed his eyes shut against the wash of bright light that engulfed him. Just before he did he saw that Kyle and Wally were little more than dark silhouettes to him, and when he closed his eyes they were outlined against the insides of his lids.

There was never a moment when he felt the

briefest sensation that his feet were not on solid ground. Yet after a few seconds the rush of static subsided. His eyes were still shut tight and he found he was breathing too quickly, bent over slightly, trying to catch his breath or avoid vomiting, he was not quite sure which one.

The first thing he noticed was the smell. Wherever he was now there was a sterile, antiseptic smell. It was warm and there was no wind, no rain. A hand gripped his arm and Ian shook his head.

"I'm all right," he lied.

"It's kind of disconcerting, especially the first time," Wally told him. "You've just made a transatlantic trip, had your molecules taken apart, and—"

Ian turned toward him, opening his eyes. "Yeah. All right. I got it. Keep talking about it and I'll puke on your shoes." He glanced past Wally to where Kyle stood, but Kyle was not looking at Ian.

Kyle was looking *past* him.

Ian had come to know Wally and Kyle fairly well. They were decent sorts, and he enjoyed their company enough that he often did not even think of them as heroes, as members of the Justice League. Now, though, Ian felt a certain trepidation as he turned to see what Kyle was staring at, knowing full well what it would be.

They were in a small conference room with a beautiful mahogany table and half a dozen chairs. A pair of speakerphones lay dormant on the table. The windows looked out at the particularly uninspiring view of the roof of a parking garage, and he could see that the cars on the uppermost, open level were American. If nothing else, the fact that the sun was still out and the sky a beautiful blue would have given it away.

But it took Ian only a fraction of a second to take all of that in, and then it was forced from his mind completely by the presence of the fourth person in the room.

For years he had seen news reports with still photos or video footage of Superman. Nothing had prepared him for the reality. The newspapers called him the Man of Steel, and in his presence it was easy to see why. Certainly he was a large man with broad shoulders and sculpted musculature, and he had a strong jaw and eyes that were somehow both kind and implacable.

More than anything, however, it was the man's mere presence that made him so remarkable. Ian could not imagine him walking into any room, not even the United Nations General Assembly, and not having the eyes of everyone in the room drawn to him. He exuded a confidence and a gravitas that commanded attention.

"Superman," Ian muttered, feeling awkward and stupid.

The Man of Steel offered his hand. "Ian. I've heard a great deal about you. On behalf of the League, thank you for coming."

"Yeah. Yeah, of course," Ian replied, the whole scene completely surreal to him. He shook Superman's hand and had a fleeting moment where he wondered if his own would be crushed in the other man's grip. Ridiculous, of course. Superman would never do such a thing.

All eyes were on him and Ian shifted his weight from one foot to the other like a schoolboy. "So, Wally and Kyle said you wanted to see me, that you needed my help."

"Yes," Superman replied, brows knitting together. "Yes, we do."

It was in that moment when Ian Partington began to feel afraid.

CHAPTER NINE

It was raining in Boston when Wonder Woman materialized in the air above Tremont Street. The Watchtower teleportation unit took a great many variables into consideration when it transported a member of the League. The traffic in downtown Boston on a weekday afternoon would be clogged at every intersection. The people who had left work early would be hurrying to get out of the city before the real exodus began. The appearance of any woman as statuesque as Diana in the midst of the swarming downtown would create a stir, but the abrupt materialization of Wonder Woman, a member of the Justice League, was likely to cause a string of car accidents.

And she could fly. So there was no need for her to appear at street level.

The wind whipped Diana's hair in front of her eyes and the cold spring rain streaked her face like tears. She glanced around, orienting herself. Wonder Woman had spent a great deal of time in this city but still had not availed herself of all of the things it had to offer. Two blocks along Tremont Street she saw the darkened marquee of the Friedle Theater, where a revival of *Medea* was set to open in less than a week.

Even as she began to fly in that direction, gliding along the wind currents, moving down over the traffic, the front doors of the theater slammed open and several people rushed out onto the sidewalk. A blond woman was screaming and she fell to her knees, sobbing, on the sidewalk. A huge, powerfully built man crouched at her side as another man, thinner and older, glanced frantically around the street as he pulled a cellular phone from his pocket.

Too late, Wonder Woman thought grimly.

There was shouting from below. Several pedestrians had noticed her, and a man whistled appreciatively as she flew down over them. Diana ignored them all, no longer thinking about the traffic or potential accidents. She alighted in front of the theater, and the man with the cellular phone cried out, startled by her arrival.

"How many people are inside with her?" Wonder Woman demanded imperiously.

"You're . . . you're . . ." the thin man muttered, his hands jittering. The day had clearly been too much for him, and it wasn't over yet.

Diana turned her attention to the woman kneeling on the rain-slicked sidewalk. She sobbed quietly, though her tears were lost in the rain. The muscular man at her side had bright, alert eyes.

"There are twenty-five, maybe thirty people in the theater still," the man said, standing. "But they're all fine. They're safe. Maggie and Ethan just needed some air, that's all."

"And what of Ms. Hillier?" Wonder Woman asked.

The man lowered his gaze. The answer came from the sobbing woman, Maggie, who glanced up at Diana with the most forlorn expression the Amazon had ever seen.

"She's *gone*."

Cursing silently, Wonder Woman left them on the sidewalk, pushing through the front doors of the Friedle Theater at a run. She sprinted through the foyer and past the concessions. It was beautifully refurbished, the ceilings painted and the grand staircase ahead carpeted in lush red. To the left were the entrances to the galleries, and Diana took the first door. Inside was a corridor with doors that were parallel to those that led off the foyer. Through the first of these doors, she finally emerged into the theater proper.

It was breathtaking. The frescoes on the ceiling were meticulous recreations of ancient works, and the detail on the balcony railings and on the edge of the stage had been expertly done. All these tiny observations infiltrated Diana's mind in an instant, but she dismissed them. On the stage, the set for *Medea* had been destroyed. Whatever craftsmen had built and painted them would have wept to see the wreckage that had been made of their efforts.

But inside the theater there was no weeping, only stunned silence. People were gathered around, some leaning upon one another, others curled up in theater seats, still others just standing there, staring at the broad hole that had been dug through the floor just in front of the orchestra pit. Wonder Woman ran to the hole, ignoring the astonished exclamations of the actors and stagehands who were gathered there.

"Back away, all of you!" she snapped. They complied, of course. When she spoke so commandingly, anyone with good sense did as she instructed.

The ground began to rumble beneath her feet. Wonder Woman spun to look at a dark-skinned elderly man who was staring at her.

"How long ago did this happen?" she demanded.

"Five, six minutes," he replied. "Gina already called the—"

She pointed at the ground. "And the tremors? They've been going on all along?"

The elderly man nodded.

"She's still here," Wonder Woman said gravely.

The cast and crew of *Medea* let out a collective gasp and backed away from the hole immediately. Wonder Woman pushed past them, leaping through the air at impossible speed to land at the edge of the hole. The rubble down inside of it heaved, shuddering as the monstrosity that was burrowing beneath the theater— through earth and stone and possibly into Boston's subway tunnels—continued to dig.

Diana glanced around quickly. "Take cover. All of you. Get behind seats or out of the theater. The authorities should be here momentarily."

"But . . ." the old man began, frowning as he

looked at her, his eyes full of curiosity. "How did you know?"

Without responding, Wonder Woman leaped down into the hole and began excavating. She dragged huge chunks of concrete floor out and threw them onto the floor of the theater. With her bare hands she began to dig, trying desperately to unearth the creature, to catch up with it. Why it had hesitated, why it had lingered, Diana had no idea. But if she could capture it alive, the League might be able to get the biological data they needed to stop this crisis before it became any worse.

The old man did not ask her again, and Diana provided no answer. It was not her place to explain that a call had been received by the police and then patched through various checkpoints before it reached the Justice League Watchtower. Or that the call had come from the husband of Amelia Hillier, the star of this production of *Medea*. The actress's spouse had become afraid of her and for her. She had developed certain powers, he said, and she wanted to hide them. He risked her resentment by reporting it; John Hillier had seen the crisis on the news, the horrors that were unfolding around the world, and he did not want anything to happen to his wife.

But he was too late, and so was Wonder Woman.

Diana tore into the rubble in that hole, but already the rumbling was beginning to recede as the burrowing creature Amelia Hillier had become put more space between itself and the theater where the actress would never get to play Medea. For her, the final curtain had already fallen.

A mighty sigh escaped her lips and Wonder Woman lowered her head. For several seconds she stood there in the crater that had been dug into the floor of the Friedle Theater, saying nothing. The crisis had grown far too quickly for even the League to keep up with it, and though they had leads now, scientific avenues to investigate, Wonder Woman feared what might become of the transformed metas—these monsters who had dug themselves like parasites into the crust of the Earth—if those leads did not bear fruit in time.

What's happening to them? she thought. And then, far more ominously, *What's next?*

"It's all right. It happened so fast. There was nothing anyone could have done. Not even you."

Slowly, Wonder Woman turned and stared up into the distinguished features of the elderly black actor. His face was vaguely familiar, as though she might have seen him in a film somewhere. The kindness and sagacity in his gaze touched her.

"Thank you," she said. "You're right." With a thought she flew up out of the hole and alighted upon the floor beside him. The others all stared at her. In the silence of the theater they could all hear approaching sirens.

"I just want to make sure it doesn't happen again."

Diana glanced around at the cast and crew, taking them all in. Then she nodded once and tapped her Justice League commlink. "Wonder Woman. Return me to the Watchtower immediately."

Her flesh prickled as though spiders were crawling

across her skin and a vague sense of nausea gripped her stomach. Her throat felt dry. Her vision began to blur as she dematerialized, and then a moment later she blinked and she was standing in the teleporter in the League's lunar headquarters.

Voices carried to her from the corridor.

Wonder Woman walked out into the hall and followed those familiar tones. She rounded a corner and found them gathered outside the entrance to the Monitor Womb. The Flash was a splash of scarlet static in the air, so agitated that Wally was not even bothering to slow himself completely to normal human speed. Green Lantern's hair was disheveled and he leaned against the wall like a petulant teenager.

The third member of the trio gathered in the hall was Superman. With his size and the confident calm that radiated from him, he was always the most impressive of them. It had been his voice that Diana had heard, but she did not like *what* she heard. Some of that confidence and calm seemed to be missing today. Nor did she like what she saw, for Kal-El . . . Superman . . . looked tired.

"What is it?" she asked as she approached.

The three men turned to regard her. Flash and Green Lantern seemed startled by her arrival, as though she had shaken them awake from a nap, but Kal, of course, only nodded hello. He would have heard the teleporter as she arrived, and then her footfalls as she approached.

"What's happened?" she prodded.

"Superman just finished a conference call with the

President, the British Prime Minister, and the U.N. Secretary-General," Flash reported too quickly, so the words seemed to tumble over themselves and Diana had to sort them out.

"What did you tell them?" she asked.

Kal-El took a deep breath and then let it out. "I told them that the League had finished its search for new metas. That other than Ian Partington, all those we know about have either died or are missing and presumed to have undergone the metamorphosis. I told them it's quite possible there are more that just haven't revealed themselves yet. I told them we did not know what they were, or what they would do next, but that we hoped to have answers soon.

"And I told them that we wouldn't let them down."

The atmosphere at S.T.A.R. Laboratories was grave. All through the facility there was a buzz of voices, not from the researchers and other employees who worked there, but from televisions and radios that had been tuned to news stations. Batman tried to tune the noise out, to sift through it for only the change in voice modulation that the newscasters employed when they had new information. The rest of it was all simply a rehashing and analysis of what little they already knew.

The world was holding its breath.

There had been dozens of incidents in a handful of hours, metas transforming into armored horrors and burrowing into the ground. As the minutes ticked by without report of further incident, the natural questions had begun to be asked: What were the creatures, and what would they do next? What was the Justice League going to do about them?

Batman was determined to provide the answers.

The cape and cowl were too warm in the lab, despite the air conditioners, but he had trained himself many years earlier to ignore changes in climate, no matter how uncomfortable. Today he found it more difficult than it ought to have been. He stood staring at a set of X-rays, deeply disturbed by what he saw, for while it provided the beginning of an answer, it also elicited a great many new questions.

A deep frown creased his forehead as he turned to glance at the microscope upon which a sample of Ian Partington's blood had been prepared on a slide. Batman was eternally patient when it was necessary. He knew that the Atom—Ray Palmer—was brilliant and a consummate professional. But he also knew that Ray was a dedicated scientist, and that meant he would want to check and recheck his findings over and over before drawing any conclusions.

"Atom," Batman said into the commlink in his cowl, his voice a low snarl. "The clock is ticking. What have you found?"

"Just another minute," came the tinny response, the voice sounding hollow and distant.

"We don't know why he hasn't metamorphosed yet," Batman reminded the Atom, grimacing as he glared at the X-rays. "And we don't know how long he'll stay this way. Time's up, Ray."

There was a low sigh that sounded almost like what one could hear inside in a conch shell. Batman turned to regard the microscope again, forcing himself not to blink. No human eye could have seen the Atom grow slightly larger so that he could run to the edge of the slide and then leap into the air. To Batman it seemed as though the Atom appeared instantly. He was a red and blue speck one moment, and then in a rush of growth that could disorient onlookers, he went from the size of an insect to that of an infant, from the size of a boy to the height and weight Ray Palmer had reached as a man. Batman was always fascinated, watching the process. This was not alien physiology at work, nor was it an evolutionary metahuman ability. This was science, and it was remarkable.

Batman stared at him. The Atom was out of breath. Whatever he had been doing at molecular size down there in Ian Partington's blood, it had been strenuous. Ray pulled his mask back over his head, the fabric settling around his throat like the cuff of a turtleneck.

"Well?" Batman asked.

The Atom nodded grimly. "Just like the dead one."

"We have to start tests immediately. There's got to be a way—"

"What'll we tell him?" Ray asked.

Batman stared at him. "Why tell him anything? We need his cooperation."

The Atom began to reply, then shook his head, eyes darting around, avoiding Batman's gaze. "Sometimes I'm not sure if you're really this cold, or if you're just trying to leaven your disappointment that the human race can't be as logical and rational as you'd like."

Batman crossed his arms but said nothing.

Ray's jaw tightened with annoyance and he swallowed hard before focusing again on Batman. "He has a right to know what's happening to him."

At length, Batman nodded. "Fine. Do you want me to tell him?"

"God, no," the Atom replied. "Not with your bedside manner. I'll talk to him. Let's go."

There were a great many tests that needed to be done. Batman felt very keenly that every minute was valuable. Explaining to Partington would cost precious time. But though he would not admit it, he knew the Atom was right. The British telekinetic would only allow himself to be poked and prodded for so long until he demanded to know what was going on. Better to get it over with and get on with the business of figuring out how to destroy him.

The Atom left the lab and Batman followed, locking it behind them. There were guards outside the door and with a single hard glance, Batman wordlessly let them know just how bad it would be for them if anything went amiss with the lab while they were gone.

The observation room where Ian Partington was being kept was on the fifth floor in a secure wing. Despite the guards, to all outward appearance it would look to Partington like a particularly spartan hotel room or a cell in an upscale prison. Yet though most of the labs and testing facilities were located elsewhere, the room was equipped with technology that provided a constant data stream to the staff at S.T.A.R. Filters screened the air in the chamber, testing Partington's every exhalation. Heat and motion sensors and digital cameras tracked the man's movements. Ultrasensitive audio detected and recorded his heartbeat. Low-level psychic inhibitors broadcast mental static to make it more difficult for the man to focus his TK abilities.

S.T.A.R. was happy to give Ian Partington the illusion of hospitality, if not the real thing. Still, the telekinetic had grown impatient when he had been told that for security purposes, S.T.A.R. could not allow him to contact his girlfriend or call anyone else until the doctors released him.

When the Atom rapped on the door, Partington's invitation to enter was weary and edgy. When the door slid aside and Batman preceded the Atom into the room, Partington stiffened and his head cocked back.

He stared at Batman.

"Well, now things are getting interesting," Partington muttered, gaze ticking back and forth between the two costumed heroes.

Batman regarded him carefully. "If my presence is an issue for you—"

Ian waved the words away. "No, you're good. Really. It's just that I've imagined you in my mind so many times, it's a bit surreal to meet you in the flesh. Particularly under the hideous fluorescent lighting in here. Darkened back alley's more what I pictured."

The man wore a broad, friendly grin. Batman stood just inside the door, waiting patiently for his rambling to end. Partington had been spending time with Wally and Kyle, who were in the same age bracket and apparently shared certain amiable qualities that Batman did not.

The Atom glanced back and forth between Partington and Batman, shifting awkwardly from foot to foot. The smile disappeared from Partington's face and he grunted as though the sound itself were a profound observation.

"Yeah, well, I suppose fluorescent lighting or no, you are pretty much as reported," Partington said. Then he looked at the Atom. "All right, then, what've you found? Have you got what you wanted? Can I go now?"

The Atom shot a quick look at Batman, then scratched the back of his neck as he turned his focus to Partington again. Silently, Batman urged the Atom to get on with it. Ray had insisted they speak to the telekinetic and now he was hesitant.

"What?" Partington demanded, his frustration obvious. "Look, I'm not expecting good news. Not after all this. And the nice people here at S.T.A.R. won't let me watch television, or ring my Sara, so I've got to figure something nasty's going on. Let's have it."

"Ray," Batman said gravely.

"Of course," the Atom replied. "Mr. Partington, you might want to be sitting for this."

To his credit, the Englishman crossed his arms and regarded both of them levelly. "Go on."

"We've had the opportunity to examine the remains of one of your countrymen who had also recently developed new metahuman abilities. You're aware of the recent wave of new metas, so I won't bore you with that. What you are not aware of is that—"

Ian Partington was staring at him. "Remains?"

"Hmm?" Ray asked, lost in his own head.

"Remains?" Partington repeated.

"Yes," Batman said curtly.

"What you are not aware of," Ray went on, "is that a number of these metas have undergone a metamorphosis."

"Wait, what?" the Englishman snapped, brows knit in anger. "Superman said you were investigating, trying to figure out what was causing the wave of new metas."

"We have been," Batman told him.

"And we've discovered it," the Atom continued. "You are, all of you, carrying a parasite. More than likely it's an alien life form. Our current hypothesis indicates a large scale infection across the United Kingdom eight to twelve years ago. In most of the infected, the parasite was likely destroyed by the host's immune system, but in certain individuals it gestated, bonding with the host on a cellular level . . . and also growing."

Now Partington did sit down. More accurately, he staggered several steps backward until his legs hit the edge of the bed and he dropped down onto the mattress, his hands snapping out to keep him from falling over completely.

"Like . . . like some sort of tumor or something?"

"Similar," the Atom replied. "Though it isn't quite that simple. Your blood, your entire body, has been affected. The organism has subtly altered your physiology to provide itself more fertile ground in which to thrive. This is also what prompted the development of your meta abilities."

Batman stared at Partington, uncertain how to interpret the emotions that roiled in the other man's eyes. "S.T.A.R. is already trying to develop a process to destroy the parasite, but surgery isn't an option. It's attached to your spine."

Partington laughed.

The sound was chilling.

Batman and the Atom exchanged a quick glance and Batman took a step closer to the telekinetic.

"Destroy it? I don't want you to destroy it." Ian Partington stared at them, shaking his head, and now he stood up again, smiling broadly. "Look, Flash and Green Lantern must have told you how well I'm doing. I've got these powers . . . and I've been working hard to put them to good use. Why would I want to get rid of them?"

The Atom reached out and put a hand on Partington's shoulder. Batman saw the way the Englishman's muscles tensed and wondered if Ray had made the wrong move.

"That metamorphosis we mentioned before?" the Atom began. "Our examination of the remains of the other meta here at S.T.A.R.—and firsthand accounts—all lead to the same conclusion. Once the meta abilities are in use it begins a chain reaction. The parasite merges with the host body and . . . transforms it. In essence, the cells are changed so completely the parasite might as well have molted the human form as a snake sheds its skin. The others have evolved, Ian. They're monsters now. Not even a trace of humanity left. Only the parasites. Things we've come to call burrowers."

For long moments the man's head shook slowly back and forth, his mouth working soundlessly. He stared at the floor, at his shoes, at his own hands as if he had never seen them before.

"Bloody Hell," he said at last. Then he looked up, and there was a glint in his eyes that was equal parts defiance and terror. "How many of them? It can't be happening to everyone. Maybe just a—"

Batman glared at him, stopping him cold with three words. "All of them."

Ian shuddered, his mouth open in a tiny "o" of dismay.

"For the moment—unless we find more—you're the last one," the Atom said. "We don't know *why* it hasn't happened to you yet, but with your cooperation, we think we may be able to figure out how to arrest the process, to prevent you from evolving further."

Now an odd calm seemed to descend upon Partington. His expression was blank and cold. He tilted his head and studied first Batman and then the Atom.

"Truth is, if you don't know why it hasn't happened to me yet, that means you haven't found any evidence it won't. Chances are I'm just lagging behind the others, yeah?"

The Atom nodded solemnly.

Batman took a step closer to him. "If we can destroy the parasite in time—"

"You're not listening," Ian replied, staring at the floor. His clothing and hair rippled in an unseen wind, and Batman could feel the power emanating from him. "I don't want it destroyed."

Alarm bells went off in Batman's mind and he began to drop into a combat stance. But he was too late. Partington threw his head back and raised his hands, golden energy streaming from his eyes and sizzling at the ends of his fingers. S.T.A.R. had underestimated the level of his telekinetic power; the dampers were useless.

Batman tried to dive back toward the hallway, looking for cover, but it was no use. His entire body was seized in the grip of Partington's power. His teeth clacked together and he strained against the telekinetic vise that constricted around him. He saw the Atom lifted from the ground.

"You're making a mistake," Batman growled through gritted teeth.

Ian Partington was levitating several inches off the ground, his entire body wreathed in that crackling telekinetic field. "I was nothing special before," he said, almost as though he was speaking to himself. "Thing is, I didn't mind it, right? This power hadn't come along, chances are I would've been happy to live my whole life that way. Just Ian. In love with

Sara. Nothing special. But now . . . it's all different now. And I can't go back."

"But the metamorphosis," the Atom managed to mutter.

Ian shrugged, eyes distant, as though he was already a thousand miles from here. "I've fought it off this long. I'll take my chances."

With a glance, he blew out the outer wall of his room, glass and metal, brick and plaster raining down onto the Metropolis street below. Then Ian Partington emerged from the gaping hole in the wall and flew out over the city, a flicker of golden light across the late afternoon sky.

Batman felt it the moment the grip of Partington's telekinesis released him and he spun in the air so that as he dropped, he landed on his feet. The Atom was not so agile, and he crashed to the floor with a painful grunt. Batman had misread the situation, and his anger at himself for that error was like a cold flame in his gut.

"Excellent," the Atom said as he rose to his feet. "That went well."

The lights seemed dimmer in the Watchtower. J'onn was sure it was just his mood. The others were gathered around the circular table—a guest chair drawn up for Ray Palmer—and the atmosphere in the room was somber. J'onn was the only one not seated. While he had addressed them he had stood behind Aquaman to indicate that this report was in truth coming from both of them.

As the two remaining original members of the League, it was only right.

"Why didn't you mention this before?" Superman asked, his eyes narrowed as he stared at J'onn, then at Arthur. The Kryptonian had his hands clasped tightly together in front of him on the table. It was all he would show of his frustration.

J'onn nodded, accepting the tacit admonishment. "Arthur and I have had our suspicions, but separately. We only recently discussed them, at which point they seemed more solid."

The Martian Manhunter studied the other faces around the table. Wonder Woman's lips were pursed thoughtfully. Flash and Green Lantern seemed too stunned to comment. Batman only stared at him.

"It was one of the first major crises the League had to deal with," Aquaman said. He stared directly at Superman, not averting his gaze at all as he continued. "It was not one of our proudest moments."

The Atom cleared his throat. "The way you and J'onn describe it, I'm not sure what else you could have done. The League had only begun to deal with threats on that level. There was no protocol in place and very little experience. Protecting the Earth had to be your priority."

J'onn hesitated. He looked down at Aquaman, gazing at the back of Arthur's head as though the Atlantean might feel it and turn around. But if Aquaman sensed J'onn's attention—or if their telepathic link communicated any of J'onn's feelings to him—the King of Atlantis did not respond.

"We were rash," J'onn said. "It was handled badly."

Green Lantern sat up straighter, almost as though he had been drifting off to sleep, and he sighed. "All right. Let me get this straight. You think these metas—the monsters they're turning into—they might be some kind of, what, new variety of the things you guys ground into paste in the U.K. ten years ago?"

"It matches the timeline we're working with," the Atom offered. "If the metas were infected a decade ago . . . something in the air from the League's destruction of those creatures could have caused it. It gestated all this time and—"

"I don't think so," Batman interrupted.

Superman shot him a sidelong glance. "Explain."

"I've read the file J'onn and Arthur are talking about. Since I did not witness it myself I didn't make the connection to the appearance of those creatures and these new beasts. But the monsters from that crisis were not transformed humans, and they were not burrowers the way these things are."

Wonder Woman tapped her fingers on the table. "Still, logic dictates there must be a connection."

"I'm not denying there is. I simply don't think we've found it yet. If the original team had kept better records—"

Aquaman glared at him. "It was barely a team at that time. We gathered together when the situation demanded it. There wasn't very much time for writing journals."

Batman met his eyes with a steely gaze. "Maybe you should have made time."

"Guys, come on!" Flash erupted suddenly, standing and slamming his hands on the table. "The crisis is now. This is happening. These things dug into the ground. Who knows what they're doing down there? Eating the earth's crust or planning to play Godzilla—whatever it is, it can't be good. So enough of this woulda, shoulda, coulda. How about we figure out what we're going to do?"

"I know what I'm going to do," Green Lantern said. "I'm gonna find Ian and bring him back to S.T.A.R. before he becomes a burrower too."

Superman leaned forward. All eyes turned toward him.

"We've got to track the burrowers," the Kryptonian said, looking around the table. "And we've got to be ready to deal with whatever they do next. Atom," he said, turning to Ray Palmer, "we need to know everything we can find out about these things, and we need to know it last week. That includes what you and S.T.A.R. have learned from Bryan Francis's corpse and from the tests you ran on Ian Partington."

The Atom nodded slowly. "If they are related, it would help to have a look at the remains of the creatures the League faced ten years back."

J'onn shook his head. "I am afraid there aren't any."

"We were forced to destroy the creatures completely," Aquaman added.

But then J'onn brightened. He looked down at Aquaman. "All save one."

Arthur frowned up at him. "I'm sorry?"

A spark of hope raced through J'onn. Superman was right, of course. There was little they could do about the burrowers now, but they had to be ready for whatever the creatures were up to. And if he and Arthur were right, and there was a connection . . . there was one way to find out for certain.

"The final creature was destroyed not by the League but by the British military. Its body was incinerated, but the British scientists who had gotten involved by that time wanted to study it.

"They kept the head."

CHAPTER TEN

The New Palace of Westminster sprawled across eight acres of the eastern bank of the Thames River. So large was the complex of buildings that housed the nation's Parliament that it seemed almost to have grown there organically, beginning with a single stone block and then spreading in viral fashion, each new staircase and court and wall another limb of this massive architectural beast. Despite the richness of its late Gothic style or the impressive nature of the Palace's trio of towers—the grandest of which was Big Ben, the Clock Tower—there was something austere about the place.

Superman was certain it had more to do with what went on within its walls than with the aesthetic impact of those walls.

He stood alone at a podium in the midst of the House of Commons, surrounded by more than six hundred members representing the subjects of the

Queen. For centuries, the fate of Great Britain had been decided in this room. The air itself seemed heavy with age and with the solemnity of the proceedings that usually took place there. But this day there were none of the usual arguments that ensued when a vote was to be taken. A low susurrus of mutterings buzzed in the House of Commons, and Superman could have focused enough to listen to any one of those voices. He ignored them.

The Prime Minister had already assured him that the British government would do whatever it could to assist the Justice League in ending this crisis as quickly as possible. But certain protocols had to be followed and a modicum of diplomacy was always required. Britons demanded a sense of propriety in the way matters were handled in the Houses of Parliament.

What had happened a decade ago in the U.K. had been very much a public event. Lives had been lost. Property destroyed. The Justice League's involvement was well known. It was the opinion of the Prime Minister that the present efforts of the League and the British government should be public as well. Superman did not want to take a moment longer than was absolutely necessary, but he understood the workings of governments.

There had been no new developments overnight. None of the burrowers had reappeared. A few more hours was a small price to pay for the peace of mind of the population of the United Kingdom and, by extension, the world.

On the other hand, propriety was not the only reason Superman had agreed to address Parliament.

As the Kryptonian spoke he gazed around the room at the hundreds of upturned faces. Somewhere in the gallery of seats that surrounded him, there was an impostor. One of the members of Parliament had been replaced by the Batman. Even now Bruce was studying those around him, in particular a hawk-nosed man from Surrey by the name of Paul Cargill.

"Time is of the essence," Superman said, gazing about the room. He had explained the circumstances to them as briefly as possible. "The Justice League has theories, of course, but there is no way to know what will happen next, and when. For now, we can only focus on possibilities, the more disturbing of which I have outlined for you.

"Ten years ago the original League worked with your government to end a terrible threat. Now we must cooperate again. The only extant remains of the creatures that caused so much damage at that time are in your possession. The genetic information those remains could provide might yield answers we need to combat these transformed metas and, equally important, to prevent those infected with the parasite from undergoing further metamorphosis. On behalf of the Justice League, I ask you to—"

The man from Surrey, Paul Cargill, shot to his feet with a cry that spoke of purest agony, and which echoed across that vast chamber. He clapped his hands to the side of his head, groaning, muttering now, but there were no words in the sounds that issued from his throat. None that Superman was familiar with at least, in any language.

The outburst was met with stares of astonishment and a flurry of angry whispers from Cargill's fellow members of Parliament.

"Lord, the pain!" the man cried out at last, biting off each word as though it hurt him even to form the syllables.

Superman stared at Cargill as he fell across the seat in front of him, convulsing. It was disturbing to see, despite the fact that J'onn had hypothesized this very reaction. Batman's relationship with British Intelligence had turned up several members of Parliament who were rumored to have recently developed metahuman abilities. Two of them had disappeared. Paul Cargill was the last.

His reaction to Superman's words proved J'onn's theory was correct. The parasite inside of Paul Cargill was sentient, aware of everything its host experienced. Threatened by the League's intentions, it was lashing out. As Cargill twitched, drooling, where he lay across the seat, his flesh began to change, to darken and take on a rougher texture. The parasite was trying to speed the metamorphosis, to force it before it would naturally have occurred.

Why this hadn't happened with Ian Partington was a mystery, but Superman wondered if Ian's parasite had not influenced him to attack and escape as he had.

Heads turned toward Superman, gazing at him in

astonishment. The Kryptonian understood. They were wondering why he was not rushing to Cargill's side. A moment later, their question was answered as a member of Parliament shoved past several others, produced a taser from inside his jacket, and shocked Cargill—and the thing inside him—with enough electricity to render both the man and his parasite unconscious.

Cargill's arms and legs jittered and then were still.

Disguised as William Locke, the Batman put away his taser.

"Ladies and gentlemen, please stand back from Mr. Cargill at this time," Superman asked, his voice booming through the cavernous hall.

The House of Commons began to comply, all save the false Mr. Locke. When the others were clear, Batman removed a metal tube from within his jacket—a weapon that had been adapted from a design originally used by a criminal who had called himself the Icicle—and sprayed Paul Cargill with a freezing agent. Frost covered the man's body, and his hair and skin took on a blue tint. Cargill stopped twitching, stopped moving entirely, and for the moment, at least, his metamorphosis was stalled.

Thanks to the telepathic rapport the Martian Manhunter was maintaining between the members of the League during this crisis, Superman heard Batman's voice in his head.

J'onn. The package is secure. Bring us back to the Watchtower.

A moment later there came from the floor of the chamber a loud clap as if of thunder, then a roar as though from a storm. Then Batman and frosted Paul Cargill disappeared, and the noise cut out as abruptly as it had arrived.

Superman cleared his throat. All eyes were on him. "Ladies and gentlemen," he said, "the quicker you vote, the quicker we will discover if it's possible to stop Mr. Cargill from becoming one of the burrowers."

It was still dark in Metropolis, dawn a few hours away, but even this late—or early or whatever—the city was alive. As Green Lantern crisscrossed the city, weaving in among the skyscrapers, he bore witness to the amazing cross section of vibrant life that went on in the wee hours of the Metropolis morning. He would have expected garbage trucks and the handful of cars, but what amazed him were the people sitting inside all-night bookstore cafés, reading and chatting with friends. Kyle knew that there would be work crews out, but never would have imagined he would see people out walking their dogs or jogging or bicy- cling, or exercising in the brightly lit windows of a twenty-four-hour health club. He had been clubbing plenty of times, but it was going on four in the morn- ing and there were places where the party seemed to be just getting started.

It was a whole other world going on while most people slept the night away, unaware. Kyle under- stood. Being Green Lantern, being part of the Justice League, was similar in a way. He too was part of a world that most people could never understand.

Make a new friend, have him run away from

S.T.A.R. Labs, then scour Metropolis looking for him, hoping to bring him back before he can turn into a huge, earth-burrowing monster.

Nope. Not the kind of thing most people could relate to.

Come on, Ian, Kyle thought as he flew past the Daily Planet building. *Where are you?*

The muscles in his neck and back were tense. Though the uniform kept him warm, he still felt a chill along his spine, a crawling anxiety that would not leave him alone until he had found Ian. Metropolis S.C.U. was on the street searching as well, alongside the soldiers the federal government had stationed at S.T.A.R. to watch over him. Already, reporters in the city had the story. They'd be looking as well.

All night, and no luck. Which made Green Lantern wonder if Ian had left Metropolis immediately, and headed for home. The Flash was in England already, conducting a search there. Kyle hated the idea that he had wasted his entire night, but if there was a chance Ian was still in the city, he had to keep looking.

Green Lantern.

The deep, warm voice appeared inside Kyle's head like a flare in the night sky. He faltered a moment, pausing in his flight across Metropolis to take a breath and get his bearings.

J'onn. I hate when you sneak up on me like that, he thought.

It's telepathy, Kyle, the Martian Manhunter reminded him. *What sort of advance warning could I provide that would startle you less?*

Okay, point taken. What's going on?

Kyle could feel J'onn hesitate, though without any telepathy of his own he could read nothing of the Martian's thoughts. Green Lantern hovered in the air above a busy Metropolis thoroughfare. He could not be certain, staring at that indigo sky, but he thought that perhaps it had lightened just a bit, edging closer to dawn.

Batman and Superman have found another infected meta. We no longer need Ian Partington for analysis.

Green Lantern nodded to himself. "Fine," he said aloud, knowing J'onn would hear the thought perfectly well. "But you're not telling me to stop looking for him, are you?"

Not at all. I just thought you should be aware of the situation. Obviously if we can help Ian, that is part of our goal. It simply changes the priority level the League places on locating him.

"My priorities aren't always the same as the League's."

Of course not. I will keep you informed of further developments.

Then, just as Kyle had felt the bright spark of J'onn's consciousness touching his mind, he felt it recede. The contact was still there, but dormant. A dial tone, but no connection.

J'onn was as empathetic a being as Kyle had ever met, but even he seemed on edge. They all were. Some of the most powerful and most brilliant individuals on Earth were a part of the League. When there was a crisis imminent, the last thing any of them wanted to do was *wait*. At the moment they were doing everything they could, short of getting giant shovels and beginning to excavate entire cities. If something did not happen soon, Green Lantern thought he might just start digging

He continued to search Metropolis from the sky. At first it had been a logical progression. The police had checked hotels and airports, clubs and cafés. Green Lantern had searched public parks and the tops of buildings, places where a telekinetic with the power of flight might set down to consider his position and try to figure out what to do next.

More and more as the night waned and sunrise lightened the eastern horizon, he became convinced that Ian had left the city. But there was no way to be sure where he had gone. London seemed the most logical destination, home to the flat Ian and Sara shared in Battersea. But that would have been the first place the Flash checked when he arrived in London, and Green Lantern would have heard by now if it had turned up anything useful.

Nothing here, he thought. The city was really coming to life now. The morning commute had begun. Delis and newsstands were opening and the streets were filled with cars and trucks and yellow cabs. There was no sign of Ian here, and with the city so active now, he knew his chances of finding his friend were diminishing with every passing moment.

Green Lantern was so distracted by his thoughts that at first he barely registered the rumbling noise that rolled across the city. Several seconds passed before he noticed it, and even then it continued. He paused, wreathed in green, crackling energy that held him in the sky. A frown creased his forehead and his brows knitted.

Thunder. Of course it was thunder, booming through the sky, echoing off skyscrapers. But the morning was dawning clear and crystal blue. There was no storm, no lightning, and therefore there could be no thunder.

It came again, and this time Green Lantern spun in the air. The buildings of Metropolis were batting the sound back and forth, but he thought he had pinpointed it then. It was not in the sky at all, not thunder. It originated perhaps a half mile from his current position . . . and it was coming up from the ground.

J'onn! he thought. *Seismic activity in Metropolis. Doubting it's an earthquake. Going in to check on it now.*

A streak of dark green against the soft blue morning, Kyle flew at top speed, covering that half mile in seconds. The Metropolis skyline blocked his view until he was nearly on top of it. Then he was above a huge intersection, traffic snarled at the lights as a city bus tried to bull its way through. People on the sidewalks seemed paralyzed with fear, holding one another, looking up at the sky or at the buildings around them. Only a handful were looking down.

Then the street cracked. The sound was like heaven shattering. A fissure appeared in the pavement, a manhole cover blew off, and the sidewalk buckled. Several cars began to tilt and slide downward where the road was falling in. By instinct alone Kyle reached out with the power of the ring, tendrils of verdant energy appeared instantly and lifted the cars away. The streets were so busy that it took him several seconds to find safe places to put the cars back down.

Those seconds were all it took. The tremor worsened. People fell to their knees. Windows shattered in buildings all around that intersection. Then a vast sinkhole appeared in the pavement.

The thing that erupted from the ground then did not look as though it had ever been human.

Green Lantern spoke in a whisper. "Oh, crap."

Ian Partington was not in London. At least, not as far as the Flash had been able to determine. It was mid-morning already and he had spent an hour scouring the city, visiting pubs and restaurants that he knew Ian frequented, as well as the man's office at the advertising firm where he worked. The Flash had ghosted in and out of Ian's workplace so quickly all he had done was rustle paperwork as he passed. The man was a friend, and Wally did not want his co-workers either alarmed or whispering rumors to one another about what might or might not cause the Flash to seek Ian out.

The very first place he had checked when he had been teleported down to London from the Watchtower had been the flat in Battersea that Ian shared with Sara. Wally knew the story of their first date, of the teenaged Ian's fascination with the coffee shop girl. Thinking about it made him think of his wife, Linda, and how much he missed her. They'd had so little time to be together in recent days. The thought process was circuitous, for thinking of Linda made him appreciate how much Ian and Sara cared for one another even more. He was more determined than ever to find Ian before it was too late for him. Too late for the bewitched teenager and the coffee shop girl.

Wally had been by the flat in Battersea, had peered in the windows and rapped on the door. No one had answered and he had seen no movement inside. Soon he would grow impatient enough to race back there and break down the door, but he didn't want to do that. Not yet. He still believed that whatever might be happening, Ian would trust him enough at least to speak to him.

The world around the Flash was a frozen tableau. From the streets of London he decided to go below, and he slipped down into the Holborn tube station, not far from where he and Ian and Kyle had gotten together at All Bar One. Wally West, the fastest man alive, explored the subway tunnels beneath the city of London, pausing from time to time to allow his eyes to adjust, passing trains as though they were standing still, zipping past passengers on each platform. In those tunnels he saw strange things, things both unsettling and remarkable, but none of them were Ian, and none of them were related to the crisis they were currently facing.

So Wally ran on.

In every station he searched for Ian. On every bench. In every stairwell. He slowed enough to peer inside each passing train car. Eventually he surfaced once more and he began to speed through some of the tourist sites, thinking Ian might have wandered somewhere to think.

The telepathic voice of the Martian Manhunter stopped him cold, right in the center of Waterloo Bridge.

Flash, J'onn began.

Wally heard regret in J'onn's tone and he braced himself for tragic news. The Manhunter told him about Batman and Superman's capture—there really wasn't any better word for it—of a member of Parliament just as the man had begun to undergo metamorphosis. In a strange way, Wally found this heartening. It meant there were others carrying the parasites who had not evolved yet, which meant that Ian was not the lone holdout. He might have more time than they imagined.

True, J'onn spoke into his mind. *But it also means that there could be many, many more. That we may only have begun to see the effects of these parasitical infections.*

Aren't we the optimist, today? Wally thought with a sigh.

Which was when J'onn explained that finding Ian was no longer a priority for the Justice League. The Flash did not bother to respond to that, or to sign off from their communication. After several moments, he felt J'onn's mind retreat from his own.

All right, he thought. *Time to stop worrying about whose feathers I ruffle.*

Several heartbeats later he was standing at the reception desk at the interior decorator where Sara worked. The slender blonde behind the desk had high cheekbones and pale blue eyes. When the Flash appeared before her she let out a shriek that jostled the coffee mug by her left hand.

"I'm sorry," Wally said earnestly. He frowned, then reached up to pull back the mask that covered his face, thinking that perhaps seeing his face might make it easier for her to deal with him. "I didn't mean to startle you. And let me start by saying this isn't a joke. Not even close. My name's Wally West. I'm the—"

"Well, right, I *know* who you are," the woman said, staring at him as though he were insane.

The Flash nodded. "I need to see Sara Bradford. Right away."

The receptionist raised an eyebrow and then pointed toward the chairs against the wall. "Have a seat, Mr. West. I'll just tell Sara she has a visitor."

Wally opened his mouth, thinking he should say something more to reinforce how urgent the situation was. Then he decided against it. The woman had the Flash standing in her waiting room. Of course it was urgent.

Even so, the time it took him to cross the room seemed an eternity. He sat in a chair, knees together, hands upon his lap like a troubled student awaiting the judgment of a stern schoolmaster, and every second that ticked by was interminable. The receptionist picked up the phone and buzzed Sara, told Wally she would be right out, and indeed it was perhaps less than a minute before she came into the foyer through a door behind the reception desk. Still, that minute went on forever.

When, at last, she did appear, Wally saw two things instantly. First, he saw that she was every bit as pretty and her eyes every bit as bright and intelligent as Ian had said. Second, that the very fact of his arrival at her office absolutely terrified her.

"What?" she demanded, glaring at him almost petulantly, crossing her arms as though the room had suddenly grown cold. Her dark hair had streaks of unnatural red and there was a thin steel ring through her left nostril. "If you're here to tell me the silly sod's off and got himself killed, just say it and be done."

Wally stared at her a moment, and then he walked toward her, purposefully slow. "Sara, it isn't like that. As far as I know, Ian's alive. But he is in trouble."

Her right hand fluttered up to cover her mouth. She studied his face and Wally let her, meeting her gaze, glad that he had drawn the mask back to reveal his face.

"Tell me," she said, a rasp through parted fingers.

"There isn't time to explain it all. You've been following the news. The recent metas . . . they're changing, evolving."

"Oh, Christ, Ian."

Wally nodded. "Yes. But from what he told me he manifested his powers really early, much earlier than the others we've tracked. I think there could be a correlation between how long he's had his powers and how long it takes the thing inside him to *change* him. The last time I saw him he was still himself. Not one of those things. I want to try to keep him that way, but he's . . . I think it's affected his mind. He's fighting us. He doesn't want to give up the powers, so he took off. We have to find him. We've looked everywhere."

Sara's eyes stayed with him, her focus total. Already she was nodding. "Norwich. If he thought you'd find him at our flat but he wanted to go somewhere, he'd go to Norwich. We grew up there and—"

"I know. I looked there. But his parents, he . . . neither one of you have any family there anymore."

"No, but we still have history," Sara replied.

Then Flash understood. "The coffee shop. The one where you met? You think he'd go there?"

Her lip quivered. "He . . . he told you that story?"

Wally stepped forward and put a hand on her arm. He nodded slowly. "We're friends, Sara. It isn't just about powers."

She drew in a deep, ragged breath and then shrugged lightly. "He couldn't sleep there, of course. But that's the first place I'd look."

"What was the name of it?"

"Culture Shock Café. It's still there." And she gave him the address.

The Flash gazed at her a moment longer, wanting to give her some guarantee, some promise that he would return Ian to her in one piece, alive. But he never liked to make a promise he wasn't sure he could keep.

"Thank you," he said.

All Sara would have seen of his departure was a scarlet blur. But as he turned from her and started to run, out of the corner of his eye Wally saw the first tear begin to slip down her cheek.

He was in Norwich before she could wipe it dry.

Norwich, where a gaping hole had appeared in the shadow of the city's famous cathedral. When Wally arrived, the second of the monsters was lumbering from it. He cursed under his breath as he raced up to get a closer look and the thing towered over him, blocking out his view of the sky.

The larger of the two horrors was like a worm, though its hide was covered in thick armor plating and there were at least five pair of eyes along the top of its head. Its upper body swayed serpentlike fifteen feet above the street and the lower portion of it was still inside the hole in the ground, making it impossible to gauge its true size.

The smaller one was far more terrible to behold. It had vestigial limbs, arms and legs that were tiny in relation to its massive frame. Its maw gaped wetly and it darted forward on those tiny legs to snap at a BMW, shattering the windows and eliciting screams from the two college girls inside. But it was covered in dark red-brown scales just like the other, and Wally could not help but wonder if one of them had further to evolve.

J'onn, he thought, not bothering with the commlink now that the Manhunter had them all in a telepathic network. *Superman. Lantern. Everyone. The burrowers are starting to surface. I think I'm gonna need some help here.*

Yet even as these vital thoughts coursed through his mind, they were chased by another, even more disturbing.

My God, thought the Flash. *Ian?*

CHAPTER ELEVEN

Despite its practical applications, Batman hated teleportation. For the duration of the physical disruption, a handful of seconds, everything—the world around him, his body, his future—was outside of his control. No matter how much data one had, one could never be certain what the situation was going to be upon arriving at the other end of a teleport . . . what you were going to walk into.

Case in point.

Batman and the Atom had just come from transferring custody of cryogenically-frozen metahuman Paul Cargill to S.T.A.R. Labs. They had seen to it that Cargill was secure and that S.T.A.R. had everything they needed to begin the analysis. Now, as they stepped out of the teleportation unit in the Justice League Watchtower, a shrill alarm was sounding and a light on the wall was flashing red-yellow-red.

"What is it?" the Atom asked.

Batman did not even glance at him as he stormed from the room. "We're out of time."

He could hear Professor Palmer's footfalls in the corridor behind him as he sprinted toward the Monitor Womb. As it always was in a crisis scenario, the door to the Womb was sealed shut. Batman placed his hand upon the door and immediately a laser eyescan began. Seconds later the door slid open. With the Atom following closely behind, Batman stepped into the room. For several seconds, he simply took in the sight before him.

The Martian Manhunter sat in the tall chair upon the raised platform at the center of the room. The chair conformed to the shape of its user, so it seemed almost a hand holding J'onn in the air. Around the room were arrayed dozens of screens that under normal circumstances presented satellite images broadcast from all over the world. At the moment, ten of those screens showed variations of the same two images, events unfolding in what was obviously Metropolis and a second city. It took Batman only a moment, based upon the architecture, to identify it as Norwich, England.

"Of course," he said. Norwich should have been the first place Flash and Green Lantern checked. "Is one of those things Partington?" he asked, referring to the monstrous things, the gigantic burrowers that were at that moment crashing again and again into the face of a train station, attempting to get at the Flash.

"We cannot be sure yet," J'onn replied.

"You've already made decisions regarding deployment?"

Still the Martian Manhunter did not turn. "Aquaman and I will join Green Lantern in Metropolis. Superman and Wonder Woman will be on their way to Norwich momentarily. Strategically, I believe it would be best for you to take over monitor duty while Professor Palmer analyzes the remains Superman brought back from London."

"I agree," Batman replied with a curt nod. The last thing he wanted was to be left behind, out of the fight, but J'onn was right. In the Monitor Womb he would be in control of the situation and the League would be able to rely upon him for strategy.

"Have you notified the reserves yet?" Batman asked.

"This began only a few moments ago," J'onn replied. He stood up and the platform automatically began to lower to the floor. "We'll rely on your discretion."

Batman nodded again. "Fine. But we'll use commlink and psi-net whenever possible. I want to be certain everyone knows what is going on at all times. You realize this is just the beginning."

"Of course," the Manhunter replied. "All the more reason why Ray should begin his analysis immediately."

J'onn and Batman both turned to look at the Atom, who was staring at the many screens, watching the unfolding events in horror and fascination. After a moment he blinked and held up both hands.

"No problem. I'm already gone."

With that the Atom turned and ran back the way he had come, headed for the Watchtower's laboratory. The Martian Manhunter followed without bothering to look back or wish Batman luck. He had passed beyond such superstitions long ago.

Batman rushed to the monitor chair, slipped into it and felt it conform to the muscles in his back, legs, and neck. It rose of its own accord. Fingers on the controls at the arms of the chair, he began to manipulate the images on the screens in the room. The satellite feeds from Norwich and Metropolis shifted to the side, one city's disaster on the left, the other's catastrophe on the right.

One by one he ran through the index of reserve members of the Justice League, activating locator beacons for those with the greatest power or experience, those he knew he could rely on in the field. Files began to appear on screen and beside them, other images as satellite cameras started to shift, tracking the locator beacons.

Green Arrow and Black Canary in Star City. Together. Stationary. No surprise there. Steel in Metropolis, probably already on his way to the scene. Captain Atom in Australia. No wonder he hadn't turned up in Norwich yet. Batman would have to arrange a teleport. Hawkman and Hawkgirl in motion in St. Roch. Firestorm. Zatanna. The Ray. Power Girl. Red Tornado.

One by one, he began to call them in.

*   *   *

As Aquaman materialized on a street corner in Metropolis he was assaulted by the sounds of a city in chaos. Police sirens screamed. Tires squealed and from nearby came the crunch of metal on metal, a car accident in progress. The city was swept by a sulfurous stink like nothing he had ever smelled before. It was carried on the breeze and instantly he knew which direction to head.

Even without the stench on the wind, he could not have failed to locate the melee in progress. For as he began to sprint along the pavement, a wave of panicked humans came around the corner ahead. For a moment, even as he ran, Arthur was overwhelmed by the expressions on their faces, the fear that was engraved upon each countenance. The wide eyes. The screaming mouths. The tears.

He shook it off. The only way to help these people was to ignore them, to push through, to run right by.

Some of them cried out to him, thanking their God. Others began to grab at him, pleading for him to help. Aquaman ripped their hands away or shook them off, forging his way through the thickening crowd, inhaling the odor of terror that exuded from them, choking on it. Police sirens grew louder, and abruptly several Metropolis P.D. vehicles came to a halt on the street nearby.

Aquaman glared at the humans who had stopped, these helpless, vulnerable souls who were clutching at him for succor. "Get off me!" he shouted. "You're in more danger every moment you remain here!"

But they would not listen. He pushed past them as

best he could but they gathered closer around him, strangling him like a forest of kelp. A fragile-looking, redheaded woman wrapped her fingers in Arthur's long, thick blond hair, as though somehow touching him, pulling him close would make her safe.

That was the final straw. Aquaman's nostrils flared, his lips curling back in anger. His huge chest expanded with drawn breath, and then he roared at them in the voice of a king.

"Enough!" he bellowed.

The crowd fell silent and stepped back. Even the police officers who had begun to usher the people frantically along the road, away from the scene of destruction, blinked and stared at him.

Without another word he began to shove them roughly out of his way. Arthur knew what they would say later, knew what his reputation was in the human world already. This was not going to help. Aquaman cared not at all. There was no time for diplomacy at the moment. Not if these fools wanted to have a city left to return to.

Ahead the crowd cleared a path for him at last and he began to sprint, golden hair whipping across his face. There were still people streaming out of buildings that he passed but now he was moving too quickly for them. Aquaman wore a look of such fury upon his features that no one would have dared stop him now.

He ran to an intersection where cars had slammed into one another and been abandoned, their doors hanging open. The ground trembled beneath his feet, pavement quivering. The air was filled with a new sound, a roar that came not from engines or voices, but from some terrible, unnatural monstrosity that did not belong on this world. It was joined by another familiar sound, the sizzle of energy that sometimes accompanied the power ring of the Green Lantern.

Aquaman rounded a corner, and he had arrived at the epicenter of this catastrophe. It was all laid out before him. In the midst of a large intersection, cars had been crushed, a hotel had a two-story hole in its northwest corner, leaving sparking wires and draining pipes dangling, and a full view into the interior of rooms and hallways and a health club. A post office building had been almost completely demolished, leaving only the brick façade that identified its purpose. It looked like an old-time movie set. A chill ran through Arthur as he looked at the debris. There were people in there. There must have been. Which meant that most of them were likely dead.

There was a crater in the middle of the intersection.

Half a block away was the thing that had emerged from that crater. Its appearance froze Arthur for a moment. It was a monster. No other word applied. With its scaly, brick orange, armor-plated body and the spines that jutted from the back of its head, the thing looked like nothing so much as a sea serpent out of ancient legend.

Aquaman knew better than anyone that many such creatures really had existed and some of them lived still. But to see something of such enormity and hideousness here, in the midst of a human city, rather than in the depths of some Pacific trench . . . here he could truly appreciate the scale of the thing.

Monster, yes, but once it was human.

In the midst of a clear blue sky, the power of Green Lantern seared the air. Cloaked in the emerald energy that poured from his ring, Kyle flew high above the spires of a Gothic church that seemed out of place amidst the high-tech office towers of Metropolis. Tendrils of power—faded to bottle green by the sun and the blue sky—snaked from the ring like rodeo lariats. The monster—the burrower—was caught from half a dozen angles by those emerald tentacles. Green Lantern had snared the thing, but it thrashed against those restraints, bucking its entire length, tail slapping downward to eradicate the glass and steel square of a bus station from the corner of the intersection.

In the seconds it took Aquaman to analyze the situation, one of the snares shattered and dissipated, and Arthur saw Green Lantern tugged twenty feet downward, nearer to the burrower. It was too strong. He wasn't going to be able to hold it for long.

Arthur.

The voice spoke softly in his mind. Aquaman glanced around and spotted the Martian Manhunter materializing in the sky above the ruins of the post office.

J'onn. There isn't time for much of a plan.

He felt the Manhunter's hesitation at this suggestion.

Do you remember what happened the last time we acted rashly? J'onn asked.

Yes. We saved lives. Arthur was not in the mood for a debate. *Lantern, are you with us?*

Immediately he could feel the strain Kyle was under, the intense focus it was taking for Green Lantern to hold the burrower in place. They had seconds before it would break free. Even his thoughts were little more than a grunt.

Barely.

Aquaman began to run. His legs pumped beneath him, the ground shaking under his feet as the burrower thrashed against its bonds. *J'onn, hang back. Be prepared to attack with everything you have. For now, see if you can amplify my telepathy.*

He could feel the understanding that dawned upon the Manhunter in that moment. While J'onn was a much more powerful telepath, Aquaman had a primal understanding of marine life. He could communicate mind-to-mind with everything that lived in the oceans, from the highest form of life, to the lowest. His first impression of the burrower was that it had the look of a mythical sea serpent, and now he was hoping there was some truth to that, that wherever it originated— whatever planet had spawned the parasite that had merged with and transformed its human host—it had an aquatic origin.

I will stand by, J'onn replied.

Arthur glanced up and saw him floating there, cloak billowing in the fetid breeze, and the Atlantean king marveled at how the Martian could appear to be so calm in the face of such a crisis. Aquaman himself was not afraid . . . not for himself, at least. But he was hardly calm. Adrenaline surged through him as he ran toward the gigantic, armor-plated serpent.

Kyle, get me up there, Aquaman demanded.

I don't know if—

Now!

The faded green tendrils that held the burrower in place shuddered and thinned slightly. Another of those bonds snapped and then dissipated completely. Aquaman came to a car that had been crushed. He leaped on top of the roof of the vehicle, nostrils filling with the stench of the creature that loomed above him. It was there, fifteen feet away, rising above him. With a sharp intake of breath, Aquaman leaped upward.

Like the hand of God, a glittering, sizzling emerald fist caught him in the air. The power of the Green Lantern enfolded him and his skin prickled with static at the moment of contact with that power. Then he was lifted up and up. The burrower saw him, its slitted yellow eyes swung around and glared and its jaws snapped and gnashed as it darted toward him, trying to snatch him up.

The tendrils of green energy held it back, but only just.

Stop! he thought, focusing his psi abilities, attempting to telepathically reach the mind of the monster. *You are doing harm here. You have killed living creatures. You must stop.*

Nothing. He sensed nothing of the creature's mind, not as though it had no thoughts, but as though they were shielded from him.

J'onn, are you—

Aquaman's communication with the Manhunter was cut off abruptly as the burrower opened its maw—jaws lined with jagged teeth of the same brick orange substance that plated its body—and let out a thunderous roar. It shrank down, body twisting beneath it, and then lunged for Aquaman again.

Kyle could not hold it captive any longer. The green tendrils shattered into shards of emerald light and were gone. Green Lantern could barely hold onto Aquaman. Arthur heard Kyle's mind, the surprise and the exhaustion and the desperate effort to hold him aloft. Green Lantern did not realize that simply holding him there was not going to be enough.

The burrower's jaws widened as it lunged for him, prepared to swallow him whole.

"Kyle, up!" Arthur shouted, both with his lips and with his mind.

The burrower missed him by inches, its plated skin scraping along the outside of the green, shimmering fist of energy that held Aquaman in its grip. Arthur knew there was only one plan of action left to them.

J'onn, he began.

But he need not have bothered. Already the Martian Manhunter was flying down toward the burrower. Red beams blazed from J'onn's eyes, searing the creature's back. Smoke rose from those armor plates, but the burrower did not even seem to notice the attack.

Aquaman stared down at its head, swaying just beneath him as it began to twist around to come after him again.

Lantern, drop me, he thought.

This time, Green Lantern did not argue. Kyle was no longer a rookie. He might question strategy when he was under stress or confused, but now that he no longer had the strain of holding the burrower back, he was following Aquaman's lead.

The emerald fist disappeared. Aquaman began to fall. The burrower was in motion, twisting its head around, and if he did not time the fall perfectly he would miss, plummeting toward the pavement. Arthur tucked his legs in and then extended his entire body, knifing through the air. The burrower was in motion, but he landed on the back of its head, barely avoiding impaling himself on one of the spikes that jutted sharply like a broken crown.

The Martian Manhunter's power beams continued to sear the monster's armor plating, to no avail.

"Aquaman!"

He heard the amplified voice over the rumble of the ground and the sirens in the distance. Arthur glanced up and saw the sun glinting off a metal man, a silhouette against the sun, with a red cape whipping in the wind.

John Henry Irons. Also known as Steel. An associate and friend of Superman's, and a reserve member of the Justice League. His arrival was more than welcome. Steel had taken Superman as his inspiration during a time when Metropolis had badly needed heroes. He was not a metahuman, but his courage made him far more than an ordinary man.

Steel dropped down from the sky, a missile on a direct course for the head of the burrower. In his hands he held the massive sledgehammer that was imbued with all the power technology could provide. He swung the hammer down.

Aquaman held onto the burrower's crown of spines.

The hammer collided with the monster's head and it was knocked sideways. Aquaman was slammed into one of the spines and it cut into him, slicing across his chest, drawing blood. He gritted his teeth with the pain and then, even as the beast began to right itself, stunned but not badly injured from the hammer blow, Arthur grabbed hold of one of those spines with his cybernetic left hand, and bent forward, putting all of his strength into it. Every muscle in his body tensed with the effort.

The spine snapped.

The creature reared up, trying to shake him off.

Green Lantern, Martian Manhunter, and Steel continued their assault upon the burrower. Crimson eye beams and emerald energy burned and pummeled the monster. Steel struck it again and again.

Aquaman held onto it with his legs, lifted the spine high, and then stabbed it downward, striking precisely at the place where two of the monster's body plates came together. The point of the spine slipped beneath that bricklike armor. Using the spine as a lever, Aquaman shoved it deeper and let out a roar of effort as he pried that plate off of the burrower.

J'onn! Arthur thought, as the plating tumbled away, falling toward the street far below. *Here! Now!*

No. There must be another—

The monster squealed in pain from the wound and thrashed backward. Aquaman had been holding on only by clamping his legs tightly, and the burrower bucked him off. He plummeted toward the pavement, tipping end over end, and then an iron hand gripped his wrist, catching him ten feet above the ground.

Aquaman looked up into the metal plate that masked the face of Steel. Then both heroes turned to see the Martian Manhunter dart across the sky toward the burrower. J'onn made himself a target, drawing its attention. The burrower's jaws gnashed and it tried to snatch him out of the air with those teeth.

But the Manhunter was intangible. The burrower passed right through him. The moment had provided all the distraction that Green Lantern needed. Darting behind the burrower, Kyle focused on the foot wide gap Aquaman had made in its armor plating. A lance of green energy erupted from the Lantern's power ring and rammed the monster's exposed flesh.

And then it fell.

Timber, Kyle thought, and the rest of them heard it over the psi-web J'onn had created amongst them.

The burrower crushed several other cars when it fell—all of them empty—but the bulk of it landed on the ruins of the already destroyed post office. The façade that had remained standing was demolished beneath its trunk. Dust rose from the debris around it. A car horn was sounding endlessly, set off by the collision and somehow stuck.

The monster did not move.

Steel set Aquaman down and then landed heavily beside him. J'onn and Kyle joined them. The four men strode cautiously toward the motionless monstrosity. Then they paused and for a long moment just stared at it.

"It appears to be dead," J'onn said, no emotion in his voice at all.

Green Lantern swore. "This wasn't . . . I mean, I wasn't trying to kill it. I thought I could just daze the thing, maybe knock it out."

Arthur said nothing. Of course he knew that this was not the outcome J'onn had desired. So now was not the time to tell Green Lantern that it was for the best that the thing was dead. This was only one burrower, and if their theories were correct, there were well over a hundred more of them somewhere, deep in the earth.

The ground beneath their feet rumbled.

"Gentlemen," came the deep voice of John Henry Irons, muffled by the helmet he wore as Steel. "I think we have a situation."

Aquaman, Green Lantern and Martian Manhunter all turned, just in time to see the second burrower beginning to emerge from the crater in the midst of that Metropolis intersection. As it pushed upward, more of the pavement around the edges of that hole was torn away.

This one was bigger than the last.

The Flash felt empty inside, as though a hollow had formed within him. The world stood still around

him as he raced in a circle. His circular path had created a whirlwind, a tornado that was completely
within his control. He crafted it with the engine of his
speed just as though he were shaping clay on a pot-
tery wheel. But even as he ran, Flash knew that what
he was doing was merely a holding action. The tornado he was creating was little more than a cage.
Lightning danced across his chest and darted from his
feet and he glanced inside that tornado as he ran,
studying the monster within.

Its skin was not skin at all, but red-brown armor
plating that looked more like it had been dug out of
the earth than grown. The burrower's vestigial limbs
were still useable and as he ran, the thing tried several
times to lash out at him with its talons. To that creature, Wally West was nothing more than a blur, but its
timing was excellent and twice he had to speed up to
avoid its claws.

The burrower was more than thirty feet long and
its body reminded him of a salamander, with its long
tail and those thin limbs. But Wally was chilled every
time he glimpsed the thing, for he wondered if this
monster had once been Ian Partington.

A single word crackled over the commlink in his
ear. "Reinforcements."

Wally glanced quickly around. It had been Wonder
Woman's voice and now he took in the melee that was
unfolding in Norwich. He had contained one of the
creatures, but the other, a ten-eyed serpent that was
longer and more hideous than the first, had torn into
a building that had apartments on top and a book-

store on the ground floor, ramming its head through walls, snapping its jaws at people inside. The Flash could not be sure if anyone had been eaten, but he hoped not.

Fortunately, Superman and Wonder Woman had arrived.

The Flash had assumed the battle was over then. But as Wonder Woman rained blows down upon the thing's armored hide and Superman's heat vision seemed to have no effect, he started to doubt. Wonder Woman tried to bind the creature but it shook her off. Superman tried to lift it, to remove it from the populated area, and the thing darted at him with such speed that the Kryptonian could not get in close enough. He struck the burrower again and again, and it was clearly dazed.

But it would not fall. It would not surrender.

Superman and Wonder Woman had managed to trap the beast between them so that other than the way in which its armored trunk tore at the pavement and the sidewalk, it could do no more damage to Norwich. But Wally was uncertain how long that stalemate could last. Superman was going to have to try again to get a grip on it. He could haul the burrower out of there, fly it high enough that the thinning atmosphere would knock it unconscious—maybe. Or he might simply be able to move it to a location where there weren't so many civilians to endanger.

All of these things had gone through Wally's mind as he continued to forge the tornado that trapped the smaller burrower. It had just snapped at him again when he had heard Wonder Woman speak that one word over the commlink.

Reinforcements.

The Flash turned to look toward the other burrower, to see which member of the League had come to help them. In the sky between Superman and Wonder Woman, Wally saw a silver-gray figure he would have recognized instantly, even without the deep red atomic symbol on his chest. Truth was, he had been surprised the man had not shown up previous to this—surprised, and glad at the same time.

It was Captain Atom.

The chill that ran through Wally went deeper now, all the way to the bone. Atom was American, but had lived in England for years, ever since he had been a part of the League's now defunct European branch. His body was coated with an alien alloy through which he could tap into the quantum field, channeling energy into devastating power blasts.

Atom was a maverick. He did things his own way.

Even as the Flash raced around the burrower he was caging in that whirlwind, he saw Captain Atom raise both hands, quantum energy spilling from his closed fists.

Wally came to a complete stop. He clapped one hand to his ear and shouted into the commlink.

"Atom, stop!"

But it was too late. The air seemed to fold in upon itself around Captain Atom and the quantum blasts burst from his fists. He timed it perfectly, just as the burrower had begun to open its mouth. The quantum energy churned across the sky, shot into the burrower's throat, and blew out the back of its head, complete with several of its pairs of eyes. Flesh and black blood and brick-red armor plating showered across Norwich.

"Noooo!" Flash screamed, rage and grief spilling out of him with that one word. He did not know if the burrower had been Ian, but he knew it could have been, knew there had to be another way to handle this.

Then Wonder Woman's voice was in his ear again. "Flash, look out!" she snapped, the words tinny over the commlink.

Wally spun around, so many thoughts sifting through his mind at once. He had forgotten. The sight of Captain Atom attacking the burrower had drawn him, had distracted him enough that he had stopped running. The tornado was gone. The cage had dissipated.

He turned just in time to see the smaller burrower lunging at him, claws slashing the air. The thing drove him to the pavement, talons slicing through the solidified Speed Force that comprised his scarlet uniform. Its jaws opened wide and viscous, fetid drool slipped from its teeth as it began to bend its maw toward him.

Golden light shimmered around the burrower, enveloping it completely, and then it began to float. The burrower levitated off the ground and for just a moment the Flash gaped at it in wonder and confusion.

"Close your mouth, Wally. You're going to catch flies."

The voice was impossibly familiar. The Flash leaped to his feet and spun around to find the source of it. There, fifteen feet above him, Ian Partington hovered in the air, floating in a shimmering golden sphere of telekinetic energy.

"Ian?" Flash said, amazed. "But I thought . . . I thought you were one of them."

The Englishman nodded, a bittersweet smile on his face. "Not yet, mate. Not just yet."

Ten years ago . . .

One thought resounded through J'onn's mind, echoing over and over. *There are ten of them.* The British military were doing their best to keep the invading monsters out of the cities, and thus far had been able to hold them back with shelling and RAF missiles. But just holding them back was not going to be enough; there had to be a way to stop the things or to reason with them. J'onn analyzed the situation, turning it over in his mind, trying to find a better solution. Between the military and the Justice League—which at the moment was himself, the Flash, and Green Lantern—they could hold the things back for a while. And in rural or even suburban areas, that would do for the moment.

But it was already too late for that in London. Two of the monsters had made planetfall in the midst of the city. One of them trudged through the Thames even now, and the other had destroyed half a city block in Islington. Lives had been lost. J'onn could not escape that fact. He did not know how many, but given the time of day he estimated as many as one hundred.

Outwardly, the Martian Manhunter always presented a tranquil countenance, a serenity that nearly always reflected the way he felt inside. But now he was in turmoil. There had to be a better way than this, had to be a more viable way to handle these creatures. Yet there was simply no time to find it. If they had been smaller, less powerful . . . if the armor that plated their bodies was not so completely impervious and they might have been drugged . . .

But there was no time for wishful thinking. Not when lives were in the balance.

High above the rowhouses of Islington, the too-narrow street jammed with cars, J'onn hovered for just a moment. The alien towered over the homes, forty-five feet tall or more. Its footfalls cracked pavement and sidewalk, its many eyes blazing. The monstrosity did not focus on the street or the cars or the screaming people who fled at the sight of it. The sirens did not bother it, nor did small arms fire. It could be staggered, but little more than that.

And yet, J'onn thought, studying its gaze . . . *And yet. It doesn't even seem to notice.* The alien had waded through a block of rowhouses, tearing them down with its tread, but its attention had been elsewhere, as though it followed some distant beacon.

What do you want here? J'onn thought, trying for perhaps the tenth time to probe its mind, to communicate with the alien telepathically. Yet there was only static, as though its mind was shielded as well as its flesh . . . or perhaps it had no mind to speak of. Only instinct.

Though he had attacked it only moments before, now that he had retreated into the sky above it the alien ignored him.

A crackle sounded in his ear over the Justice League commlink.

"J'onn, this is Aquaman," came the Atlantean monarch's strangely accented voice.

"I'm here," the Martian Manhunter replied, watching as another car was crushed by the alien. He tensed, knowing he had to stop it.

"I have a report from the area outside Coventry. The R.A.F. missiles have managed to shatter some of the armor plates on the invaders. Witnesses on site say the dermal layer underneath doesn't look armored at all. They can be killed, J'onn."

Regret whispered through his mind, but the Martian Manhunter flew down to block the alien's path. It swung at him but he was prepared for its speed, expecting the attack, and he made his body intangible so that the blow passed right through him. An instant later he lunged at its head, pummeling it with his fists.

"J'onn?" Aquaman prodded over the commlink.

"I heard you. Thank you for the update."

So they could be killed. A cold knot formed in J'onn's gut. He was determined to find a better way. If he could only get this beast out of Islington, or freeze it somehow . . . but Green Lantern had attempted to contain one of the creatures with his power ring and it had only worked briefly. The Flash had managed to whip up a gale powerful enough to drive one of them back, but nothing more.

Sirens screamed in J'onn's ears. He heard the shriek of jet engines as R.A.F. pilots scraped the sky above. They wouldn't attack here, not in the midst of the city . . . not unless they had no other choice.

The alien swiped a talon at J'onn again and once more he let it pass through him harmlessly. He had to hurt the invader, that much, at least, he could not avoid. Perhaps if he could wound it, he could stop it long enough to discover more, to find a more effective way of dealing with them, or even to learn what their presence signified.

J'onn grabbed hold of one of the invader's horns with both hands. Crimson beams of laser energy erupted from his eyes and seared the armor plating at its edge, at the very place where it touched the horn. The giant alien staggered and roared, those beams burning down inside that gap. With all of his strength, J'onn grasped the horn in both hands and he pulled.

It tore loose with the crack of bone and the rip of flesh and the alien screamed. As J'onn dropped the massive horn to the ground, where it cracked the sidewalk and destroyed a wrought iron fence, he flew up and away from the creature. It staggered, its wail of agony now almost pitiful. A pink rivulet of viscous fluid dripped from the hole where its horn had been.

Fall, J'onn thought. *Just fall down.*

But then the sky lit up with emerald light and the Martian Manhunter glanced up to see Hal Jordan—the Green Lantern—streaking down toward him. Toward the alien invader. The energy from Green Lantern's power ring rippled and shimmered and a sudden arc of verdant light lanced out from the ring. Hal dove toward the alien, that emerald lance slicing the air until he drove it into the exposed, tender flesh where the monster's horn had been torn away. There was a wet, popping noise and the alien let out a small sigh. When it fell, it shattered the face of a building, window glass and brick erupting outward and showering into the street and across the alien's corpse.

"Well done, J'onn," Hal said as he raced across the sky, emerald power crackling around his body, to where J'onn came softly to rest on the edge of a rooftop.

Hal tapped his commlink. "This is Green Lantern. Good news, people. It takes some doing, but they can be killed."

The Martian Manhunter shivered, then, suddenly so very cold.

CHAPTER TWELVE

Ray Palmer was torn. The entire world was in danger and though he loved science, the last place he wanted to be right now was in a laboratory on the moon, so far away from the action that it seemed almost like fiction to him, like something that was happening on television. His commlink was on and he was part of the psi-web that J'onn J'onzz had set up, so he heard the entire play by play of events unfolding in Norwich and Metropolis. Things were going from bad to infinitely worse.

If I was there, he caught himself thinking, *I might be able to enter the burrowers' bodies, to shut down their brains from inside without killing them.* He did not know this for certain, but it would not have been the first time he had accomplished such a feat. He was a scientist and a member of the Justice League, and the combination had given him some extraordinary missions over the years. The Atom could shrink himself down so small that his existence passed from tangible to theoretical, explainable only by particle physics and quantum theory.

He could do something. Down there, on the Earth, with the abilities of the Atom and the amazing strength that was part of that gift, he could be a hero.

But the Justice League needed him far more here in the laboratory than they did in the midst of the destruction in Metropolis or in Norwich. As the events unfolded and he listened in, Ray was also working. The lab was silent save for the humming of life support systems in the walls and the strange buzz that came from the ultra-microscope.

The temperature in the lab was far below freezing, but Ray's costume gave him thermal protection. The cold was necessary to preserve the samples of the dead metas' DNA, blood, and organs that he had brought back from S.T.A.R. labs. They were still working on their analysis down there, now that they had Paul Cargill to work with.

On a steel table in the corner of the lab sat the massive alien head that Superman had retrieved from London. Even beneath the layer of ice that was crusted over it, the thing was frightening to behold. The head alone was nearly as high as Ray himself. There were three eyes in the monstrosity's face and numerous holes in the plated, stonelike flesh all over the skull. He was trying to make sense of its physiology, but that was less important at the moment than other tests he had to run.

J'onn and Aquaman had been correct in suspecting

a similarity with the burrowers. Ray could see that with the most superficial examination. But the real question was the nature of the relationship between the two. There had been the chance—though highly unlikely after ten years—that thawing out the alien's head would bring it back to life, allow it to grow a new body. Thus, it had seemed prudent to drill through the ice and its skull and take a sample of its tissue and that armor plating. Even that posed a limited threat, but there was little choice.

Fortunately, the flesh was dead. Well preserved by the ice and cold, but it had been deprived of its other organic systems for too long to survive or regenerate. It had taken Ray a while to even cut through that armor-plated skin, and some small amount of time to prepare the samples from both the mutated humans and the aliens.

Tissue. Blood. DNA.

The ultra-microscope had the capacity to examine all of them at once, the various samples arranged side by side and labeled. As Ray bent to peer into the eyepiece of the scope, he could still hear the cacophony of words and thoughts, that matrix that connected all the members of the League at the moment. He heard Wonder Woman tell Superman and Flash that reinforcements had arrived in Norwich, and heard Batman's thoughts as he informed the Martian Manhunter that Captain Atom was in England. He was aware of the moment when Steel arrived to aid the others in Metropolis, and he heard J'onn telling Aquaman there had to be another way to fight the burrowers, some way other than killing them.

In the moment when Kyle Rayner thought the word *timber*, Ray Palmer paused in his work. Green Lantern's sadness was evident in the word and the feeling that came with it. Just as Flash worried that one of the monsters in Norwich was Ian Partington, Kyle also feared that he might just have killed his friend.

In the midst of that chaos that swirled in his mind and echoed in his ears, it took Ray a moment to realize what he was looking at. He frowned, slid his hand along the barrel of the scope and clicked the selector. After a few seconds of staring at the tissue sample beneath he pulled back and double-checked the label on that sample. Then he pushed his eye against the scope again and clicked the selector back to its previous position.

Then back again.

And again.

And again.

As he had expected, within each cell taken from Bryan Francis, the meta who had committed suicide to stop his transformation, there were minute organisms that did not belong in the human body. The tiniest of organisms, things that were likely alien in origin. Each of the transformed metas had been host to these tiny parasites which it seemed had prompted their bodies to manifest certain metahuman abilities, then merged with them and turned their bodies malleable, transforming them into the burrowing giants that even now were bursting up from the earth.

All of that supported the theory they had been working with, that something alien had somehow infected a portion of the population of England. With no other connection, the victims would have had to contract the parasite at widespread locations. The idea that they had filtered into the Earth's atmosphere and seeded a rainstorm, falling with the rain and beginning to infect people, seemed more like a certainty than a possibility now.

The thick plating that covered the alien's hide was not just similar to the bricklike substance that armored the burrowers' flesh, it was *precisely the same*. Beneath that plating, however, on a sub-atomic level the two species differed substantially, which he had expected from creatures with different origins. It had occurred to him that perhaps their origins were not so different, that the aliens that had invaded the Earth a decade earlier and been destroyed by the Justice League might have been otherworldly victims of the same infection, the same parasitical race.

It would have been simple. It seemed likely, in fact. There was logic to the idea that these microscope parasites that could drift through the universe as little more than space dust and fall upon a planet, mutating those organisms it came into contact with . . . it just made sense that if they had done it on Earth they had to have done it elsewhere as well. And perhaps they had.

However, when Ray clicked the selector to the other sample and stared at the ultra-magnified tissue from the alien creature, the core sample he had taken from its head, everything was different.

"Nothing," he said to himself.

The alien cells showed zero trace of those minute organisms. The alien creature whose head sat on a steel table in the Watchtower's laboratory had never carried those parasites.

"So what's the relationship?" Ray asked aloud.

He stepped away from the ultra-microscope. With a sigh he ran his right hand across his head, pushed his fingers through his hair. His mask was pulled back, bunched up around his neck, but the commlink was still in place. The voices were gibberish to him now, everyone talking on top of everyone else. Things were getting even worse. And of course they would. They had found four of the burrowers. There were well over a hundred more.

The Atom tapped a button on the commlink and it shut down.

He pressed several fingers to his right temple, brow furrowing. *J'onn*, he thought. *This is Ray. Drop me from the psi-net, please. I need to think.*

Dropping you now. I will continue to monitor you, should you want to reestablish contact, the Martian Manhunter thought in return. Ray could feel the tension in J'onn's mind as the battle in Metropolis continued to unfold. *If you discover anything, please inform me immediately. If we cannot find a more efficient way to combat the burrowers—*

The Atom sighed. *I get it*, he thought. *Be a hell of a lot easier if we could just call the exterminator, maybe put out a roach motel.*

But J'onn wasn't listening anymore. He had other things to worry about.

Ray went back to work. He wanted to take a fresh look at the samples he had prepared. After that, he was going to have to begin trying to unlock the secret of the burrowers' metamorphosis to see if it provided any clues as to how they could be weakened, or possibly killed. He knew, however, that the latter option would not go over well with some of the members of the League, particularly given the bad feeling about how the original situation had been handled.

The Atom had already established with as much scientific certainty as possible that the mutation was irreversible, than these things might once have been people but there was no trace of humanity left in them. The human bodies had been hosts, nothing more, and now the host bodies had been destroyed. The people who had been infected had not been caterpillars undergoing the metamorphosis to butterfly, but merely the cocoon from which the butterfly emerges.

Ray had told Batman and the Manhunter that, and presumably they had passed it on. But it was obvious that J'onn was still hesitant. Whatever they were now, these things had once been human. Killing them was not going to be the first option the League chose. But it might be the only viable one.

In a few moments he would contact S.T.A.R. and see if their analysis of Paul Cargill had turned up any new information about the parasites. Now Ray walked back to the ultra-microscope and, taking a deep breath, pressed his face against the eyepiece.

The sample from the alien, clear of parasites.

The Atom frowned. Where before the sample had been large, it now seemed smaller and thinner, almost smeared to one side. It was possible it could have run off the slide he had prepared it on, but the ultra-microscope had its own equilibrium. It was impossible for there to be an angle on the thing. Its display was always entirely flat.

The solution that he had used could *not* have run.

And yet it had.

A tingling began at the base of the Atom's neck. His chest felt tight and without realizing it, he was holding his breath. *Something,* he thought, a spark of suspicion forming in his mind. *This is something.*

He pulled his face away from the eyepiece and examined the display of slides. The solution from the alien sample had run. Impossibly, but it had. A trickle of fluid followed a single line from that slide to another. Upon closer examination, it seemed as though the fluid had gotten *onto* the other slide as well.

Quickly he put his face to the eyepiece again. Ray rotated the selector, bringing the affected slide into focus. It was the cell sample taken from Bryan Francis.

The alien sample had leaked across the display and mixed with this one. The only way for that to happen is if the alien cells moved *of their own accord*. The two had mixed, on a cellular level.

The parasites from Bryan Francis's tissue sample were still there.

But they had stopped moving.

They were dead.

* * *

Ian Partington felt his every heartbeat, was keenly aware of its rhythm, of the knowledge that each beat of his pulse brought him closer to something that truly was worse than death. He stared at the horror that he had captured within a telekinetic net as it thrashed against his power, its huge jaws snapping again and again. Unless he did something, unless the Justice League could help him, this was his future, his fate.

Every time he inhaled, the air tasted sweeter.

He thought of Sara and wished he had called, wished he had gone to see her, so that he could have caressed her face and looked into those eyes one more time. If this was the end, he so wanted to tell her, to make certain she knew what she meant to him, what she had always meant to him. She *was* his life.

But right now, in this moment, his place was here. He had come to Norwich to hide away, to think, but once the burrowers had come he could not sit calmly and sip coffee and wait to die. The time for action had arrived.

Ian would stand with the Justice League.

Whatever came afterward, he was not going to run from the future—from the truth—anymore. He was going to fight.

He felt feverish, now. Sweat ran down his face despite the chill in the air. The effort it took to hold the burrower aloft seemed to drain him all the more. Superman was the first to join him. Wonder Woman and Captain Atom followed, all of them gathering round.

"Well done, Mr. Partington," Superman said.

"Ian. Just Ian's fine," he replied, feeling foolish speaking that way to Superman. *Superman, for God's sake!* "You might want to take over now, though. Not sure how much longer I can hold onto the ugly sod."

As Ian watched in amazement, Superman flew behind the burrower. Even as the creature thrashed against its telekinetic prison, Superman grabbed it by the tip of its tail, put it over his shoulder as though he were jolly old Saint Nick, and began to rise. Captain Atom followed him, but Wonder Woman lagged behind a moment. Gracefully she floated across the sky until she was only a few feet away from him.

"You're Ian?" she asked.

He could barely breathe. Ian loved Sara more than his life, but that did not prevent him from being awestruck by Wonder Woman's presence. It was not merely her beauty, though with those extraordinary eyes and regal features, that was certainly substantial. More than that, it was her bearing. She wasn't an ordinary woman. She was a goddess.

"Yeah. Yes, I mean."

Wonder Woman nodded gravely. "Well done. The League appreciates the help. But maybe it's time now to see to your own ailments."

Ian nodded slowly and she turned and flew in pursuit of the others. Over the rooftops of Norwich they had already become little more than black dots on the horizon. Sadly he glanced around at the damage that had been done in Norwich, and he hoped it would not take too long before the city was able to make the necessary repairs.

Below him, the Flash stood with his arms crossed, tapping his foot impatiently on the pavement.

Despite his exhaustion and the nausea that had begun to roil in his stomach, Ian smiled as he flew down to the street. He alighted on the road just beside the Flash.

"Hello, Wally."

"Hello, Wally? That's it? That's the best you can do?" Flash asked, half-smiling. "You know I was afraid you were one of those things."

Ian nodded. "I'm sorry about that. I just . . . it wasn't the easiest thing in the world to accept."

Now Wally's smile was gone. He let out a short breath, his expression grim. "No. No I guess it wasn't."

Ian glanced at the horizon above the city again, but he had lost sight of the other members of the Justice League, as well as their monstrous captive.

"What will they do with it, do you think? Captain Atom seemed to have no trouble killing—"

"They're monsters, Ian," Flash replied, a dark understanding in his eyes. "The analysis says they can't be changed back. There's nothing more human left in them. Even so, our strategy is to avoid killing them if possible. If we can immobilize them at all, we might be able to relocate them."

"To where, Antarctica?" Ian asked, incredulous. "They'll only burrow deeper."

"To another planet, maybe. It's not impossible."

"Might as well be. You know how many of these things there are. You're the one who told me. There isn't time to be gentle, not when so many lives are at stake."

Flash glanced away then, unable to meet his gaze.

Ian smiled. "Surprised to hear me say it? 'Cause I'm one of them, yeah? Look, Wally, if I turn into . . . turn into one of *them* . . . I'd want you to do me in."

Eyes narrowed, Wally glanced up angrily. "It's not going to come to that. And even if it did—"

"Right," Ian said, nodding. "I'll get Captain Atom to do it. Don't think he'll even blink, from the look of him."

"No, listen, it won't be necessary," Flash replied. "I just heard over the commlink. The Atom's figured out a way to kill the parasite, to eliminate it from your body completely. It can't save the ones who've mutated already, but—"

"What if I can't live without the parasite?" Ian asked, almost too frightened to hope that what Wally had said could be true.

"Then you'll die. But at least you won't ever become one of *them*." The Flash stared at him, gaze unwavering. "On the other hand, if you survive, you get to go back home. Home to Sara."

Ian closed his eyes and let his head roll forward. He bit his lip slightly, feeling his eyes burn with unshed tears. It was too much to hope for, and yet he could not stop himself. And then, before he could say any more, the strength went out of him and he dropped to his knees on the pavement, swaying, his equilibrium completely shot.

Wally's hand clamped on his shoulder, steadying him.

"Batman, this is Flash," he heard Wally say, the voice echoing strangely as his vision swam and the center of Norwich blurred around him. "I've got Ian. Teleport us to S.T.A.R. Now!"

Even as the last of those words drifted to his ears the world began to fade to black.

The situation in Metropolis was under control, but only barely. J'onn had pulled back to the rooftop of a bank to survey the battle. The new burrower that had erupted from the ground was much larger than the previous one, and this one had razor sharp fins that lined the length of its body. The fins were made of that same brick-colored armor plate, and even an attack from Steel's hammer could not shatter them.

Aquaman, J'onn thought, sending the message telepathically, *see if you can pry an armor plate loose from this creature as well. This time, however, perhaps we can avoid killing it.*

Green Lantern flew above the burrower and by this time had erected a barrier that corralled it within that intersection, keeping it away from other buildings at least for the moment.

It isn't as if I did it on purpose, J'onn, Green Lantern thought. *I mean, what if it had been Ian?*

It wasn't, Aquaman's mental voice broke in. *Batman just told you that. Now focus on what you're doing, Kyle. I see some wavering in the walls you've got up.*

Doing the best I can, Green Lantern replied.

J'onn could feel Kyle's relief. There was still chaos in Norwich, but moments earlier, Batman had reported that Ian Partington had arrived at the scene there, and his final mutation had not yet begun. This was good news, but barely a footnote in comparison to the crisis at hand. Though harsh, Arthur was right. Kyle needed to focus.

Steel flew in behind the creature and, once again, swung his hammer with both hands. Despite the strength in his technological armor, the blow staggered the burrower, but nothing more.

Nothing was working now.

Green Arrow and the Black Canary had arrived, teleported from Star City via the Watchtower. But Green Arrow's presence was useful only for strategy and to help with those people still evacuating the buildings around them. The arrows in Oliver Queen's quiver would be beneath the burrower's notice. Black Canary, on the other hand . . .

Gentlemen, get out of the way, J'onn thought. *Let Dinah have a shot at it.*

Thanks, J'onn. Don't mind if I do, came the response from the mind of Dinah Lance, aka the Black Canary.

Steel and Aquaman immediately retreated, giving the Canary a clear path to the monstrosity. The thing slithered against the ground, its fins slicing pavement and concrete as though they were gelatin. As she ran toward it, it spotted her and slid swiftly toward her over the street.

Dinah stood her ground, threw her head back, and screamed. But this was no ordinary scream. It was the Canary Cry, the power that made Dinah Lance more than a gifted martial artist. The sonic blast pummeled the burrower, knocking its upper body back hard enough that it coiled upon itself, and blowing out windows on the upper floors of the buildings around the intersection.

Steel and Green Lantern followed that with attacks of their own, John Henry's hammer crashing down upon the burrower's head and Kyle attempting to pry the thing's armor plating loose with a spike of emerald energy from his power ring. Neither attack bore fruit.

The Black Canary opened her mouth and loosed another Canary Cry. The waves of sonic power swept across the burrower, knocked Steel backward, and shattered more windows. But the burrower was barely fazed this time.

It was precisely what J'onn had feared.

The burrower was adapting. They could evolve. These monstrosities might well be able to adapt to almost anything, and he suspected that they had a way to share that knowledge, that when one of them changed, they were all affected. If the creatures had been benevolent, and he'd had time to study them, he would have found it fascinating. At the moment, it was rather alarming.

A voice filled J'onn's head, then, interrupting his thoughts. It was in his ear as well, coming over the commlink with a delay that was a sliver of a second.

Batman. Manhunter. This is the Atom.

Go ahead, Ray, came the Batman's response.

I hope everyone can hear this. I have news.

"Good news or bad?" J'onn asked aloud, so that

those who were on the commlink but not part of his psi-web could hear him.

You'll have to decide for yourself. The alien invaders, the ones the League destroyed . . . they weren't attacking Earth. I believe they were here in pursuit of the real invaders. The microscopic parasites that infected these people . . . the things that used human hosts to evolve into the burrowers. They weren't our enemies. They were exterminators.

J'onn shuddered to hear this. Though those aliens had caused a great deal of damage in the United Kingdom, he had always felt that the League had acted rashly. But there was no sense of victory in being proven correct. Only sadness.

I think I can create a kind of antivirus from the exterminators' DNA that will kill the parasite in the human hosts, the Atom continued. *It won't help the burrowers. There's nothing that can be done for them now. But it may be possible to cure Paul Cargill and anyone else who hasn't mutated completely.*

"That is good news, Atom," J'onn replied, even as he watched the action unfolding in the Metropolis street below him, as Aquaman, Steel, and the others continued to attack the burrower. "But I'm afraid there's bad news as well. I believe the creatures have been adapting to our attacks. They are far from identical to begin with, but I think it may only be a matter of time before nothing we can do will stop them."

Another voice entered the conversation. "I hope you're wrong, J'onn," Batman said.

His tone alone was enough to set off alarm bells in the Manhunter's mind. But then, rather than try to describe it, Batman let J'onn see what he was seeing, look through his eyes at what was unfolding. Through the eyes of the Batman, the Martian Manhunter surveyed the many screens in the Monitor Womb on the Justice League's lunar Watchtower. Satellite feeds of locations all over the world.

Hong Kong. Los Angeles. London. New York. Glasgow. Montreal.

The burrowers were surfacing.

With the psi-web he had set up, J'onn shared those images with the rest of the League. He felt their horror sweeping over him in waves, and it mirrored his own.

My God, came Green Lantern's voice in all of their minds. *How do we stop this?*

Actually, the Atom replied, *there may be one way we haven't considered.*

CHAPTER THIRTEEN

The Monitor Womb was swathed in darkness, the only lights those coming from the shimmering screens upon which horrors unfolded around the world. Batman preferred to work in shadow. His eyes burned from staring so long at the many screens and his fingers moved lightly over the controls on the arms of the chair.

The minutes seemed to be passing far too swiftly, rushing by as he manipulated the Watchtower's teleportation systems, plucking members of the League and their allies from locations all over the Earth and redepositing them in crisis areas. Still, he was far from tired. Rather, he was edgy with frustration at his captivity here in the Monitor Womb. He had remained here to organize the benevolent forces of the Earth against the burrowers, to focus strategy, to call in reinforcements.

Now, all that was done, and he was ready to join the fray.

When the datascreen that scrolled the teleporter activity registered the Martian Manhunter's return to the Watchtower, Batman did not wait. He touched his foot to the control that lowered the observation chair to the floor, then stepped immediately out of the conforming seat. Batman quickly checked the contents of the pouches on his belt and the concealed pockets in his cape. He stole a final glance at the wall of monitors.

There came a beep from the door and it slid open. J'onn J'onzz was silhouetted in the light that streamed in from the corridor. The Martian blinked his eyes against the darkness but did not seem overly curious about it. They had worked together for years, and each knew the other's eccentricities.

"You've assigned reservists and volunteers to the crisis locations?" J'onn asked.

Batman frowned. They had confirmed this already via both commlink and psi-web. The situations were over in Norwich and Metropolis, at least for now, but just beginning in other cities. The burrowers had appeared in only a handful of places outside of the U.K., but there, particularly in the greater London area, it was anarchy. He did not understand why J'onn felt the need for this exchange, but he nodded.

"There are combatants at some of the locations who are mavericks, pitching in but not in communication with us."

J'onn looked at him, one eyebrow raised. "But we'll take all the help we can get."

"As long as they don't get in the way," Batman

replied. "Lives are going to be lost here, J'onn. People are going to die. Our job is to keep the number of casualties to the absolute minimum. That's going to take strategy, especially when the Atom's radical solution starts to roll out. I'm not going to let a rogue hero interfere with that."

"Agreed," the Manhunter said with a nod. "I'll coordinate with S.T.A.R. and Professor Palmer and we'll get the exterminators out as quickly as possible. I'll be in constant communication with the teams at the various sites, but the United Kingdom is in chaos. You'll take over ground strategy there?"

"I'm on my way."

The interior of Grand Central Station was a shambles. Hawkman soared just beneath the New York City landmark's cathedral-like ceiling, high above the catastrophic scene that was unfolding far below. Slightly more than half an hour earlier, the first of the burrowers had appeared in a subway tunnel, making its way toward Grand Central. Passengers on a Metro North train heading away from the station saw it out their windows in the flickering half-light of the tunnels and got on their cell phones immediately.

The burrower—from all reports much more lizard-like than the others who had previously appeared—had damaged tracks and several columns when it had emerged into the terminal at Grand Central. The station was always jammed with people. If New York's Times Square was the crossroads of the world, then Grand Central was the crossroads of New York. It was nothing short of a miracle that no one had been killed by that burrower.

But it was not alone.

Two others had appeared shortly thereafter, both of the more serpentine variety. The third had burst up through the floor of the main concourse of Grand Central, tearing up tile and stone and the clock tower that thrust up from the middle of the vast structure.

People had died.

The Justice Society of America had not arrived in time to save them. Hawkman felt the rage of the warrior surging through him, his veins pulsing in his temples. He carried a massive mace in his hands and he swooped and glided, surveying the horror beneath him. A guitar player who had been busking not far from the ticket office had been killed by flying tiles, change and dollars spilling all over the floor when he collapsed on his guitar case. The number of commuters who had been killed by that erupting floor or crushed to death beneath the burrowers was hard to calculate at this point. The front of a newsstand had been staved in by flying debris and Hawkman could only hope that the people who had been inside were alive.

"Terrific," he snarled, knowing that his voice would be picked up by the communications rig the JSA's chairman, Mister Terrific, had provided to the entire team. "Just slowing them down isn't enough. You know that, Michael."

For a long moment there was no response. Hawkman circled again, surveying the activity below, as the Justice Society attempted to hold the three creatures in their present location without any further loss of life and with as little additional destruction as possible. It was a thankless task. The JSA had been founded more than half a century earlier for precisely this sort of task, to protect ordinary citizens from extraordinary dangers. They had been the first organized team of metahumans and shared a proud legacy that still endured. But the problem the Earth was facing at the moment was too great for any one hero, or any one team.

Wildcat, the Star-Spangled Kid, and Doctor Midnite rushed about the shattered floor inside Grand Central, retrieving the injured and those who had been cornered by the monstrosities, helping to evacuate the entire station. Screams echoed all the way to the ceiling. The burrowers' armored bodies scraped against the floor, making a horrid noise.

Atom Smasher had increased his size so that he was a much more formidable opponent for the lizardlike burrower. The two grappled near the main staircase that led up to the street level, an extraordinary bit of architectural design that crumbled as the monster opened its filthy maw and tried to clamp its jaws down on Atom Smasher's face. Masonry cracked and fell. Police and fire personnel who had responded to the initial crisis stood at the top of the stairs with their guns drawn, unwilling to fire for fear of hitting a member of the JSA. Instead they had to focus on aiding the evacuation and helping the injured.

Hawkgirl darted through the air, wielding a mace nearly identical to the one Hawkman presently carried. She flew down and swung the mace with all her might, striking the burrower in the skull. The blow stunned it momentarily, allowing Atom Smasher to get the upper hand, but that wouldn't last. So far they had found no way to overpower these things. Mister Terrific was on the floor, taking field command, shouting at the others. His T-spheres—technological marvels the brilliant man had created himself—zipped across the interior of the station, lightning erupting from them as he attempted to shock the burrowers, but technology was doing no better than brute force against the creatures.

Jay Garrick—the original Flash—ran circles around one of the serpentine burrowers, keeping it in place, stopping it from retreating as Captain Marvel attacked it again and again. Marvel was a streak of red and white, pausing for single instants to strike the infernal thing, knocking it to the ground again and again. But even the incredible strength given to Marvel by the wizard Shazam could not keep it from rising once more.

The third burrower was encased in green light, the humming magic that sparked from Sentinel's fingertips. He had been the first Green Lantern and his dignity and nobility were an example to every hero who had come after him. Sentinel had it off the ground and it thrashed against his magical power, but he would not let it go. Power Girl hovered in the air close by, waiting for those moments when the thing would pause in its violent seizures, and then she would attack, trying to rip the armored plating from its body without any luck at all.

"Damn it, Terrific!" Hawkman shouted, looking for an opening, looking for a way. They weren't going to be able to hold these creatures forever. More destruction was sure to come, and more death as well.

"The League says—"

"I don't care what the League says. We've got to destroy these things now, before they escape. And what if there are more of them? What then?"

There was a burst of static in Hawkman's earpiece.

"All right. Before anything worse happens," Terrific replied. "We take them down. Whatever means necessary."

Jaw clenched in fury, Hawkman descended upon the nearest burrower, letting loose a battle cry as he swung his mace with both hands.

The Santa Monica pier was shattered. Nightwing stood on the swaying remains of a portion of the pier, its pilings still jutting from the water though sections of it had been obliterated. When Batman had contacted him and asked for help, Nightwing had known the situation must be desperate. Before he had taken the identity of Nightwing, Dick Grayson had been the first to fight at Batman's side under the name Robin. No one knew the man better than Nightwing did. Though the Titans—the group of younger heroes Dick had helped form back in his time as Robin—were a formidable force, Batman would not have brought them in unless they were truly needed. Even with that knowledge, Nightwing had not imagined precisely how precarious things really were.

The thing was hideous, a sea serpent from out of ancient myth. It had odd, jagged fins jutting from the sides of its head where ears might have gone, and similar appendages along its body. But the creature, with its reddish-brown scales, was nothing like any of them had seen before, not even Tempest, who had lived his entire life in Atlantis.

And it was thrashing the Titans.

Jesse Quick—whose father had discovered a formula that gave its user incredible speed—raced along the beachfront, keeping civilians out of the way. The shape-shifting Beast Boy was injured and Arsenal—after having found his weapons useless against the monster—had taken him to the paramedics who had in a matter of minutes set up an emergency desk on the street in front of a flamingo pink Holiday Inn.

Tempest attacked the burrower with bursts of violent magic that seemed to have no effect at all. Cyborg and Damage stood on the shore, both of them stunning the burrower with energy blasts that barely served to keep it from doing any further destruction in Santa Monica. It was still half in, half out of the water. If it got up into the city proper . . . Nightwing didn't want to think about it.

His ace in the hole was supposed to be Troia—the former Wonder Girl—but even her raw power was not enough to defeat the burrower.

Nightwing stared at it, perched on the swaying remnants of the pier, trying to force his mind to come up with another approach, a new strategy. He had nothing. What disturbed him the most about that was that for all the Titans' power, they could not stop one of these things. And Batman had told him there were more than a hundred.

Hong Kong was a city of neon, the business district a forest of glittering silver skyscrapers and multicolored industrial light shows. But those lights were as nothing compared to the flares and blinding explosions that now seared the sky over the jewel of the Orient. Streaks of red and yellow and orange scarred the heavens and were reflected off the calm surface of Hong Kong Harbor.

Buildings had collapsed. A crater had been torn out of the heart of the city's business district. There were two burrowers now, one that had come from the harbor and one that had burst up through the earth. They had drawn together here, just as they had in other locations around the world.

Ronnie Raymond wasn't a part of the Justice League anymore. Sure, he was in the reserves, but with the power in the core membership, the League rarely needed him. All of which meant that when the League *did* call upon Firestorm, the situation was dire. Batman himself had contacted Firestorm, not only for his vast atomic power, but to ask him to coordinate a group of heroes who had volunteered in this crisis. They had all been teleported to Hong Kong, so far from home, and thrown into combat as allies.

Now the sky above Hong Kong looked as though it was on fire. Ronnie rocketed through the air at such speed that he left lingering trails of flame in his passing. Far below he saw Geo-Force launch a brutal assault on one of the burrowers, lava blasts burning from his hands. Black Lightning attacked the other, doing his best to at least keep the creature from burrowing through any other buildings. The winged Black Condor and the metal man named Cliff Steele—formerly of the legendary Doom Patrol—lent their help where they could, but really didn't have the power for this sort of work.

As he gazed down at the burrowers below him and the heroes set against them, a terrible dread crept into Firestorm's gut. He scorched the air around him as he plummeted toward them. As he reached the first one, Firestorm let loose with a torrent of atomic energy. It staggered the beast, stunned it into momentary paralysis, but this was not the first time he had accomplished this and it had not done them any good. His power could transmute inorganic matter, but though the creatures' armor plating looked like brick, it was not.

"This isn't working," Firestorm whispered, not even remembering that his Justice League commlink was active.

The voice of the Martian Manhunter in his ear, and in his mind, was soothing. "Do your best, Firestorm. We are working on a more permanent solution."

My best, Firestorm thought. *What if my best isn't good enough?*

In the center of Montreal, amongst hotels and restaurants, only a stone's throw from the Old Town, which held all of the city's history, the Red Tornado fought to keep his charges alive. A group of teenaged heroes—most of them associated with members of the Justice League—had banded together to form a sort of club, a junior league, of their own. The League had asked the android Red Tornado—a former member himself—to become a mentor of sorts to the young heroes.

Now he worked side by side with them, trying to defeat the impossibly huge stone-skinned serpent that had tunneled up beneath the city. Montreal's Old Town, prime tourist destination and home to some of the most elegant structures in the city, was only a few blocks away.

Red Tornado manufactured hurricane force winds to drive the monstrosity back. Robin—sometime partner to Batman and the latest to bear the name—shouted instructions to the others over the thin black headsets they wore. Red Tornado had that in one ear and the chatter of the Justice League commlink in the other, and he could not afford to shut out either one.

Superboy and Wonder Girl hammered at the creature time and again, him hitting high and her coming in low. The young speedster Impulse and Empress worked evac, keeping civilians out of danger. Now, even as Red Tornado churned the air to keep the monster rooted to that spot—keep it from escaping Wonder Girl and Superboy's attacks—the one they called Secret moved in on the burrower. Her body was ghostly, little more than mist, and when the burrower gnashed its jaws and snapped at the air, she slipped inside it. This had been Robin's plan, a desperate ploy in hopes that Secret could find a vulnerability in the creature or somehow damage it from the inside.

Red Tornado poured it on, pinning the beast to the pavement, unmindful of the half-destroyed cars that his winds shoved out of the way. The teen heroes kept at the creature, but moments later when Secret drifted, shivering, out through the monster's mouth again, he could only stare at it.

"Whatever you're doing, J'onn," the Tornado told the Martian Manhunter over the commlink, "make it fast."

Glasgow was simply a mess.

An hour had passed since the appearance of the first burrower there. Another had appeared at roughly the same time in Edinburgh, perhaps forty minutes away, but it had dug itself into the earth again moments later and disappeared. It seemed likely that the Edinburgh creature was among the three that had rampaged through downtown Glasgow.

Museums lay in ruins.

The history department at Glasgow University had been obliterated.

An entire shopping district had been gutted.

Now, at last, outside the city, Booster Gold flew down to land beside Blue Beetle on a gently sloping hill. Booster was bleeding badly from a gash on his arm—a spine on the burrower's tail had cut right through his armor—and he found he could not breathe properly. He wondered if the tightness and pain in his chest and side had anything to do with the monster swatting him into a building with its tail. *Probably broke some ribs*, he thought. *Not the first time, probably not the last.*

He was nowhere near as casual about the prospect of broken ribs as this, but Booster always wanted to sound confident, even to himself.

The Beetle was bent over with his hands on his knees, breathing too fast and clearing his throat in a way that made Booster think he was going to throw up. Blue Beetle's costume was torn in several places and dirty from digging through rubble to rescue people from collapsed buildings. They had worked together, reluctantly taking orders from this green-skinned babe, Jade. Booster was a bit ticked that the League would have her coordinate the volunteers up here when she had never even been in the League. Sure she was powerful—all that green mystic energy—but Booster figured it had more to do with her being Green Lantern's girlfriend than anything else.

Beetle agreed. But then, Booster and the Blue Beetle agreed about a lot of things these days. They had served on the Justice League together, briefly, and now both of them were ignored by the current membership. Sure, they had made a lot of mistakes. Booster knew that. But their hearts had always been in the right place. Beetle usually had a great sense of humor, but not today.

"You look like hell, Ted," Booster told him.

The Blue Beetle looked up at him and grimaced,

still sucking in a breath. He nodded slowly. "I'm sure. You don't look so hot yourself. The good news is, we're in the clear for now. At least we got the freakin' monsters out of Glasgow. So they stomp a few sheep, maybe some cows. Fire up the grill, I say."

Booster's stomach did a nauseous little flip. "Umm, Beetle buddy, I think maybe you need to clean your goggles. We're not out of the woods yet."

Ted Kord, the Blue Beetle, tugged the yellow goggles and blue mask back over his head, revealing boyish good looks and eyes that were completely devoid of humor at the moment. "What are you telling me, Booster?"

With a deep breath, Booster pointed up the hill. "Have a look for yourself."

The Beetle glanced in that direction as Booster stood beside him, catching his breath. The burrowers were under attack, a savage melee that tore up the countryside even as it had the city. In addition to Jade, the things were being pummeled by the combined powers of Fire, the Ray, and Guy Gardner. Animal Man was up there somewhere as well, but Booster wasn't sure exactly what that guy thought he could accomplish.

The assault was slowing the burrowers down, but not stopping them. And beyond them, at the crest of the hill, was the most stunning castle Booster had ever seen. It was a rich earth color, as though it had been sculpted from copper and clay, and though it was clearly many centuries old, the circular keep that towered above the rest of the structure was intact.

"Bothwell Castle," the Beetle said.

"Is that its name?"

"Yeah. The largest and finest thirteenth-century castle in Scotland. Survived dozens of sieges in the wars with England in the early fourteenth century."

Booster frowned. "What are you, historical nut all of a sudden?"

The Blue Beetle shook his head. "We had a corporate outing here last year."

Beetle ran his own tech firm, Kord Industries, and did the adventurer thing on the side. They were best friends, but Booster had never understood that; Ted enjoyed it all too much, both the adventuring and the celebrity.

There was a momentary pause in their conversation, during which the roar of energy blasts and thundering rock serpents echoed out across the hill and down to the Clyde River not far away.

"Guess we should try to keep them from destroying it," Booster noted.

Ted pulled his mask and goggles back on. "Probably a good idea."

At Earl's Court in London there was a gaping hole in the middle of the road, an open wound in the street that still rained debris down into the tube station below, and deeper into the tunnel that had been bored through the bedrock of the British capital.

Yet that was the least of Batman's concerns.

It might not be the League's fault that all of this was happening, but it was most certainly their responsibility. Batman understood that the founding members of the League had been adventurers, not investigators. He could understand the way in which things had unfolded ten years past, the destruction of the alien invaders. The League had been a haphazard collection of heroes who had stepped in to prevent death and destruction. But it infuriated him to know that after they had stopped the invaders, they had not pursued a serious analysis of the remains or made any further investigation of the origins of the creatures.

That lapse in judgment, in follow-through, led directly to their current predicament.

Batman had not been a member of the League at that time, of course, but he still felt the weight of responsibility keenly. Even now, though, he was not at all certain that the League was pursuing the most efficient solution. The burrowers were not human. They were, if anything, the parasites that had grown inside their human hosts. Those hosts were already dead. Despite that scientific fact, many of the heroes scattered about the world in combat with the monsters at that very moment were unwilling to take drastic measures, take the steps necessary to kill the things.

Yes, they were adapting to defend themselves against the powers of the heroes who attacked them. Yes, the League and their allies were in most cases keeping the burrowers contained, limiting the damage they would otherwise have done. But Batman was not certain that using DNA to regrow Exterminators and setting them loose on Earth was the best course of action. It certainly was not the only course of action.

But he could not kill all of the burrowers himself

and there was no time to waste attempting to sway dozens of metas and other heroes to his position. There was time only to act, and hope that if things spun out of control again, the League could handle it.

Blue Beetle and Booster Gold had been almost completely ineffectual in Scotland. Fortunately, the teams Batman had assigned to burrower incursion areas in England and Wales had been more successful. Aquaman and Wonder Woman were at the Isle of Wight. Green Lantern, Captain Atom, and Green Arrow were in Manchester, where a refurbished street filled with shops and restaurants had been nearly demolished. Flash, Steel, and Black Canary were dealing with a burrower who had erupted from the earth amidst a farming village in the foothills of the Cambrian Mountains.

Which just left London.

The burrower presently plowing through an abandoned hotel at Earl's Court was one of four in the city. Two of them were at Kensington Gardens, churning up the ground as though they were building a nest of some sort. A third had destroyed Blackfriars Bridge and was currently burrowing along just under the pavement of a road in Southwark. The fourth, the one with its snapping jaws thrashing through the lobby of the Regency Hotel . . .

"I'll handle it," Batman rasped, eyes narrowed as he stared at Superman, who hovered a foot or so off the roof of the shop upon which Batman was crouched.

Superman shook his head in exasperation. In the

dark, the red and blue of his costume were shadowed so that they had become blood-scarlet and indigo.

"What are you doing? You've left just the two of us here and sent how many to the mountains in Wales?"

Batman shifted closer to the edge of the shop roof, then turned to shoot Superman a hard look. "You're prioritizing London. I don't think the Welsh farmers would appreciate that. And there are more than just the two of us here. Connor Hawke is in Southwark right now. And so is Blue Devil."

Superman stared at him, but Batman ignored his incredulity.

"Connor's a bright kid. They'll find a way to secure the area for a while. Meanwhile, the situation in Kensington Gardens is going to get out of hand unless you—"

"But what about—" Superman began, pointing at the burrower down in Earl's Court. Its armor plating was scraping the pavement with a horrible rasping noise.

"I've got it."

The Kryptonian's brows knit. "I don't think—"

"I've got it, *Clark*."

Batman stood on the edge of the roof. Thus far no one inside the hotel had been injured. When the burrower had first broken up through the pavement at Earl's Court the lobby had been evacuated. There would still be guests on the upper floors, but the burrower's obsession with the lobby had bought him a handful of seconds to deal with Superman's doubt. But now the burrower was pulling its head from the hotel's façade, coiling its massive, serpentine body, brick-red armor plating dully reflecting the lights of the buildings around it.

"Time's up," Batman said. "I can't force you to go deal with the burrowers in Kensington Gardens."

With that, he dove forward off the roof of the shop. A mid-air somersault gave him added momentum, carrying him out over the street. Batman landed in a crouch on the roof of an abandoned taxi. The driver's side window shattered with the impact.

He did not look back. Did not bother to even wonder what Superman would do now. Batman was certain he would already be on his way across the city to Kensington Gardens. In their history together, he and Clark had not always gotten along, but they had built up a grudging respect and trust. It was natural for Clark to wonder how Batman—who had no metahuman abilities—planned to take on a burrower by himself. But forced to decide between trusting Batman's judgment or taking the time to confront him, Superman erred on the side of trust.

Just as Batman had known he would.

Superman doubted his ability to combat a burrower alone because his approach to this crisis was so very different from Batman's. All of them had their minds clouded by the history, by the mistake the original League had made. None of them were certain that killing the burrowers was the proper course of action. Batman had no such hesitation. Rather, he had a clarity of purpose that gave him momentum. If the things could not be removed from earth simply and easily without violence, then destruction was the only option. They were parasites. Monsters. It was possible they could infect others.

Clarity of purpose.

The burrowers were very difficult to stop, even harder to kill. The others would rely upon the promised exterminators. But Batman had allotted the League's forces as best he could and now had a shortage of manpower. He was not going to able to stop this burrower, even slow it down, without killing it.

A police siren warbled nearby and he heard tires squeal. People who should have had the sense to evacuate their buildings stood silhouetted in windows. Others were scattered in both directions on Earl's Court. They should have been fleeing in terror and instead they stood around watching as if it were some kind of Las Vegas floor show. Idiots. Batman was just glad there were no television cameras. At least not yet.

The wailing of police sirens caught the burrower's attentions. The entire upper trunk of its serpentine body twisted round, rising up and turning to stared at the source of the sound. Batman was not about to allow it to pursue the police car. In a single swift motion he reached inside his cape and snatched a smooth, circular object from his belt. With his thumb he clicked a button on the sphere, cocked his arm back, and hurled it skyward.

The concussion grenade exploded mere inches from the right side of the burrower's head. With a roar the monster snapped around, swaying on its lower body, and the head rose further, jaws dipping downward to point directly at Batman. Its amber eyes found him and its teeth clacked together like stones grinding against one another.

On the off chance that heat or light would attract it, he popped the top off a flare and dropped it to the pavement at his feet. With his left hand he snapped another concussion grenade off his belt—this one containing forty-seven times the explosive power of the first one.

The burrower roared low in its throat, the sound like tires on gravel but at earsplitting volume. Its jaws opened wide, baring rows of needle fangs each the length and width of a human femur. Batman did not wait for it to descend, to try to snap him up in those jaws. He raised his grapple-gun in his right hand and fired the retractable grappling hook into the monstrosity's mouth. It was more than thirty feet above him, but the grapple-gun had enough velocity that it went into the thing's open maw and punctured the interior flesh of its throat. Claws popped open on the grapple. Batman tugged the line and the burrower reared up, stunned by the sharp pain. With its armor plating, he suspected the monster wasn't used to pain at all. Not of any kind.

It whipped its head back, tugging him off his feet. Batman retracted the hook, which served to pull him upward at such speed that the wind whistled past his face. It felt the weight of him, glanced down again and saw him speeding upward, hanging by a line that dangled from its own mouth.

Enraged, the burrower opened its maw again just

as the Batman had nearly reached the top of the grapple-rope. He felt the warm air that rushed from its mouth, smelled the fetid stench that wafted from its gullet.

He threw the concussion grenade. Let go of the grapple-gun. His boots were planted firmly on the bottom jaw of the behemoth and now he sprang away from it in a backflip. His hand went to his waist where he grabbed at a second grapple-gun. Upside down, he fired it into the stone face of the damaged hotel where it scraped and held. Then he was swinging down and away from the monster, and the burrower was snarling and darting its head after him, jaws snapping as it pursued him.

It was too fast. Its jaws opened for what would be the final time. A heartbeat from now, they would snap closed on Batman himself, breaking bones and tearing flesh.

Then the burrower's head exploded.

Batman swung clear, dropped to the street, then slipped into an alley from which he could check up on the progress the rest of the League was making.

Which was how he discovered that the Exterminators were on the way.

CHAPTER FOURTEEN

The Atom felt nauseous. *Too much damn teleportation*, he thought. His stomach was churning and it certainly hadn't been anything he had eaten, because he hadn't had anything at all for hours except a bottle of spring water. He hadn't had a moment to spare.

"It's amazing," said a hushed voice.

He forced a smile to mask his discomfort and turned toward Janice Feldman, a fit, fiftyish woman who wore thin spectacles and had white hair. As Associate Director of S.T.A.R. Labs, the Atom suspected that Dr. Feldman had not let her hair go white as any kind of statement about aging or appearance, but because she simply did not have time to keep up with it. He understood.

"You work here every day, Janice. The kinds of things you've seen and done in this building . . ." the Atom said, raising an eyebrow. "I'm surprised you can be amazed by anything."

She shrugged. "Actually, I'm constantly amazed."

Together they turned to look up through the safety glass into the Crisis Chamber. When S.T.A.R. had designed this building they had created this enormous room as a kind of catch-all, incorporating security, safety and analysis functions into its design. Injured metahumans whose powers might be dangerous had been treated there, unknown phenomenon and bizarre artifacts had been analyzed there, superhuman and alien criminals had been temporarily incarcerated there. But this was the first time the Crisis Chamber had ever been used as a factory.

The Atom stared upward, his nausea subsiding. He wondered if perhaps it wasn't the teleportation at all, but stress that was causing it.

"You were able to stabilize the degenerative trend?" he asked.

He did not have to look at Janice to feel the woman's irritated gaze burning into the side of his head.

"Professor Palmer, please just trust that my people know their jobs," the Associate Director said tersely. "I told you we could stop the degeneration. I wouldn't have given the go ahead to begin cloning if we hadn't isolated the problem."

Ray finally glanced at her. "Sorry. Just anxious, I suppose. There's a lot riding on this." He was about to look back into the Crisis Chamber but he hesitated. "So, with degeneration stabilized . . . how quickly does it begin?"

The woman bit her lip and tried to glare at him, but

ended up laughing softly instead. "Twenty-seven hours, Ray. Each one of the things has a shelf life of about twenty-seven hours. Which is a hell of a lot less than it would have without S.T.A.R.'s gene-engineering."

The Atom nodded. "Point taken."

He turned and gazed into the Crisis Chamber once more. A shudder went through him, not merely from the chill of the building's air conditioning, but partially from revulsion as well. The observation ring around the Crisis Chamber was poorly lit, but inside the chamber itself a warm golden glow suffused the vast, circular room. Inside the Chamber was the severed alien head that Superman had brought back with him from London.

It was growing.

The Exterminator had three eyes set into a face that most resembled the shell of an armadillo, only on a far greater scale. The scales that plated its face—and the new bits of shoulder and neck that had grown out—were not exactly the same as those of the burrowers. They had the same reddish-brown coloring, but the plates of the Exterminator's armor were smaller and seemed more layered, like shingles on a roof. Horns like the gnarled branches of an ancient tree grew out from the sides of its head and curved forward, sharp points twisted round so that they jutted dangerously.

But the Atom had spent far too long looking at the head, before and after it had been thawed. They had determined that it was going to take the Exterminator more than three days to grow a complete body back. As such, it was useless to them.

So his eyes strayed higher. Ten feet. Thirty. Forty feet up, inside the Crisis Chamber, to the horns of the alien Exterminator who stood now, just coming awake, inside the chamber. The gas inside the room was enough to keep it calm as its trio of amber eyes fluttered open. Still, its massive chest began to heave beneath its armor plating, and all four of its three-fingered hands began to close into fists. The Atom stared at the thing's horns. They were the only things that weren't identical to the source creature. Each of the clones had grown horns whose contours and curves were different from the others. Individual.

"Ray?" Janice prodded. "Don't you think we ought to—"

"Huh? Oh, right." He shook his head. The monster was remarkable. No matter how many aliens he had met in his life, each new one was fascinating to him.

He tapped the commlink at his left ear. "Atom to Manhunter."

The answer from J'onn J'onzz came not through the commlink, but in the Atom's mind. *I'm here, Ray. Are you ready to send another?*

"Begin teleport now," the Atom replied. "Next Exterminator should be ready in . . ." He glanced at Janice.

"Four and a half minutes," she said. "It's getting faster every time. We were able to shorten the gestation period in the lab and speed the whole process. But now it's as if the Exterminator cells themselves are helping, as if now that we've jump-started them, they're increasing the speed of gestation on their own."

Excellent, the Martian Manhunter said, the thought slipping right into the Atom's mind. *This just might work.*

Ray Palmer stared into the Crisis Chamber as the massive, hulking, four-armed alien monster began to stir and stretch and glance around. There was something about its expression, a kind of dark concentration, that unnerved him.

"It just might," he said.

The Crisis Chamber was illuminated with the glow of energy that accompanied teleportation. For a moment bright light flooded the Chamber, and when it faded, the Exterminator was gone.

The Atom breathed a sigh of relief.

And then they began the process all over again.

On the southwestern edge of the Isle of Wight, off the coast of England, the ocean crashed against steep cliffs and the cold sea spray spattered the air. In spring it was still chilly, and so the area was deserted. For that, Wonder Woman thanked the gods. The burrower had tunneled up through the earth, bursting from the ground not far from the edge of a cliff, with such force that a portion of the ledge had fallen away like an iceberg calving. Soil and stone and the ancient bones of a brachiosaur had rained down upon the coastline.

For a time the burrower had dug trenches and tunnels up and down a half-mile stretch of land atop those cliffs. Wonder Woman and Aquaman had arrived just as it had begun to rumble across the island toward the more populated areas. Princess Diana was very pleased they arrived in time. It would have been much more difficult to deal with the creature in the midst of such a popular vacation spot.

But there on the grassy coast above the ocean cliffs, there was nothing to hold her back.

Wonder Woman soared across the night sky, the cold air embracing her, whipping past her as she dove toward the burrower. It had no eyes that she could see and its face was studded with sharp spines, but still it snapped around toward her as she rode the wind. Wonder Woman darted downward and the burrower's head lowered, following her, its jaws opening, teeth gleaming.

But she was Diana, princess of Themyscira, and she was faster than any such monstrosity. She reversed direction, willing herself through the air so swiftly that she rose above its head before it had time to react. Wonder Woman flew over the burrower's spines and then dropped down behind them. She brought both fists down as she landed on the back of its skull. A war cry tore from her lips and her entire body reverberated with the blow.

The burrower shuddered and its upper body began to collapse, dropping toward the ground. The earth shook with the impact. But Diana was not about to celebrate her attack—this was the sixth time she had knocked the beast down, and each time it recovered far too quickly. Even now it began to slither across the ground, the armor plating on its belly tearing up the grass.

Aquaman rode the burrower's back. Even as Wonder Woman took to the sky again to gain perspective on the creature's movements, she saw Arthur there, his good hand holding onto the monster's armor plating while the cybernetic one—now in the form of the harpoon he sometimes used in battle—tried to pry up one of those red scales.

The burrower stopped its forward motion. It began to bunch its body, coiling its tail. As the creature tensed, Wonder Woman realized what was about to happen. She was about to shout a warning, but was too late. The burrower coiled further, thrusting the center of its body upward, bucking Aquaman off its back. Arthur tumbled through the air end over end.

Diana would have caught him, but in an instant she noticed two things. Aquaman was going over the edge of the cliff. He would tumble down into the ocean, his home, his element, and would surely return to the fray quickly. But the burrower was already moving off, much more quickly than it had moved before. It was heading inland, toward more populated areas. She could not let it get there.

Once again, Wonder Woman swept down out of the sky to attack.

She never reached the burrower.

The air began to hum. The ground to quake. A cascade of bright light illuminated the southwestern coast of the Isle of Wight. Wonder Woman knew what it was immediately—someone was teleporting in. But it was the biggest teleport effect she had ever seen.

And then she saw why.

Wonder Woman had lived a life filled with gods and monsters, yet even she was impressed by the size of the Exterminator. Still, simply because it *looked* formidable . . .

Any doubt was erased as the massive, four-armed, ram-horned alien tromped across the island, shaking the earth, and reached down to grab hold of the spikes that jutted from the burrower's face. The burrower roared and its serpentine tail whipped around to encircle the exterminator, tightening snakelike around the new arrival.

The Exterminator snapped one of the spines off of the burrower's head, held its snapping jaws away, and then impaled it with its own sharp appendage, shattering that armor plating with a crack like shattering glass.

Booster Gold lay sprawled on the hillside below Bothwell castle, more than a little dazed. He could taste the copper tang of his own blood on his split lip and every time he took a breath, his cracked ribs sent jolts of pain through his body. He could not move his right arm without searing, stabbing agony, so he tried to pretend he didn't have one. The last thing he wanted to do was speculate how many places the arm was broken.

The ground shook beneath him. The cold wind carried on it a kind of static smell, like there was an electrical fire nearby. He heard the shouts of his comrades and the roar of the burrower, heard the sizzling sound of the Ray's energy blasts as they scorched the air.

Then something else. The ground shook hard enough for his broken arm to spike pain into his brain again. The air lit up for just a moment as though the sun had risen and fallen in a heartbeat.

Nearby, he heard the Blue Beetle swear loudly.

With a grunt of pain, air hissing through his blood-stained teeth, Booster tried to turn his head toward the castle, tried to get a look at what had caused Beetle to curse. He couldn't manage it. But he didn't have to. A moment later the Blue Beetle came around him, wounded and bleeding, costume torn and filthy.

But there was a big smile on his face.

"What?" Booster demanded. "What is it?"

"The cavalry," Beetle replied. "The biggest, ugliest, scariest cavalry you ever saw. When J'onn said they were sending an Exterminator, I was thinking pest control."

Booster grimaced. Beetle obviously hadn't been paying much attention to the ongoing conversations on the Justice League commlink.

The ground trembled. There were monstrous screams.

"What's it doing?"

Beetle grinned. "Kicking burrower butt. Moving it away from the castle."

With a sigh, Booster tried to sit up. It hurt like hell but he held his broken arm against his abdomen and sat on the hill, staring up at the Blue Beetle.

"Great. Now let's go home. I don't want to be here when someone asks how come we didn't stop the thing before it trashed half of Glasgow. I need pizza, beer, and the Spice Channel. Oh, and possibly some immediate medical attention."

Sitting up had been too much for him. The pain from his broken arm and cracked ribs was too much.

Booster fainted.

In the Monitor Womb, the Martian Manhunter took a deep breath and relaxed back into the chair, feeling it wrap its conforming embrace more tightly around him. The kaleidoscope of colored lights from the dozens of viewscreens danced across the walls and for a long moment he pressed his eyes closed tight against them. He took another deep breath, and he watched with cautious optimism as the satellite feeds showed Exterminators arriving at the last of the crisis points. Thus far it was going well. The burrowers in Montreal and Hong Kong were both being severely thrashed by the Exterminators. In Santa Monica, it was already over. The city was clear of burrowers and the Exterminator was wading into the Pacific Ocean.

"J'onn, this is Nightwing."

The Manhunter raised an eyebrow. No matter how often he had contact with the leader of the Titans, he was always fascinated by the young man. There were ways in which he was so very like Batman, who was his mentor and in a way his surrogate father as well. As Nightwing, Dick Grayson had a commanding presence and a dark determination of purpose that reminded J'onn of Batman. And yet when the battle was over, Nightwing was open and warm in a way that was so completely unlike Batman. It was the younger hero's saving grace, really. Batman was the most formidable non-meta human being J'onn had ever come into contact with, and yet there was the inescapable air of tragedy around him.

"I'm here, Nightwing."

"Do you see this? Where's it going? Should we try to track it?"

The Manhunter watched the satellite feed from Santa Monica. On screen he could see the ruins of the pier and members of the Titans standing at the edge of the water. Tempest was chest deep in the ocean and he kept glancing back to shore, waiting for Nightwing's instructions. Meanwhile, the Exterminator was further out, its horns just disappearing below the waves.

The alien clone would rapidly deteriorate in just over twenty-four hours, at which point it would cease to be a concern. For the moment, however . . .

"Yes. Please ask Tempest to follow it and report back. I expect it may be heading toward the nearest extant burrower, but once they're all destroyed, we believe it will fall dormant until deterioration sets in."

"But just in case—" Nightwing said, his voice dark and resonant over the commlink.

"Yes. Just in case."

That done, he turned his attention to a trio of monitors showing visuals that did not come from a satellite. It was a view of the inside of Grand Central

Station in New York, provided by cameras in several of Mister Terrific's T-spheres. The Justice Society were still in combat with burrowers inside the station. The first Exterminator to be teleported to the site had been outnumbered by the burrowers there.

It had been killed.

J'onn had been anxious about this. The burrowers were capable of killing the beings who had come to Earth specifically to destroy them. That did not bode well. Now, even as J'onn watched, a second Exterminator was teleported into Grand Central. For a moment he tensed, but then the forty-five-foot monstrosity grabbed the nearest burrower and tore its head off and J'onn glanced away from the screen, simultaneously relieved and disgusted.

Awful as it was, the plan was working. It was, in its way, little different from owls hunting field mice or spiders trapping flies. From what he and Ray Palmer had been able to determine, the Exterminators were the natural predators of the alien parasites that had evolved into burrowers. But that did not mean it was pleasant to watch.

It's working, he thought.

J'onn sent that message out telepathically to the entire psi-web he was using to connect the members of the League and the reserves. In the morass of thoughts he constantly sifted through, the words and ideas and intuitions, he felt the relief that swept through them.

All of them but one.

Batman? J'onn thought.

It isn't over yet, came the reply, which resonated through the psi-web to all of the others. *Save the celebration until both the problem and the solution have been dealt with.*

Superman felt nauseous, conflicting emotions roiling within him. He hovered in the darkness above Kensington Gardens, the starlit ebony sky reflecting back the chill of the night. But the cold wind brought the stench of death and an acrid stink that could only have been the alien blood of the burrowers. The Exterminator had done its work. Superman had continued to fight and only pulled back when the cloned destroyer had killed the first of its prey and moved on to the second.

Relocation. That was the thought foremost in his head. That would have been better. The human hosts that had fostered these massive parasites were dead, but the burrowers themselves were still living creatures. Destructive, possibly even malevolent, yes. But he wished the League could have spent more time considering relocation for them. Superman himself could think of several planets within the same space quadrant as Earth that could have supported the creatures.

But that would have taken time. More people would have died. More damage would have been done. The Justice League had been forced to go with the most expedient plan instead of the most merciful in order to protect the Earth and its people. He understood that there hadn't really been a choice. Yet hovering there above the Exterminator as it tore the head off the second burrower—as though to make absolutely certain it was dead—he could not help but feel regret.

A sadness came over him. The League was going to win this one. But as happened all too often in a real crisis, there would be no true victory, no triumph. Even *win* was a poor word choice. Together, the League and its allies were in the process of averting greater catastrophe. The tragedy was, that was the best they could hope for.

Superman turned away from the carnage below him and began to fly from Kensington Gardens, cape whipping against his back in the wind.

You'll continue to monitor the Exterminators? he thought.

Of course, Kal, came the Martian Manhunter's telepathic reply. *Those who have already dispatched their targets seem to be heading for the nearest surviving burrower. Though there are a few—*

The pause in J'onn's stream of thought troubled Superman. High above the trees he stopped, floating in the air.

A few what?

Well, the Exterminator you've just left behind, for instance.

Superman turned and narrowed his eyes. The alien clone had turned away from the dead burrowers and set off across Kensington Gardens. Even as he watched, trees cracked and toppled. It was frustrating. He was going to have to stay with this creature to make certain that it did not cause any further damage between now and the time it naturally degraded and died. Nearly an entire day.

What about it? Superman asked as he flew back toward the monstrosity.

It's headed due west. But the nearest living burrower is to the south. I have no idea where it's going, or why.

Kyle Rayner had never been to Manchester, England, before, but from the look of the place it was a charming, cosmopolitan city with a lot more going for it than the ferocious loyalty its people gave its soccer team. He had regretted almost instantly upon arrival that his first visit to the place had been as Green Lantern.

At the moment, however, he had more serious regrets. Despite their best efforts, he, Captain Atom, and Green Arrow had been unable to prevent the burrower from doing serious property damage in Manchester. Kyle didn't want to think about the age of the structures that had been demolished, nor about the cost of replacing them. The center of Manchester was a warren of curving streets with boutiques and restaurants, almost a labyrinth of shopping. On the street below him, where half a block lay in ruins, Captain Atom and Green Arrow were helping sift the rubble for those who might be trapped beneath it.

The only bright side, if there was one, was that it was the middle of the night and the shops were empty.

Green Lantern held himself aloft in a sizzling sheath of energy from his power ring. By the sheer force of his will, the mechanism that controlled his ring, he aided with the cleanup, clearing as much of the debris from the street as he could so that emergency vehicles could pass. All the while, however, half his focus remained on the strange monolithic figure of the Exterminator that had been teleported to Manchester. Kyle had already moved the remains of the dead burrower, and now the Exterminator seemed confused. It stood in the middle of a public street, the area cordoned off by police, and it kept turning in fits and starts, facing east then north, west then south. All he could think of, watching its clockwork turns, was radar.

"But what's it looking for?" he wondered aloud, knowing the question would be carried over the commlink to all JLA members and reserves. Kyle had been listening to comments and conversation from Superman, Batman, and the Martian Manhunter. He wanted to know what the Exterminators were going to do for the next twenty-four hours or so.

"J'onn, what's the plan? I know there's no room for all of them at S.T.A.R. Labs, but why not teleport them to the moon, or the Sahara or something until entropy sets in?"

The commlink crackled as dozens of heroes awaited the Martian Manhunter's response. A chill raced through Kyle.

"J'onn?" Superman prodded. "Kyle's got a point. The Exterminator you 'ported to Kensington Gardens is out of control. We've got to get it out of here."

The commlink rasped with static. Green Lantern

focused on the neural net, trying to get a feeling for what was going on with J'onn.

There is a problem, my friends, came the Manhunter's telepathic voice.

They can't be teleported back, can they? Batman thought. *You could teleport them here, but now the system can't get a fix on them. They've adapted . . . something in their genetic structure is jamming the teleporter.*

That is correct, J'onn replied. *How could you have known that?*

I didn't know. I wondered. They're adapting, like the burrowers did.

Almost simultaneous with this thought, the Exterminator towering above the buildings in downtown Manchester stopped turning. Its massive, stone-plated head rotated to look past the spot where Kyle hovered in the air. On the street, ambulances and trucks carrying emergency response personnel were rolling in toward the demolished area, coming to the aid of the Justice Leaguers who were already trying to clear the debris. The Exterminator had ceased its searching. All of its attention now was on the rescue workers. Green Lantern did not like the look of that at all.

This doesn't bode well, he thought.

"What doesn't, Kyle?" Superman asked, having picked up Green Lantern's thought on the neural net.

"Hang on," Kyle replied.

He left Captain Atom and Green Arrow to their work with the rescue crews and flew toward the Exterminator. Whatever was going on with the alien, it would be best if he could get it out of the city. Kyle raised his fist and emerald energy spilled from the ring. With that power, driven by his mind, he reached out to grab hold of the Exterminator.

But he could not.

The ring's power slid right off the monstrous clone. Green Lantern frowned, alarm bells going off in his mind. Again he wrapped the Exterminator in bonds of verdant power, and again when he tried to lift the monster, his power was useless.

"Guys," he said slowly. "I've got a really bad feeling about this."

"They're going AWOL, J'onn!" Superman shouted over the commlink. "The situation in London is out of control. These things might have been made to destroy the burrower parasites, but they'll kill anyone who gets in the way. We've got to stop them. We put them here and—"

Green Lantern was only half listening. He watched in horror and astonishment as the Exterminator reached for an ambulance, its sirens wailing.

"Captain Atom! Green Arrow! We've got to stop the Exterminator! We have to take it down!"

"On it, Lantern," Captain Atom replied.

"Wish somebody'd make up their mind," Green Arrow added, his angry muttering low but still audible on the commlink.

Green Lantern was in action immediately. Captain Atom began firing energy bursts at the Exterminator as Green Arrow shouted at the driver of the ambulance, forcing the other rescue workers away from the battle. They were all possible targets. Kyle knew he could not hold the Exterminator with his power ring, but he had another idea.

"Kyle!" J'onn called, both on the commlink and on the neural net.

"What's going on there?" Batman demanded, from wherever it was he had ended up. His voice on the commlink sounded so close, as though he were standing right behind Kyle.

Green Lantern used his power to snatch the ambulance from the Exterminator's grasp. It roared, teeth gnashing, burning eyes glaring at him. Then it came for him, ground shaking under its bulk.

"Kyle!" J'onn snapped again.

"It's going after civilians," Green Lantern explained as the Exterminator lumbered down the street. "I don't understand. I thought it would only hunt burrowers and . . . and metamorphs, the people with the parasites."

"This is going south," Batman said. His tone was grave and yet unsurprised, as though he had expected something very like this. "We miscalculated. Now that they're almost done exterminating the burrowers, they're going after humans infected by the parasites . . . people who are infected but haven't begun to evolve yet. It's got to have some way to track them."

"Apparently there were more parasite hosts than we realized," J'onn observed with maddening calm.

Green Lantern soared quickly over Manchester, flying away from the city with the ambulance towed behind him in a sphere of green energy from his power ring. The Exterminator was swift, but not as swift as he was. He could lead it out of town and hopefully at that point Captain Atom and Green Arrow would catch up and be able to deal with the alien.

Kyle had somewhere else to be.

"J'onn, emergency teleport."

"Where are you going, Kyle?"

Before he could respond, the Atom broke in with a distress signal.

"Ray Palmer to Justice League. I'm at S.T.A.R. Labs in Metropolis . . . send the cavalry. We're under attack."

CHAPTER FIFTEEN

Alarm bells wailed, echoing off the walls of the offices and corridors of S.T.A.R. Labs. Emergency systems had kicked in, casting the entire facility in the reddish hue of urgently flashing lights whose illumination demanded the immediate evacuation of S.T.A.R. personnel. Or most of them, at least. Far beneath the ground level lobby that opened onto a busy Metropolis street there were sublevels below sublevels, laboratories and experimental holding cells whose contents could not be abandoned, even though staying by their posts might cost the lives of the technicians and security guards who remained behind.

There were rooms there, deep beneath S.T.A.R., that locked down completely, sealed so tightly that even an earthquake would not crack them open.

Wise of them, the Atom thought as he shouldered his way through the panicked throng attempting to evacuate the structure. The floor beneath his feet trembled. Every few moments the entire building seemed to buck as though attempting to throw its occupants off their feet. Nobody wanted to think about potential catastrophe, but he was very pleased to know that S.T.A.R. *planned* for it.

Of course, they never could have planned for this.

The alarms continued to screech. The public address system crackled with a mechanical voice whose evacuation and lockdown instructions were garbled at best. Not that it had stopped people from heading for the exits. The Atom tried his best not to hurt anyone, but just to avoid being swept along by the flow of the frightened scientists and administrators he had to force his way through the crowd. People swore. For the most part, though, they were wide-eyed with fear and paid him no mind at all, despite the red and blue costume he wore.

That was another thing he was grateful for. The costume. Beneath it he was just Professor Ray Palmer. Teacher. Physicist. The outward packaging reminded people he was more than that, but truth be told, it worked on himself as well. A reminder. He was the Atom. He was a member of the Justice League.

He didn't get to evacuate.

The ground trembled beneath his feet again. Walls and ceilings that had been constructed to withstand disaster began to crack. Plaster rained down from above. The Atom cursed under his breath and tried to see over the heads of the fearful exodus that rushed around him. He considered willing himself to shrink down, but then dismissed the idea. Certainly it might be easier for him to move quickly through the tide of humanity he was working against, but it was also possible he would be trampled.

"Out of the way! Let me through!" he shouted.

Some people focused on him then. He saw their faces shining with the red flickering emergency lights, saw their eyes as their gazes locked with his. A few even tried to get out of the way, but they were being tugged along in the current now, and could not move if they wanted to. Their only possible destination was *out*.

With a thunderous crack, a fissure appeared in the wall to his right. A woman screamed in shock and terror and abruptly, others seemed to notice him. It became easier for him to pass through the evacuees, and then they began to thin out. Down the corridor, over their heads, was a set of steel double doors. On the other side of those doors was the Crisis Chamber. Its name was disturbingly apropos.

The Atom twisted sideways to avoid colliding with a burly security guard who was one of the last of the people in the corridor. The man shot him a doubtful glance, obviously wondering what he was thinking going in the wrong direction, but said nothing. Then they were all gone, retreating behind him, and Ray was alone in the corridor. His whole body was tense as though he were on board a sailboat, waiting for the next wave to throw off his balance. But in this case it wasn't the surf that he had to worry about.

He never made it to the Crisis Chamber.

When he was fifteen feet from the double doors a

massive tremor ripped through S.T.A.R. Laboratories and those doors exploded outward in a devastating eruption of concrete and steel that tore out the walls and the ceiling. In the space between heartbeats, the Atom shrank from six feet to six inches. He heard the rush of wind against his ears as a two-foot square of steel door sliced the air just above him. Other debris rained down, clattering across the floor, and he held his breath as he leaped and rolled to avoid being crushed.

For just a moment, the cataclysm subsided. The Atom glanced up and saw that the end of the corridor had been demolished and the ceiling torn away. He could see torn and bent girders and the ragged edges of the floors above where they had been collapsed. In the midst of it all, moving in the rubble of the destruction it had just wrought, was the Exterminator. The alien clone was single-minded, slowly tearing at the structure around it. The Crisis Chamber had held it for a time, but now it had shattered that room and the glass enclosure and was ripping its way through S.T.A.R. Labs, trying to get to Paul Cargill and Ian Partington, the two men who were still infected with the burrower parasites.

Even at Ray's full height, the monstrosity would have towered above him. At six inches tall, he could barely see its head. With plaster raining down around him, fissures appearing in the wall, and cracks splintering the floor, the Atom ran toward the Exterminator. No matter how much stronger he was than a normal man—even at this height—there was no way he was going to be able to stop this thing alone.

But he had to try.

We've got to put an end to this, J'onn.
The thought echoed through Superman's mind and he knew that the rest of the League would be picking it up on the neural net. That was fine with him. *We've traded one enemy for another. All we've done is react, just the way the original League did ten years ago. We knew it was handled badly then, and yet we haven't done much better. We're scrambling to keep people alive and it's meant we haven't had a chance to formulate any real plan of action. We've got to stop it . . . now!*

Superman felt J'onn's reaction even before the words formed in his own mind. *Easier said than done.* And the Martian Manhunter was right. Even now, Superman was in the midst of a struggle that was devastating Kensington Gardens. He'd thought the burrowers had done damage, but his own combat with the Exterminator was worse. The alien was extraordinarily fast.

It opened its mouth and let out a roar that sounded like an avalanche. Its eyes followed Superman no matter how swiftly he moved. Even now he was little more than a blur of red and blue. With his fists out in front of him he sliced through the pre-dawn sky above the treetops, aiming for the Exterminator's neck, thinking it was possible he might be able to hurt it, to incapacitate it.

The massive alien swung its right hand up and batted Superman away as though he were an insect. As he collided with the impervious brick-red plating of the Exterminator's flesh, Superman grunted in pain and surprise, the wind knocked out of him. He was knocked backward, somersaulting end over end through the air, and he barely felt it as he crashed through the rear wall of a hotel. Rubble fell all around him as he threw out his hands, trying to grab hold of something, to stop himself, worrying all the while about civilians he might collide with. The impact drove him through the outer wall and a guest room, tearing through wood and metal and plaster as though a missile had struck the hotel. When Superman crashed through into the elevator shaft, his momentum had finally slowed enough that he could stop himself. His fingers caught the edge of a girder and though the metal began to tear, he found his grip.

By then he had the beginnings of a plan. It wasn't much—in fact it had enormous holes in it—but it was better than what the League was doing now. They had gathered dozens of metas and advanced humans, some of whom had brilliant minds in addition to powers and skills, and yet in the face of impending catastrophe all they had managed to do was limit the number of casualties and the amount of property damage. They were the Justice League. They ought to have been able to do better, and it frustrated him to know that they had not.

Superman made sure the damage to the elevator shaft was not enough to cause the lift itself to fall, then he slipped through the hole his impact had made and out into the empty guest room he had crashed through. There was an open suitcase on one of the beds and a laptop computer on the desk. He frowned and glanced around to see a man in a white T-shirt and underpants peeking out from the bathroom.

The room wasn't as empty as he had thought.

"Get dressed and get out in the hall. I'm not sure how much structural damage has been done," he instructed the man. "Security will be up here in a moment, I'm sure, but phone down right now and tell them I said not to use the elevator."

The man straightened up, brows knitting with gravity now that he had been assigned this task. "Tell them . . . tell them Superman said . . ." he repeated, as though testing the words out.

"Do it now," Superman told him.

Then he was gone. The Exterminator wasn't going to wait. The world blurred around him as he flew over several buildings and then was above Kensington Gardens again. All he could hear was the whistle of the wind in his ears and his own heart beating in his chest. There was no need to search; the Exterminator was too large to hide, and had no inclination to do so even if it could have. It was headed west but Superman narrowed his eyes and focused. Thin beams of blazing light erupted from his eyes. The attack struck the Exterminator's back and the air sizzled and popped with the energy from those beams. They ought to have sheared the alien in half, but Superman had tried them before and knew what the outcome would be. The Exterminator's armored hide protected it.

But he had gotten its attention.

With another of those avalanche roars, it spun, the trees rustling as its feet pounded the ground, and it started toward him again.

It had taken two steps before another figure slid swiftly across the indigo sky. The Exterminator was fast, its vision unerring, but it had been focused on Superman. Wonder Woman took it by surprise. With her raven black hair flying behind her, she swept through the air and brought an enormous Amazonian battleaxe down across its face.

One of the armor plates on the side of its head cracked.

"J'onn," Superman said aloud, not relying merely on the neural net this time. He wanted to make certain the message was carried on the commlink as well. "We can't stay in this holding pattern forever. But if we work at it, we might be able to spread the League out enough that we can keep them penned in while the others gather up the people who are still carrying the parasite. We can't teleport the Exterminators out, and there are too many of them to take them out into space until the deterioration starts. But if we can control where the parasites are, we can control where the Exterminators will go."

Wonder Woman was engaging the Exterminator one on one, dodging its furious attacks and attempting to land another blow with that devastating axe. Superman darted forward, cape fluttering behind him, and he struck upon that same spot on its head, shattering the already cracked plate of armor. Shards of it fell away, revealing pink, vulnerable flesh beneath. There was the smallest spark of triumph in his heart, but in his mind he knew full well that this was merely one of many.

And the Martian Manhunter had not responded. When a voice did come—both in Superman's ear and in his mind—it was that of the Batman.

"Too imprecise. It won't work."

Superman grimaced. "I'm open to suggestions."

Batman was doing rapid calculations. He had asked Aquaman to keep track of the Exterminators who had gone beneath the ocean surface, though he suspected he knew where they were headed. In a room that had been provided to him days earlier by his M.I.5 contact, Batman stared up at a holographic map of the Earth, a direct linkup with the same map J'onn J'onzz would be looking at even now in the JLA Watchtower.

Some of the Exterminators were still busy doing the job they had been created to do. The alien clones were eliminating the burrowers, destroying them. All along the question had been what to do with the Exterminators after they had served their purpose, which was why S.T.A.R. had built genetic deterioration into their systems. But twenty-seven hours was too long. Four hours would have been sufficient. So many variables had not been taken into account. For instance . . .

"We have no idea how many are still carrying the

burrower parasite," Batman reminded the rest of the League, his voice echoing in that small room, which was dark save for the greenish glow of the holographic world. "We'll need to keep one Exterminator alive as a bloodhound afterward, so that we can track them and administer the serum. But it will be sloppy and destructive if we just let it happen now.

"Some of the Exterminators are still occupied dealing with burrowers. We need to do this quickly. Professor Palmer and S.T.A.R. were working on the serum. Several doses must have been developed by now, but they haven't been administered to Partington or Paul Cargill, or the Exterminator there wouldn't be rampaging."

Batman paused, letting the communication sift through both commlink and neural net. Thanks to J'onn, he *felt* the Atom's mind brush against his own. There was panic there, but there was also understanding.

There's a safe room on sublevel four, the Atom thought in reply. *If I can get down there—*

"You can administer the serum to Cargill and Partington, ending the situation in Metropolis for the moment," came Wonder Woman's voice over the commlink. "But that is a fleeting solution and a localized one."

Batman stared at the hologram of the Earth that spun and flickered in the air in the darkened room. He could smell the cigar smoke of an M.I.5 agent who had used it before him and a bit of mold in the carpet. There were blinking lights all over the holo-globe. Gold for Exterminators. Blue for burrowers. Green for known parasite carriers. Red for locations where other carriers were suspected. Violet for the League and its allies.

Chaos. Certainly, up until now it had been controlled chaos. But it was chaos, nevertheless.

And it was time to bring order to it all.

Batman is not suggesting using the serum on humans, J'onn replied.

"What?" Superman asked, his voice a grunt that was followed over the commlink by the sound of something roaring in a terrible voice and the thud of impact, of a devastating blow, though whether Superman had delivered the blow or received it, Batman could not tell.

One voice cut through the chatter then. It belonged to the Atom. "That makes sense, Batman. There's no empirical evidence to support it, but theoretically it could work. I'll get the serum—"

From somewhere deep in the ocean, Aquaman's mind-voice entered the neural net and interrupted. *What about the Exterminator there, Atom? Should J'onn teleport me to S.T.A.R.? You can't do this alone.*

"Thanks for the offer, Aquaman, but I'm not alone."

In the darkened room, in the emerald glow of the holo-globe, Batman smiled. Of course he wasn't alone. Aquaman had obviously not been paying attention or he would have noticed two members of the Justice League had been uncharacteristically silent throughout this entire exchange.

"This is Batman to all League members and allies,"

he said into the commlink. "Do whatever is necessary to limit the Exterminators' movement. Help is on the way."

In New York City, in the midst of a devastated Grand Central Station, Mister Terrific leaped out of the way of a thunderous blow from the fist of an Exterminator. It shattered marble and granite and he felt several shards of stone strike the protective padding on his back even as he dove over the edge of a balustrade and fell twenty feet to the floor below. He landed hard and fell into a roll to take the brunt of the impact.

When he stood up again, brushing off his jacket, he glanced up to see Captain Marvel hovering just beside him, making certain he was all right.

Which was when he heard Batman's words in his earpiece. Mister Terrific shook his head and glanced up at Marvel. "Whatever is necessary," he muttered. "Easy for him to say."

A war cry tore from Wonder Woman's lungs, echoing across the ruined Kensington Gardens. She brought the golden battleaxe down and felt it crack another plate of armor on the Exterminator's brick-red hide. Its massive fist raked the air, attempting to bat her away, but now that it was injured, the Exterminator had slowed some and she danced out of its range.

Superman glided up to fly at her side in perfect tandem as they kept a distance from the alien.

"What do you think they have in mind?" he asked.

"I think you know," she replied.

His jaw was set in a grim expression and he nodded slowly. "We created them just to kill them."

"They would die in less than a day if we left them alone. But the death and destruction in the meantime would be—"

"I know," Superman replied. "There's just something obscene about it."

The Exterminator lunged at them and Wonder Woman dodged, flying off to her left even as Superman went the opposite direction. They reconvened a moment later and thirty feet higher, needing to keep out of the thing's reach but not get so far away that it lost interest in them. Not that she thought that was going to happen now that they had hurt it. It had identified them as a threat and it would not depart until it had eliminated them.

"I will not say I am without regret, but we've done what has been necessary. There's no shame in that. No shame in protecting the world we've vowed to defend, in saving the lives of its people. This may not be one of the League's most glorious moments, Kal, but we were never in it for the glory."

The Exterminator was glaring up at them. Wonder Woman saw the gap on the side of its head where the plating had been shattered. If she could strike at that with the axe, she could wound it further. On the other hand, if Batman and the Atom were correct, that would be unnecessary. If she and Superman could hold it off for a few more minutes, that would be enough.

"You're right, Diana," Superman said. When she looked at him, she saw regret engraved upon his features. "But I cannot wait until this is over."

In Scotland, Captain Atom felt as though he had been fighting forever. Exhaustion was beginning to drag at him. He raised his hands and felt the power erupting from him, staggering the Exterminator that was slowly advancing toward Glasgow. The city had endured enough this night, though, and he would not let the monstrosity pass.

Whatever the League's planning, they'd better do it fast.

In Hong Kong, Firestorm burned streaks of flame across the sky, frustrated at his inability to do more. *J'onn*, he thought, knowing the Martian Manhunter would hear him on the neural net, *isn't there something—*

Be patient, came the instantaneous reply. *You'll be needed momentarily.*

The Flash stood completely still in front of the cryo-tank that held Ian Partington. His friend's face was frozen in a grimace of fear, the expression completely foreign to his own memories of amiable, confident Ian. It was a face he knew he would see in unsettling dreams. They were on the west side of the S.T.A.R. Labs facility, on sublevel two, and yet the entire building bucked and shook with the efforts of the Exterminator to tear through it. Plaster rained down from the ceiling but the walls had not begun to crack in here. Not yet. This room was supposed to be impregnable, just like so many of the labs down here.

But this was the Exterminator's destination; the alien was being drawn here by whatever sense it used to track the burrower parasites. And Wally had little doubt that it would have no trouble tearing into this room when it arrived.

He gazed at the frozen rictus of Ian's expression.

Then the Flash was gone from that room as if he had never been there, speeding up his molecules enough that he was able to sift himself right through the walls of that impregnable chamber. The wall exploded as he moved through it, a side effect of his passing. He only hoped flying debris would not damage Ian's cryo-tank. A red blur, he moved through corridors and up stairs and emerged into the center of S.T.A.R. Labs only a few seconds after he had left Green Lantern there to take on the Exterminator alone.

Kyle was like a small jade sun in the midst of the decimated remnants of the building's core. Energy seethed around him, his imagination and willpower tapping into the ring's power and creating columns and support beams that kept the upper floors from collapsing down on top of them. The Green Lantern sent tendrils of verdant energy out to cap the exposed ends of electrical cables, where the upper floors had already been torn away. And all the while, Kyle held the Exterminator back with a solid wall of shimmering emerald light, a barrier not unlike the Crisis Chamber that had held it before.

But the effort was taking its toll. Even as the Flash arrived he saw the sweat on Green Lantern's forehead, saw that the Exterminator was forcing its way, driving itself against the barrier.

And Kyle's boots were slipping, scraping backward along the ground amidst the debris.

The Flash stopped right beside Green Lantern and raised both hands. "Drop it," he said, even as he began to whip his fists in circles, thrust out in front of him. The shimmering barrier of energy disappeared and the Exterminator would have staggered forward and then begun to tear its way deeper into the building, except in that moment it was struck full on by the wind the Flash had created and instead of moving forward, it staggered back three steps, its arms snapping out, claws tearing at the internal structure of the building around it.

Green Lantern glanced at him. "How is he?"

The Flash raised an eyebrow. "Wasn't even sure you'd notice I was gone."

Under normal circumstances they would have bickered then. It was part of who they were, and the friendship they had established. But Kyle said nothing and so, after a moment, Wally nodded.

"He's fine. For now."

The Exterminator had regained its balance. It threw its head back and its mouth hung open impossibly wide. The roar that erupted from its chest shook the damaged building and Flash saw Green Lantern clap his hands over his ears. Then the alien started forward again, lunging across the massive hollow it had torn through five stories of the building. It thrust one arm into a fourth-floor corridor and tore downward, collapsing steel and concrete that showered down, crashing through the ceiling above them.

The Flash grabbed Green Lantern and the two retreated twenty feet. The dust cleared and above the rubble, there was the Exterminator . . . that much closer to Ian Partington and the other infected man, Paul Cargill.

Green Lantern threw up that barrier again, but the Flash knew neither of them believed it would hold the Exterminator for long. Wally shot Kyle a dark glance.

"I should have gone with the Atom."

Through gritted teeth, struggling to hold the Exterminator back, Kyle returned that grave look. "Not too late. Go find him. Make it quick."

The lab where the serum had been stored was sealed, but in the event of catastrophe, it had life support systems. Air recycling. Heat. Ray did not even have to go sub-atomic to find a way in. Microscopic, certainly, but that was a walk in the park. He blew into the lab on the cool air rushing from a vent high on the wall and began to grow instantly. He somersaulted through the air, getting control of his fall, and by the time his feet hit the floor he had returned to his full height.

A scream echoed off the interior of the laboratory, ululating in synch with the flashing of the emergency lights that glowed in the otherwise dimly lit room.

The Atom spun around in alarm and saw in the

strobing red and yellow glow a lab-coated figure huddled on the floor against the wall. The scream had stopped but now she—for it certainly was a she—held a hand across her heart. Dr. Janice Feldman looked up at him with a furious glare.

"Dr. Palmer, if you ever do anything like that to me again, I swear to God I'll wait for you to shrink and then swat you like a fly."

"Janice, I'm sorry," he said as he walked toward her and offered her his hand. She took it and he helped her to her feet. "I didn't realize you were down here."

Her features were drawn and though the emergency lights made it difficult to tell, she looked pale to him. "Believe me," she said, "I wish I was anywhere else. I was informed of S.T.A.R.'s emergency procedures when I was hired, but I never imagined—" Dr. Feldman glanced around and shuddered. "It's terrible, being down here like this, feeling the building falling apart and knowing you've got nowhere to hide."

Ray smiled. The building had stopped its trembling, at least for the moment. That meant Green Lantern and the Flash were holding the Exterminator back for now. But probably not for long.

"Janice, listen, I know there's nothing you want to do more than get out of here, but I'm afraid I need your help. You said the serum was ready to go. I need a double dose, immediately. And I need you to get to work preparing more."

Dr. Feldman licked her lips as though they were dry and she stared at him. "How many more, Ray?"

"A lot. A lot more. As many and as fast as you can. I'll be back to help you, just as soon as we stop that thing up there from bringing the whole complex down on top of your head."

She sighed, a little shudder passing through her. Then Dr. Feldman pushed her hair behind her ears and went across the lab to a massive steel refrigeration unit. She opened the door and took two glass ampules from a rack inside.

"You do that. Stop that thing up there and you've got me until you have all the serum you need or until I pass out from exhaustion, whichever comes first."

The Atom reached out to take the two ampules from her. The lab was suddenly filled with a crackling hum. Janice Feldman gasped and the Atom turned around to see what had affected her so. He was just in time to see the Flash phasing through the laboratory wall, before that wall shook itself apart from his passing. He turned his back and shielded Janice Feldman as best he could.

When the dust had settled Ray stared at the Flash for a long moment. Despite all he knew of physics and of metahuman physiology, he was still amazed whenever he saw Wally perform that particular parlor trick.

"I swear to God, the Justice League is going to give me a heart attack!" Dr. Feldman snapped.

"Did you get it?" the Flash asked.

The Atom took the two ampules from Janice and handed them to him. Ray stared in Wally's eyes, remonstrance as clear as he could make it. "*Don't* drop them."

"Not a problem," the Flash replied.

Then he was gone, a red blur whipping out of the room through the hole in the wall with a sound like a small firecracker exploding.

The Atom turned back to Dr. Feldman and nodded once. "All right. Let's get to work."

The Flash was not quick enough.

Green Lantern cursed under his breath, teeth gritted, trying desperately to hold the Exterminator back. His mind was filled with recriminations. What the hell had they been thinking, manufacturing these things like they were action figures? A little forethought would have been nice. But the League had been backed into a corner.

Honestly, the original League had dealt with the arrival of Exterminators on Earth ten years earlier, and he had privately judged them harshly. They had dealt with the situation poorly, acted without thinking things through completely. With people dying and entire cities in jeopardy, they had also been forced to think short term.

Kyle wasn't judging them anymore.

The corridor was crumbling around him. The support beams he had erected with the verdant energy from his power ring were flickering. He was growing tired, his will was weakening. Green Lantern stood there in the ruins and the chaos and held his ring aloft, using his free hand to brace the one with the ring. Beneath the faceplate that covered his flesh around the eyes, he squinted in anger and frustration and glared at the Exterminator. It raised its huge fists and slammed them against the crackling energy barrier he had made. Green Lantern felt every blow. The massive alien clone rammed its head against the barrier and Kyle grunted in pain as the impact echoed through his power ring and up his arm. His bones ached.

"Wally!" he shouted, furious with himself for the surrender this signified. He was calling for help, admitting that he wasn't going to last much longer.

The Green Lantern held both hands out, fingers twined together now, and he leaned forward as though trying to walk in a gale. He muttered beneath his breath. Swore aloud. Plaster cracked in the ceiling and showered down upon him. The Exterminator rammed the barrier again, its grim eyes blazing as it stared at him with determination that mirrored his own.

The floor beneath Kyle's feet began to crack.

For an instant . . . only an instant . . . his focus weakened. But in that instant, the Exterminator rammed the barrier a final time. The ring was an extension of Kyle's mind, of his imagination and his will. The barrier he had erected with that power shattered and the backlash threw him off his feet, tumbling him end over end along the debris-strewn corridor.

"No!" he shouted.

But it was too late. Even as Green Lantern leaped up from the rubble, raising his fist again, the ring sparking with jade energy, the Exterminator was free. The gigantic creature lunged forward, throwing its entire body into the already devastated structure. It tore at several stories of S.T.A.R. Labs from the inside. The impact threw Green Lantern to the floor again. He scrambled to his knees as the Exterminator ripped steel beams from their moorings, as walls and floors collapsed. The ceiling above his head split open and Kyle barely had time to register the danger he was in when hundreds of tons of debris crashed down upon him.

Commanded by instinct, a ripple of green energy surged from the ring, sheathing him in a bubble of power that saved his life. Rubble rained down upon him but despite his exhaustion, adrenaline shot through Kyle and gave him one last burst of strength. He stood, forcing the tons of steel and concrete and wood off him, rising up through a mountain of debris twenty-five feet high as though he himself were burrowing through it. When he burst from that mound, he hovered above it, staring at the Extermintor. It was tearing away at a promontory of third-floor construction that jutted toward it, trying to clear its path.

"Okay," Kyle said softly. "That was my last nerve."

He raised his fist and fired a blast of energy into the alien's face. When its head snapped back and it staggered two steps and let out a roar of pain and surprise, Green Lantern smiled with satisfaction.

And immediately the smile slid from his face. He was tapped out. Just keeping himself aloft was tiring him now. More than anything, Kyle needed a nap. Instead he shook his head, stretched, and reached down even deeper inside him, searching for reserves of energy he was not at all certain he would find.

The Exterminator roared again, but this time there was no pain in it. Only fury.

Kyle raised his fist. Power crackled and shimmered around his hand.

"Hey. Miss me?"

The Flash stood on top of the heap of rubble, arms crossed, a smile on his face.

Green Lantern glared at him. "Tell me you brought it."

The Flash extended his right hand and opened his fist to reveal two glass ampules. The entire mound of debris shook and shifted, and Wally had to struggle to keep his footing as the Exterminator began to ravage the building again. Green Lantern did not want to think about how much further it was to the chamber where Ian and Paul Cargill were being kept. But he no longer had to worry about that.

"We'll never get it through the armor. Not fast enough, anyway," the Flash said.

"That's not the route we're using," Green Lantern sneered.

A tendril of power licked up from his hand, darted from the ring to scoop up the two ampules from the Flash's hand. Green Lantern stared at the Flash.

"Go on, Wally. Piss him off."

The Flash frowned. "What?"

"Piss him off."

Flash nodded. With the blinding speed that made him the fastest man alive, he began snatching up pieces of debris and pelting them at the Exterminator's face. At the speed with which they were thrown, the projectiles struck with the force of bullets. With its armor plating, the Exterminator wasn't hurt by them, but it *was* annoyed.

It bared its teeth, gazing down at the red blur that was attacking it. Then the Exterminator opened its mouth to roar.

With all the power his ring afforded him, Green Lantern shot the ampules of antivirus into the Exterminator's open maw. The glass shattered upon impact, slicing into the soft flesh inside the creature's mouth, spilling their contents into its throat.

When it threw back its head to roar again, its fury was even greater. The bellow that erupted from its throat was enough to shake loose debris from shattered walls and girders. The Exterminator bent and its massive claws shot out, reaching for the Flash and Green Lantern.

Its eyes were bleeding. Its mouth drooped open and it staggered forward and crashed into the remains of the interior of the S.T.A.R. facility. Then it stumbled back and toppled. The impact of its fall brought more rubble crashing down.

The Exterminator twitched once.

Then it was dead.

Green Lantern felt no satisfaction whatsoever.

When he looked over at the Flash, he saw that Wally also seemed strangely subdued. Several seconds ticked by in the silent aftermath before he finally tapped the side of his collar, activating the commlink there.

"All right, J'onn," he said quietly. "We're in business. Let's get this thing done."

It was dawn in London, yet the golden light of the sun was dimmed, filtered through a gray shroud of cloud cover. Superman stood upon the wreckage of a metal gate at the very edge of Kensington Gardens and gazed down upon the rapidly dessicating corpse of an Exterminator. The antivirus had worked. They would be able to cure those who were hosting the parasite before they metamorphosed into burrowers . . . if they could find them first.

Of course, the fastest way to find them would be to have S.T.A.R. genetically engineer a new breed of Exterminator. One that could be controlled. One that was bred with a failsafe, a self-destruct.

But Superman thought that in this case, perhaps it would be wiser to avoid the fastest way, to eschew expediency in favor of caution. They would find another method of locating those carrying the parasite. It was a risk, of course; others might metamorphose while the League and its international allies were still trying to track them.

But that was a risk they would have to take. Wonder Woman and Firestorm had already teleported to other locations to assist the League's efforts to halt the

Exterminators, but Superman had stayed behind to keep the curious from becoming involved before the proper authorities arrived. Now Superman gazed around at the destruction that had been wrought here and could only imagine the damage that had been done in Manchester and Hong Kong and Glasgow and Metropolis. Yes, choosing caution over expediency was a risk.

But it had to be better than this.

EPILOGUE

The Watchtower was filled with the hum of machinery but otherwise all was quiet. J'onn gazed around the table and found it remarkable that this group of individuals, these extraordinary people, could sit still even for a few minutes while the world they worked so hard to protect spun far below their lunar headquarters. The clock was ticking. Yet this was not wasted time. The tension in the room was evidence enough that a meeting had been absolutely necessary.

Aquaman sat rigidly in his chair, eyes distant, mind very likely already elsewhere, focused on the concerns of Atlantis more than of the Earth as a whole. As it should be. Arthur was a king, the monarch of an entire nation. His own people's welfare had to be his first priority.

Green Lantern slumped in his chair, nodding slightly, not troubling to hide his boredom in any way.

Beside him, the Flash sat with his eyes closed, apparently trying to focus inwardly to fight the urge he must feel to run, to *move*. J'onn always admired Wally's ability to stand still for even a moment, given his speed.

Superman leaned forward in his chair, his fingers steepled beneath his chin. His expression was grim and expectant. Beside him, Batman leaned far back in his own chair, arms crossed, and though the room was sufficiently lit, what shadows there were seemed to pool about him as though drawn magnetically. He seemed, as ever, to be on the verge of getting up and leaving.

When the door to the conference room slid open and Wonder Woman stepped inside, J'onn could sense the relief that exuded from the other members of the League.

"The Secretary-General sends his regards and his gratitude," Wonder Woman said.

"Yet again," Green Lantern sighed. "Look, it's done. It's over. I'm sure we all have other things we could and should be doing right now."

As J'onn watched, Kyle glanced over at Batman. Under normal circumstances, the detective would have been the first to suggest that they had other responsibilities to attend to. In fact, quite often he would not have bothered to come to the Watchtower at all, preferring to focus his energies on fighting crime in Gotham City, the same way that Aquaman tended to his subjects in Atlantis. But this time, Batman made no sign that he agreed with Kyle. On the contrary, to J'onn's surprise, he frowned as he leaned forward and gave Green Lantern a hard look.

"No. This is exactly where we should be." Batman glanced around at the others, his gaze lingering at first on Superman and then coming to rest on Aquaman for several long seconds before returning to Wonder Woman. "Diana, I don't envy you the diplomatic duty of dealing with the United Nations. But the Secretary-General doesn't owe us any gratitude."

The Flash opened his eyes and his brow furrowed as he looked over at Batman. He pulled upward on his mask, peeling it back from his face so that it pooled like a turtleneck around his throat.

"I'm not sure I heard that right. I mean, admittedly, this thing got messy. But they're already inoculating people against the parasite. There's no telling how many lives we saved. Both from the virus and from the burrowers and the Exterminators."

Superman let out a long breath. That alone was enough to draw the others' attention. "Batman and J'onn assisted, but without the Atom and the scientists at S.T.A.R., there wouldn't have been an antivirus to fight the parasites. We did damage control, Wally. And not a very good job of that, I'm afraid."

"We did our best," Green Lantern said. "This was a no-win scenario. We all know that. There was no way we were getting out of this thing easy. All in all, I'd say—"

"All in all?" Batman interrupted. He stared harshly at Kyle, then turned that same look upon the rest of the League. "What we did was repeat the same foolish errors the original League made a decade ago. We knew the past, and we still repeated it. When the Exterminators first came to Earth . . ." Batman's words trailed off a moment and he looked first at Aquaman and then at J'onn.

The Martian Manhunter stiffened.

"When the Exterminators first came, the original members of the League made hasty decisions. Dangerous decisions. All of this could have been avoided entirely if the League had bothered to investigate the Exterminators, to find out what they were and what they were here for."

J'onn raised his chin slightly and felt a spark of ire in his heart. "You'll pardon me, Batman, but none of the original members of the League were detectives. Given the destructive nature of the Exterminators it was presumed—rashly, yes, but I don't think surprisingly—that an invasion was in progress."

"Just because they were aliens, J'onn?" Batman asked dryly. "So what are we to make of your presence here? Or Superman's?"

J'onn hesitated a moment and then nodded. "You are right, of course."

"Is he?" Aquaman asked angrily. He stood up, fists upon the table, leaning over to glare at Batman. "You weren't there. You sit there in judgment of us. The League didn't do a great deal of soul-searching in those days. It was about saving the world back then, not understanding it. But just to be clear, J'onn was the one person who was against destroying the Exterminators before we figured out what they were here for. He was outvoted. But he was wrong then, just as you're wrong now. No one likes the fact that this situation became as out of control as it did. None of us even wants to discuss the lives that were lost during this crisis, lives we all wish we could have saved. But Lantern's right. We did our best."

Batman only stared at him.

It was J'onn who spoke up. "And when our best is not good enough, Arthur? What then?"

Wonder Woman turned to J'onn, a grave expression on her face. "Then cities fall. And people die. But if *our* best isn't good enough, J'onn, then the world has only prayer and hope to rely on." She glanced at Batman. "Perhaps you're right. Perhaps we should have waited, taken the time to investigate from all angles. It's possible that the serum would have killed the fully grown burrowers just as it did the Exterminators. Probable, even. But we have no way of knowing if that solution would have occurred to us, or how many people would have been killed, how many made bankrupt or homeless, before it did."

Superman looked around the table. "Every day," he said. "Every single day for me is prioritization. With my senses I can hear crises unfolding minute by minute, from gunshots in the street to a husband and wife screaming at one another. J'onn's telepathy is even more widespread. If he focused it keenly enough, he could probably prevent crimes before they happen . . . something I'll bet he has done in the past. With the Monitor system we have, every moment, even this meeting, is a matter of prioritization.

"I can't be everywhere at once. Neither can any of you," Superman said. Then he looked at the Flash. "Not even you, Wally."

His iron gaze tracked over to Aquaman, and then to Batman.

"Prioritization is a necessity for us even to exist, to survive. We do what we can. Despite what some people may believe, none of us is infallible. In this case we erred on the side of humanity. Maybe there was another way to go about it . . ." Superman's voice trailed off a moment, and then he focused on Batman.

Batman stood. They watched him in silence as he took several strides toward the door, cape draped over his shoulders. He paused and glanced back at them.

"Despite all the power you have, the strength and the brilliance, you can't be perfect. Of course you can't. But both on your own and together, as a team, you have to strive to be as close to perfect as it is possible to become. That's the job. That's what we do, what the Justice League is. The biggest mistake the original League made was in not following through, not investigating afterward. So much could have been avoided.

"I only hope that this time, we didn't make any mistakes that we're going to regret later on."

With that, Batman turned and strode from the room. J'onn knew that he would go immediately to the teleportation chamber and return to Gotham City. He would be anxious by now to get back to his own struggle for perfection, his battle against the darkness and cruelty that existed in that troubled town.

It was a struggle Batman would never win.

In that moment, realization dawned on J'onn. He understood, then, that Batman knew that he would never win, that he had not chastised the other members of the League for the way they had handled this crisis. Batman had antagonized and admonished them not because he expected perfection of them, but because he expected them to demand it of themselves.

Rain pelted the windshield and the rhythm of the wipers made Ian want to sleep. But he had done enough sleeping—enough resting—in the past couple of days. It was not especially cold but he shivered with a chill and huddled down into the seat. Sara was driving and that in itself was a clue that he was not at all himself. Whenever they went out together, Ian drove. It wasn't a gender thing, not some sexist control issue; rather it was simpler than that. Sara hated to drive.

But today she did not mind at all.

His plane had arrived at Heathrow at half past three in the afternoon. The representative from S.T.A.R. Labs who had helped book the trip had thoughtfully arranged for the rare daytime flight, not wanting him to have to deal with the typical overnighter. He had spent the entire trip in a kind of daze, numb from everything he had experienced in recent days.

Ian Partington just wanted to be home. With Sara. In their flat in Battersea. In their bed, warm and close, her cheek resting on his chest while he kissed the top of her head and just held her there.

Without looking at her he snaked his hand across the space between the seats and slipped it into hers, their fingers twining together. She squeezed so tightly that it almost hurt, but he didn't try to pull away. At the airport she had been all business, this woman who had once been that girl behind the counter at the coffee shop, the girl who had stolen his heart. Her hair was dyed a respectable auburn now and she had fewer piercings than she'd once had. But she was still Sara. She still took his breath away.

God, he was glad to be home.

"You had me worried for a while, Mister Partington," Sara said, her voice tight.

Ian glanced at her, but she kept her eyes on the road, navigating toward home. "I'm sorry. I . . . you know I never—"

"I know. It's only that I . . . well, you're home safe now. I don't mind telling you I was frightened."

He did not have an easy response for that and so the windshield wipers kept beating out their tempo, squeaking as they scraped the rain from the glass. At length, Sara did finally glance at him. Her fingers tightened in his.

"You miss it, don't you?"

Ian blinked and glanced away. "I'm not sure what you mean." It was one of the very few lies he had ever told her.

Sara let his fingers slip out of hers, grabbed the wheel again with both hands. "I can't begin to imagine what it was like. Being up there. With them. Being one of them. Still, I suppose I understand that even with what it could have done to you, even though it could have killed you . . . maybe you still feel as though you've lost something."

There was a stop light ahead and she slowed the car carefully, wary of the rain-slicked street. Waiting for the light to change, Sara glanced at him again.

"I don't want you to ever forget that you were an extraordinary man before all of this started. You're still that man, love."

Ian nodded slowly. "I know, Sara. I do. But with the power I had . . . I could have done so much more. So much good. And there was something about it . . . the camaraderie . . ."

He let the words trail off. Ian knew Sara would understand without elaboration. Kyle and Wally—Green Lantern and the Flash—had become his friends. All his life he had seen men share an easy bond that allowed them to sit around a table at a pub and have a pint, trade stories, and laugh together. That had never been as simple for him as it seemed to come to so many others. And yet he had been comfortable with Wally and Kyle; he had enjoyed their friendship. Ian had had to overcome the temptation to see them as something other than ordinary men, and he had suspected that his having powers had enabled them to connect with him the way they might not be able to with the average civilian.

"What now?" he said aloud.

The light changed. Sara actually chuckled as she accelerated and the car began moving again.

"Now you come home. You get back to your job, your real job, if they'll have you," she said in a tone that was just short of scolding. Then she softened and reached out again for his hand. "And you remember that you have always been *my* hero. There was a time when that was enough."

Ian squeezed her hand. Sara turned onto their street, a block of renovated rowhouses, and despite the rain he was cheered by the sight of home.

"It's more than enough," he said. "At the end of the day, it's really all that matters."

Sara smiled, her gaze upon the rain-slicked road. "Good," she said without turning. "And now that we've got that sorted . . . have a look . . . I think you've got company."

As she pulled the car into the short narrow drive in front of their flat, Ian stared at the two figures huddled under a single umbrella on the front stoop. A pair of pitiful creatures in blue jeans and sneakers, a couple of ordinary blokes who just happened to be two of the most powerful people in the world.

Ian grinned.

They looked ridiculous.

"Shall we have them in for a cup of tea? I made scones for you this morning."

Ian glanced at Wally and Kyle again, huddling there together in the storm.

"I'd like that," he told her. "And I think the lads will, too."

About the Author

CHRISTOPHER GOLDEN is the award-winning, *L.A. Times* bestselling author of such novels as *The Boys Are Back in Town, The Ferryman, Strangewood, The Gathering Dark, Of Saints and Shadows,* and the *Body of Evidence* series of teen thrillers. Working with actress/writer/director Amber Benson, he co-created and co-wrote *Ghosts of Albion*, an animated supernatural drama for BBC online.

Golden has also written or co-written a great many books and comic books related to the TV series *Buffy the Vampire Slayer* and *Angel*, as well as the scripts for two *Buffy the Vampire Slayer* video games. His recent comic book work includes the creator-owned *Nevermore* and DC Comics' *Doctor Fate: The Curse.*

As a pop culture journalist, he was the editor of the Bram Stoker Award-winning book of criticism, *CUT!: Horror Writers on Horror Film*, and co-author of both

Buffy the Vampire Slayer: The Watcher's Guide and *The Stephen King Universe.*

Golden was born and raised in Massachusetts, where he still lives with his family. He graduated from Tufts University. There are more than eight million copies of his books in print. Please visit him at www.christophergolden.com

JUSTICE LEAGUE of AMERICA

BATMAN

THE STONE KING

ALAN GRANT

From Pocket Books available wherever books are sold

JUSTICE LEAGUE of AMERICA

THE FLASH
STOP MOTION

MARK SCHULTZ

JLAF